BROKEN ANCHOR HERITAGE

E.M. BURTCHEARD

My Best to You Always

Evelyn Burtcheard

LifeRich
PUBLISHING®

LifeRich Publishing is a registered trademark of The Reader's Digest Association, Inc.

LifeRich Publishing books may be ordered through booksellers or by contacting:

LifeRich Publishing
1663 Liberty Drive
Bloomington, IN 47403
www.liferichpublishing.com
1 (888) 238-8637

ISBN: 978-1-4897-1857-0 (sc)
ISBN: 978-1-4897-1858-7 (e)

Library of Congress Control Number: 2018908770

Print information available on the last page.

LifeRich Publishing rev. date: 08/07/2018

DEDICATION

This book is dedicated to several people who encouraged me to keep writing after the death of my son and my husband. These people became part of my family: Terri S., Dianne, Marilyn, Debbie, Cheryl, Jan, Glenda, Judy, Rosie.

1

BROKEN ANCHOR REVISITED

The old man Hamish Kevin MacDougall lay silent and small in the large sturdy built oaken bed. The furniture in the room was heavy, large pieces of the last century. The dark heavy drapes had been drawn to darken the room of a dying man. Gavin and his brother Gideon entered silently, entering over the protest of their aunt Fiona who was whispering they must not disturb Hamish. Old Hamish had long ago taken the English spelling MacDougall of his Scottish name of Mac Dhaggaill when he left Scotland at the age of fourteen going to sea. He came from a family of prodigious Scotsmen that could trace their lineage back hundreds of years. Many of his family were of royal blood and counted nobility and Statesmen among their kin.

"You cannot go in there, it's against the Doctors orders," stated an emboldened Fiona, sister of the man lying on his death bed.

"You don't understand aunt Fiona Da sent for us. My ship just got into port. I went to Gideon's home and we came as soon as we got word he wanted to see us. We didn't even know he was ill," answered Gavin.

The old man raised his hand and motioned his sons to come to his bed side. "Fiona, leave us I have to talk to my sons." With a voice that belied his weakened body old Hamish began to talk to his sons.

"I have to tell you of the land I have in the mountains in the Utah Territory. I won that land in a poker game. I won half of a ranch from one of two Marsh brothers Caleb and Daniel. I won the ranch on the south side of the Copper River. Caleb called the fifteen thousand acres of grassland he owned the Muddy River ranch. There is also some five thousand acres of timber land. You have known of this land but what you do not know is how valuable the land is. I spent all the time I was there looking for gold, and I found enough to start building your mothers and my home we had always dreamed of, the house we would call the Heritage. I never found enough gold to make the loss of time with her and you boys to be worthwhile. I did not realize there was so much more value in the family and land than in gold." Out of breath his face grey from the effort to talk the old man lay back onto his pillows appearing to be asleep but instead dwelling on the irretrievable lost time with his family.

"When the ship came into San Francisco to dry dock for repairs five of my mates and I went to the Parker House it had the reputation of being an honest house for whiskey and cards. I got into a card game with several men and one of them was a rancher named Caleb Marsh. It got down to just the two of us at the table and I put almost everything I had on the game. He laid the deed to his part of the ranch on the pile. I beat him by one card, he was angry and started to remove the deed but someone had called the sheriff since Marsh had a habit of getting angry and violent when he lost while gambling."

The sheriff said "leave it and was ready to stop him, he told me to take the winnings and leave." "Within a few days my mates and I left and went out into the territory to see what I had won. Your mother and you two boys were home back in Scotland. The men and I went to the ranch by way of old Dry Diggings and Eagle Station. The quickest route was over the pass at Coburn Station but we had heard stories of how rough that route was, of early or late snows that stopped all travel. Travelers had been known to become stranded.

"We reached the ranch and it was a two by twix outfit not much more than a rawhide camp. The men on the ranch were living in two dilapidated shacks. One was a leaning log cabin and the other was a picket cabin and the mud chinks had mostly fallen out. One of our men decided he wanted to return to San Francisco so I sent a letter to the lawyer I had hired before leaving San Francisco, and had him hire eight men to come out and start building a house that we would live in while the house we wanted was being built. I had seen this house your mother and I wanted in Scotland. I would have to find a knowledgeable carpenter to build this very special house. When the men arrived there were eight cowboys with them looking for work and I hired them to round up the cattle on my range. The carpenter that was the foreman knew of the house I had seen and began work immediately. He remembered the house in Scotland."

The old man leaned back on his pillows and closed his eyes. His sons sat silently waiting for their father to go on. Gavin was shocked at the sight of the man he had known all his life but had spent very little time with. He remembered his Da as being a stone solid man with a booming voice. The man in the bed appeared to be smaller and much older. His hair was thin and the auburn red had turned white. There were deep lines in his face, brown spots on his hands that shook constantly as they lay on the top of the coverlet.

Finally able to continue old Hamish took a deep breath and went on with his story. "I sent word home that I was starting a ranch and told your mother to get ready to come to California. It would take two years for her brother to settle my affairs to the point I could bring my family to the ranch. During this time there were men rounding up the cattle and men building the house. We named our new home the Heritage and I named our brand for the ranch the Broken Anchor."

"Some of the men who stayed with the ranch when I got it told of gold being found in the Big Thunder Mountains. I began going into the mountains for longer and longer periods of time. I found gold enough to keep the ranch going for several years. I missed the sea but since I had brought you boys and your mother over here I thought I had to stay. Your mother was carrying a baby, Fiona named after my sister. The baby died during that first harsh winter, your mother never recovered. She was inconsolable in her grief"

"I returned to the mountains more and more in search of the elusive yellow treasure. I could not see the natural treasure in the form of timber and the grazing land. The cattle that came with the ranch had not been culled or sold or even properly cared for. With water, grazing and natural shelter the herd prospered but they were of poor quality. I hired a man named Fletcher to manage the cattle and he moved his family to the ranch."

"The more gold I found the longer I stayed in the mountains. I spent weeks on end searching but never found the mother lode. I searched the cold mountain streams and learned that the heavy gold flakes were found where there was black sand and the banks of the streams were colored with yellow or orange stains. The heavier gold would stop at the bend of a stream where the water slowed. I knew the gold came from a lode high in the mountains so that's where I began searching on the mountain. I found a cave but could not explore it at that time. There was a mountain lion with cubs living there and she was not going to give the cave up. This was no pussy cat it looked like one of those great mickle beasts from Africa, the largest cat I ever saw. I was sure that's where the gold came from. I named what I believed to be a possible strike the Panther mine. One day in my constant search for the elusive yellow treasure I became careless and fell while in the mountains."

"I was found by a Shoshone Indian that nursed me back to life. The Shoshone people kept me alive by feeding me a cabbage soup and to this day I cannot abide cabbage. Later I was given corn Wa sna` also called Indian candy and also something called Tin`psi-la they pronounced teem`see lah that was made of dried beef, wild turnips, wild potatoes and dried corn. They took care of me by feeding me and doctoring my wounds until I could return to my family. I was gone so long your mother and Fiona believed I was dead. The Indians were the kindest, most gentle people I have ever known in all my travels. During my recuperation an old Indian told me of his relative who was Sacajawea also called Grass Child who had been born and lived in his village. The very young girl had been stolen from their village by the Minatare and traded to the Hidatsa's. He told me the story of this same Indian girl that guided the Louis and Clark expedition to the west coast. He told me of Toussaint Charbonneau a fur trader born of a Sioux mother and a French Canadian father. He said Charbonneau was not a good man, he told of the man winning the very young girl in a game of bones, and later of the child she carried on the trek west to the big water, and how she saved the expedition books and instrument in a river crossing. She taught the explorers how to build a bull boat. Baptiste was the son of Sacajawea and Charbonneau. Her brother was Chief Chameshwait. After Sacajawea left Charbonneau who treated her badly she returned to her people for a time. She later adopted her nephew Basil a member of Old Man's village. When I asked what became of her the old Indian did not know. He said it was a very old story, passed down through the years."

"I would have died in the Big Thunder mountains had it not been for the Indian Black Thumb and what remained of his tribe who spent winters in the Gotome Canyon. They had been driven far south by the Blackfeet tribe, a fierce war tribe. Old Man was the name of several long ago chiefs and the remaining of the tribe was all that was left when they escaped south. You will find this same said canyon on the ranch. The Gotome is a long deep canyon that runs through the east side of our range, there are stories that seems more myth than truth but don't take the stories lightly. There was an old Navajo Indian that has worked on the ranch for years and he swears the mountain lion is a shape shifter, something that can change shape into whatever animal or person it wants to. I laughed when I first heard it, but the longer I was in the Big Thunder mountains the more I believed. The mountain lions seemed to appear at very odd times and then vanish. The Indians know things we white men will never know. Don't discount anything you hear, I did and it was a mistake," said Hamish slipping back into his reverie again.

Gavin and Gideon sat silently mesmerized until their father began to talk again even though his story appeared at times disjointed and hard to follow.

"By the time I got back to the ranch there was word that your mother, my sister Fiona and you boys had gone back to San Francisco. I left to bring you all back to the ranch. You boys were five and seven and your mother had not weathered the trip across the sea very well. When we got back to the ranch the first floor of one half of the house was closed in so we could live there. The old cabin that Caleb had lived in became the chicken house. The men on their time not working the cattle had built a log bunkhouse that first winter. It had been three years since I won the ranch. Caleb and his brother continued to try to get the ranch back but I had taken care to have the deed made legal and there was no way they could break the deed. Finally we heard that Caleb was killed when he got caught cheating at a card game over in Fort Baker."

"Your mother continued to remain ill more so after our second baby daughter died and Fiona took over the care of the house. A few months after arriving back in the Utah Territory your mother died. As you remember she is buried on the hill with the babies behind the house on the ranch. Your aunt Fiona and I brought you boys back to San Francisco to this house I bought and I returned to the sea. I continued to be a sailor long after gold was discovered in California. I could not see the natural treasure on the ranch in the form of timber and grazing land. The cattle that came with the land had good water, grazing and natural shelter and with the good management of my foreman Fletcher the herd prospered. There are some twenty thousand acres of ranch land and another three thousand or so acres that is useable to graze. It was free land then, I don't know how it is now."

"You have known of this land but you do not know how valuable the land is. I spent all the time I was there looking for gold, I will never forgive myself for the loss of time with your mother and you boys to be worthwhile, he said again." Out of breathe the old man lay back into his pillows and appeared to be asleep. Gavin and Gideon sat silently waiting for their father to continue his story.

"I don't know how much of the house is finished. I kept in touch with Fletcher over the years but I lost interest in the house after your mother died. I continued to pay for the house to be built and for the ranch to continue but I could never return to the ranch once I returned to the sea. Like me Fletcher is an old man but I believe his son is foreman now. There is money deposited in a ranch account every fall but I have never given it any attention. With that money I believe the ranch could get back on its way to making money."

"I cringe to think I spent all the time I was there looking for gold he said dwelling on the past and repeating himself, when your mother died I brought you boys back to San Francisco. I have not been back to the ranch since. I now believe that the real treasure is in the land. If new cattle blood was mixed with the range cattle I think the ranch would easily support your families. This is what I wanted to talk to you about."

"My time here is short. I don't care what that old sawbones says, open the drapes, I want to see the sun I'll spend a long time in a dark place soon enough. Now I gott'a rest but send in Fiona I have some things to talk to her about. As you know I don't have all that much to leave to you but that ranch is free and clear to you boys. This house and what money I have will go to Fiona, she has been a faithful sister and she raised you boys when I went back to the sea. Although he was young I knew Captain Horacio Dunbar to be a good man and was glad when he agreed to take Gavin on his ship when he was sixteen years old. A friend of mine taught Gideon the real estate business," said the old man apparently reminiscing to himself as though he was alone reliving the past.

Suddenly aware his sons were still in the room he said, "Come back tomorrow and I will tell you what I can of your mother." Out of breathe the old man lay back and appeared to go to sleep.

Talking with their aunt the brothers asked what they could do to help, it seemed there was nothing to be done. Fiona told the men that Hamish had set up an account for her and she needed nothing. She wished them luck but stated she had no desire to return to the ranch. It had not held any good memories for her.

Gavin and Gideon left going to Gideon's home to discuss what their father had just revealed to them. Gideon's wife Isobel left the men who remained closeted for several hours to work out plans for going to the ranch. Their final decision was that Gavin would leave the sea and Gideon would postpone his investment business and together go to the Utah territory and attempt to make a go of the ranch, they would be equal partners. Isobel was just happy that Gideon was going to be away from San Francisco. She said her sons needed their father's strong hand.

The men talked far into the night. Gavin would return to Scotland and buy the red longhorn Highland cattle their father had suggested. As a last gesture to their father they would make the ranch prosper.

The following day they returned to their father's home to tell him of their decision and to ask his advice on the best route to take the cattle. The old man seemed stronger and in better health than when they arrived the day before. He was sitting in a chair by his bed with his feet on a footstool and a blanket over his legs. He was excited as he began to talk.

"Earlier I contacted young Fletcher and asked his advice on the best route to the ranch it has been several years since I was last there. I had even had hopes of going out there myself then my health got bad and I could not make the trip now. His letter is in that little wooden chest in my trunk with his route and suggestions for taking a herd and wagons to the ranch."

In part the letter read, "Take the southern route it is a little longer but safer with good water. Don't go over what is now called the Donner Pass. Donner Pass is said to be good on either side but it is known for severe storms and the pass can close quickly in unexpected snow storms. The Donner wagon train from Illinois was lost there because the pass filled with snow and trapped them in it. Also I believe it would be hard to drive a herd of cattle through there. You will be told it is closest to the ranch but do not go that way. Go southeast from San Francisco to Stockton it used to be called Mudville and some folks still called it that when we went through there on our return to San Francisco after your mother died.

"Then keep on that trail to Eagle Station. Go through Grimmes Point and turn north. There are military forts all along the route. You will come to a beautiful little valley where there is good grazing to rest the herd for a few days. Go on northeast to Red Lodge." The letter continued. "It was a trading post when I was last there and it is the closest town to the ranch. It is on our southern boundary. The post is west of Ft. Cameron. I just wish I could go with you, but I lost my chance and I want your families to have the experience of the western country." It was apparent he had studied Fletchers letter carefully.

◆

After their visit with their father and the decisions made Gavin went to tell the captain that he was leaving the sea and going into ranching with his brother. When he arrived at the Dunbar home the Captain insisted he have supper with his family and tell him all he knew of the ranch Gavin was going to. It was a pleasant but anxious evening. He was very nervous when he was introduced to Moria the Dunbar's daughter. Gavin fell in love with her on sight she was beautiful, with long golden blonde hair sparkling blue eyes. She was tall for a woman and spirited and she carried her slender willowy frame with a grace seldom seen in a girl so young and she was strong willed. It was apparent that Moria's feelings were the same for Gavin. During the next three weeks while waiting for the ship to sail to Scotland and after meeting Moria Gavin told her of his feelings for her. He had fallen deeply in love with her.

"I am going to return to Scotland to buy cattle and when I return back here will you marry me and wait until Gideon and I can get the ranch started again? It has been several years since my parents lived there so I don't know what we will find. Will you wait for me until I can send for you, asked Gavin?"

"I will marry you on one condition that we get married before going off into the wilderness to the ranch. And I will go with you! If we are going to start a life together it will not be one of us here and the other somewhere else. Do you not think your mother waited and watched for your father and wished to share his life more fully, not just occasionally?

I have seen my own mother watch and wait for my father to return from the sea and that is not the life I want for myself."

Stunned Gavin asked, "Are you certain you want to go out there now? It may be very rugged for a while. I don't know what condition the house is in. It may not be fit for a new bride."

"I am certain! Gideon's wife is willing to take a chance and so am I. When may we speak to my parents?"

The following evening Gavin was invited to dinner at the Dunbar home. Gavin and Moria were nervous as they approached her parents when they returned from a walk in the garden. The two older Dunbar's Horacio and Mavis were seated in the parlor when the young couple asked to speak with them. Gavin had never been so anxious before in his life as he prepared to seek permission to marry their only child. Finally summing up the courage he asked their permission to marry Moria.

The parents were not at all surprised and gave their blessing until Moria announced she wanted to get married when Gavin returned from Scotland with the cattle. She told them she wanted to go with Gavin straight away to their western home. The Dunbar's were anxious but did not put up any road blocks for the young couple. They were used to the strong willed actions of Moria. While not headstrong she did have certain opinions, marriage was one of them.

———◆———

Gavin had gone to Scotland and was returning with a hundred head of the shaggy, long horned Highland cattle born and bred for the harsh life in Scotland. The ship would land in one week. The Captain had known Gavin since he was a cabin boy at the age of sixteen. While he approved of Gavin as a son in law he was dismayed at the demands of his daughter but she was the daughter of himself and his wife who were both independent people. With the approval of her parents Moria made plans to leave her parents' home. As a gift to the young couple her parents hired a crew of builders to finish the interior of the home started by Hamish.

———◆———

Moria sat at her mother's desk in the morning room of her parent's home. She was going over the list of items her mother had made for her soon to be wed daughter to Gavin MacDougall. Moria smiled as she came to the new bed room suit which her parents had contracted to be made. She had visited the furniture maker and listened closely as he explained how the dove tail fittings in the dresser and bed would go together. Each piece was labeled and numbered. It would be assembled at the ranch. He instructed her on how to put a second coat of varnish on the beautifully carved set.

Mrs. Dunbar a tall beautiful woman with golden hair like her daughter stepped to the door of the room. "Moria your father would like you to come outside."

Laying the papers aside Moria went through the back of her home to the stable where her father stood in the door smiling. Turning to her mother she saw a smile on her face also.

"What are you two up to?" asked Moria.

"Come through the stable to the paddock in back."

Moria went through the barn and stepped into the paddock to see two splendid black mares standing shoulder to shoulder. They were magnificent animals, their coats were silky, brushed to a sheen. They were not tall horses standing fourteen hands tall with well-defined intelligent eyes in beautifully shaped heads.

"Dad they are beautiful horses," said Moria hurrying to touch the beautiful animals.

"Moria these are Morgan mares and both will foal in the spring. They are trained to ride and drive. They are for you, we want you to be well mounted up there at the ranch."

"I have never seen such horses" said Moria who was used to riding gaited horses.

"They are Morgan and they are special horses. All true Morgan horses can trace their lineage back to a horse named Figure that was owned by a man named Justin Morgan. Figure, the foundation sire was born in the late 1700's. Figure was known for his legendary exploits of out-performing other breeds at that time. They are known for their smooth gait stocky build and strong endurance. They are a favorite mount of the cavalry. We hope you like them."

"Oh I love them and have not even ridden or driven them! Thank you, Thank you! This is too much, you have gone beyond love for me and I love you for it. I could not have better parents. I love you both and we, Gavin and I both appreciate all you have done for us but you must stop now. You have done too much already. Dad, mother the horses are gorgeous and I love them already. Thank you both," said Moria rubbing the face of first one then the other of the horses.

"Do they have names?" she asked.

"We thought perhaps Queen and Duchess said her mother but we will leave that to when the registration papers are done. You can choose."

"Queen and Duchess are wonderful names for such beautiful animals," said Moria. She could not wait to show the horses to Gavin. He had given her a new padded saddle since she had indicated she wanted to ride horseback to the ranch.

She had several riding skirts made that she had seen pioneer women wearing. She had asked for her saddle to be made so she could ride astride over rough terrain going to the ranch. She had borrowed her father's saddle and discovered she felt safer riding astride. After all this was not a walk in the park and certainly no gossips to judge her. She was so excited to begin the trek to the ranch her excitement infused Isobel to excitement.

———◆———

2

GAVIN

I was the eldest of Hamish and Maeve MacDougall's two children and I was the steadying influence in the care of my brother after our mother died. Aunt Fiona had the care but I calmed the waters. I seldom lost my temper and saved Gideon from getting his head busted more than once during the years after our father returned to the sea.

An imposing man of medium height I stood five foot eight with broad shoulders I had built working on the rigging of the Dunbar ship. My soft voice and benign manner belied the strength of an earnest intelligent man; I was considered by some as a handsome and rugged outdoors man. I was the proverbial man that could be led to water but not made to drink. Stubborn if forced, willingly if asked. Once I went to sea I believed the sea was in my blood and I was happy as a sailor for the Dunbar shipping line.

From the first moment I saw Moria Dunbar her face was indelibly imprinted in my mind and my heart. I could not believe my good fortune when Moria agreed to marry me. At the age of sixteen I had become a cabin boy on her father's ship and stayed on as a sailor. I knew he had a family, the picture of a beautiful woman holding a baby was fastened to a shelf above the table in the Captains quarters. I saw the picture when I took coffee to Captain Dunbar late at night when he was bent over the huge maps for the sea and cargo. He was a jovial honest man and I liked working for him but at this time I had begun to think of a life that did not center on the rolling of a ship at sea. My own father was in poor health and my brother and I were not that close in our adult years. When I arrived at the Dunbar home it was with regret that I was going to tell Captain Dunbar I was leaving the sea.

When Gideon and I were summoned to Da's bedside and told of his wishes for us to go to the Utah Territory to the ranch he owned I had no idea how much I would fall in love with the land. The fact that Moria felt the same and that we loved one another was beyond my wildest dreams.

I was surprised that my sister in law Isobel took to the idea of living on an isolated ranch so quickly. I believe Moria was a great influence. Her quick wit and happy demeanor kept everything in balance. Shortly after arriving in San Francisco I began to hear rumors involving Gideon and other women. I was surprised myself as I truly began to look forward to going to the mountains and beginning a new life.

———◆———

The Union Pacific Railroad had reached Promontory Point Utah on May 10, 1869 and some day it would go to the very edge of the Pacific Ocean. For the time being we would have to drive the cattle to the ranch. I had discussed with Gideon the possibility that by the time we had cattle to ship the railroad would be far enough west that we could ship the cattle by rail. But to get to the ranch with this herd it would be necessary to hire men and drive the wagons, horses and cattle overland.

Moria and I were married in a small country chapel near her parent's home. Our guests were her parents and some of her friends, Gideon, Isobel, their sons and Aunt Fiona. I was afraid that without a longer engagement there would be talk. Moria answered that those who really mattered knew the circumstances of our marriage and they were folks that counted. I arrived at the church early and tied the carriage horse to a tree. I then went to sit in the shade of a large oak tree, more than likely as old as the nearly two hundred year old chapel. A tall bell tower reached skyward above the adobe structure. California was hot even in the shade of the tree. I went inside the chapel and was met by an aged priest. "Are you nervous son?" he asked. My teeth chattering I answered yes. Going into the large main room I saw my Aunt Fiona and my brother's family.

Quietly almost with reverence an elegant carriage drawn by a pair of beautiful white horses stopped at the door of the chapel and Moria stepped out behind her father. In all my life I had never seen anyone so lovely. She took my breath away. By this time there were several other carriages tied up but I did not recognize any of them. I stood with the Priest at the front of the Chapple. Captain and Mrs. Dunbar escorted their daughter into the building and down the aisle to me.

And so I married the love of my life.

We began our journey to the ranch shortly after our wedding. Moria and I took two wagons of our belongings including furniture for our new home especially Moria's beautiful piano. Gideon and I hired men to drive the cattle and horses and to drive our extra wagons.

There were times at night when Mark, Stephen and Philip would come to our wagon when we heard Gideon and Isobel quarreling. There were several times I found one or more of the boys asleep rolled in a blanket near the fire beside our wagon. I loved Gideon's sons but at times I felt overwhelmed with the need to protect them from their parents.

◆

3

GIDEON

We left San Francisco at dawn, the sun a slight glow over the mountains to the east. Gavin had gotten into port with just over a hundred head of Scottish Highland cattle. He hired an army scout and two soldiers that were on their way to Fort Halleck north of our ranch and the Copper River to act as scout and to help with the wagons. He had hired six more men to work on the ranch once we arrived. Tater Fletcher had written to him that the ranch needed more riders.

Gavin was taking his bride of only a couple of weeks with their two wagons. There were two ranch wagons one to have the men's bed rolls and tools and a specially built chuck wagon. We, myself, Isobel, Mark, Stephen and six year old Philip followed with our two wagons and two provision wagons, eight wagons in all. We were on our way to the property my father and mother had settled on when I was a youngster. I could not clearly remember the house, the house Da called the Heritage had started being built as a mansion our father had seen in Scotland or England I forget which. This was not what I wanted but my wife Isobel had nagged until I had agreed to leave San Francisco. She had discovered my uh….liaison with a wife of one of my friends. I love women and this one was special. I was considered handsome, I was taller than my brother Gavin by four inches. I was of slim build with a smile that melted the female heart. I was blessed with dark auburn curly hair that kept falling forward, I looked like a tall version of my father in his young days.

I would attempt to operate my real estate and shipping interest from the ranch. I refused to divert all my energy into the ranch. There was a stage line from south of the ranch to San Francisco so it wasn't like I couldn't be in San Francisco within a few days. I had no intention of burying myself on the ranch and this was the cause of many of mine and Isobel's quarrels.

I was considered a severely practical man, and I lived to enhance my wealth. I believed wealth lay within the real estate and shipping not in ranching. I had married not for love but to gain material benefits from Isobel's wealth. We fought about everything even the most minute subject. I was never close to my son's especially Mark. I was so busy with my business the boys were outgrowing me, and I never considered what they wanted. I viewed them as pottery clay that I would mold. As time passed we became farther apart on all instances which I squarely place the blame on Isobel she poisoned the boys against me. If I said yes she said no and vice versa.

The trip to the ranch was not a pleasant one for any of us. Living in such close quarters Isobel and I fought constantly, more so when she realized she was once again pregnant. I was happy to have Gavin and Tater Fletcher make the decisions for the ranch and I could sequester myself in my office at the ranch to plot and bargain for my first love-business. At times I would work into the wee hours of the night on plans and schemes.

———◆———

4

ISOBEL

Gideon and his brother were summoned to their father's bedside. When they returned to our home the two of them spent several hours together. Later that night Gideon told me that their father wanted Gavin and him to go to the Utah territory to settle on the ranch he owned and was turning over to them. Gideon did not want to leave San Francisco and I believed I knew why, he was involved with one of his partner's wives. I didn't think it was serious yet, I knew the woman and she had a history of playing around but never serious. It was humiliating and I would not stand for it. So I talked in favor of the move to the ranch. At this time I was not aware of his Spanish interests.

We had three sons about two years apart in just ten years. I was five years older than Gideon and at times I felt so insecure. I could not always accompany Gideon to business functions but mistrusted him when he went alone. This was a very different person from the popular girl and considered a beauty I had once been however I was also considered flighty because I refused to be married until it was my idea. There were those who were jealous and spread gossip that I was wanton but I let it roll off me like so much water off a duck. I knew who I was and what I had to answer for. But I had made a mistake in marriage. The only good to come from that union were my sons.

I believed I was in love with Gideon as soon as I met him. He was tall, very good looking and several of my friends were already in love with him. I needed to prove I could win him from them.

I knew I was beautiful. My greatest asset was my long luxurious black hair, but I also had a well-endowed figure that was eye catching. Never shy I seemed to make friends very easily. I loved to flirt at social events. My skill to entertain at dinner parties became the talk of the town. Gideon relied on me to help him in his business, I could make or break a business deal and I did very well until I began to have children. With the birth of each child I lost something of myself. I was also losing Gideon. I believed he had become a lascivious creature no longer hiding his affairs. I had no direct proof but I just knew it.

The difference in our ages was something that Gideon brought up when we quarreled, he would throw my past into my face, and we quarreled often and vicious. The year before we left for the ranch I lost a still born baby. Something happens to a woman when she loses a baby and she is never the same again. I resented Gideon his stamina and vigor in life while I had become a fading rose. I was aware that Gideon was very attractive to women and drew the attention of women wherever we went. I resented the fact men could grow old almost with grace while women just grew old. No longer were there as many looks of admiration as I had once enjoyed. I believed that going to live at the ranch I could avoid some of the aging process and the resentment of the young beautiful women.

We left San Francisco with two wagons loaded with our belongings. Within two weeks from the time we left San Francisco I realized I was with child again my fifth pregnancy within ten years. I was not pleased and began to resent Gideon even more. By the time we reached the ranch I was almost sorry I had persuaded Gideon to come to the Utah Territory. My sons at the time were Mark ten, Stephen eight and Philip six. I was hoping for a girl, however Gideon was wishing for another boy, one he could mold to be like himself, he had never managed that with his other sons. Perhaps the women in his life took up too much time, I don't know. Quarreling could be heard from our wagon often. Our life was far from serene.

———◆———

5

MORIA

I knew from the moment I met Gavin MacDougall I would never love anyone as I loved him. It truly was love at first sight. As we spent time together I began to be afraid he would not ask me to marry him. I had other beaus but no one measured up to Gavin. I was afraid Gavin would think I was too tall to be his wife. I was the exact same height as he and while my friends were petite I knew I stood out in a group. At least two young men informed me it was off putting for the woman to be as tall as her escort. Oh how I prayed Gavin would not think so. While Gavin was dark I was fair complexioned with an abundance of golden blond hair that curled around my face and was almost waist length.

Mother had invited Gavin to dinner and the two of us went into the garden and sat on our favorite bench to watch the sun set. We could see the Pacific Ocean far out. Gavin had been unusually quiet and nervous acting and my heart sank when I thought he was going to break off our relationship.

And then it happened he asked me to marry him but to wait until he had the ranch house ready for me. I had watched my mother wait days at a time for my father to return from the sea and I did not want to start married life apart. I made demands of Gavin, one being I would go with him to the ranch the first time. I was so looking forward to a new life with Gavin and our future. Ours was a hurried wedding and I am certain there was talk but the important family and friends knew the truth and so we had a very small ceremony and my dreams of being Gavin's wife came true.

I was so excited when the trip began, I was truly happy. I loved the open prairie, and the mountains but was very anxious about the rivers although we had no problems. I loved the evenings sitting around the camp fire, Gavin had a wonderful singing voice and Isobel's sons and I joined him and we sang every song we knew. There were few times Gideon and Isobel joined us, those were very special evenings. I truly enjoyed the trip to the ranch and I loved Isobel's sons, especially Mark who in so many ways was like Gavin. I wanted children desperately. I was certain that when we got to the ranch and settled I would begin to have the family we wanted. I wanted at least six children and I believed that to be a very attainable number.

———◆———

6

THE TRAIL TO THE BROKEN ANCHOR HERITAGE

Gavin hired men to drive the cattle and horses as the two brothers and their families set off for the wilderness with one hundred head of cattle, a string of twenty five head of horses and eight wagons each pulled by large draft horses loaded with household and ranch goods. Two of those wagons were loaded with provisions. A wagon had been outfitted as a chuck wagon according to specifications designed by the ranch cook, Cricket. He would also cook on roundup for the ranch hands. Cricket had certain built in boxes, shelves with doors that closed and locked and a drop down block table top that he had designed. We had a light wagon we used to carry the men's bed rolls and ranch tools. We would use it later to bring supplies from Red Lodge to the ranch. Gavin planned to sell the heavy wagons once we reached the ranch and no longer needed all the large wagons. We were leaving one life and starting a new one. The draft horses would be needed to make winter hay.

The MacDougall families left San Francisco shortly after Gavin arrived from Scotland with the cattle. The cattle, horses and eight loaded wagons pulled out at sunrise on a mild late winter day.

The cattle still tired from their ocean trip proved no resistance as they fell into line behind a big red shaggy cow that had taken over dominance of the herd. Even the young bulls deferred to her dominance. The horse herd was half a mile ahead of the cattle and a short distance behind the last of the wagons. Driving the next to last wagon which had been built as s chuck wagon for the ranch was Cricket, the only name he ever gave, not even a last name. He was a man of rather short stature, of fastidious nature and unknown origin. He had been hired to cook for the bunkhouse and to go on the roundups. He kept a wash pan near the fire and could often be seen washing his hands which was much appreciated by Isobel and Moria.

The small wagon outfit did not encounter any problems the first three weeks of their journey, other than a couple of severe thunderstorms that left animals and humans tired and sleep deprived for a couple of days. The weather and trail had not been noteworthy although Moria kept a detailed journal since the day she married Gavin MacDougall.

Gavin, Moria, Isobel and the boys had driven into Stockton also known by many old timers as Mudville and renewed the supplies they had used. Gavin noticed a young woman and four men who had paid particular attention to their wagon and team of four horses. It was true their wagon was well cared for and the MacDougall family did not appear to be the disparate souls that had given up on the California gold dream and was heading back east.

Gavin had gone to the hardware and feed store and the blacksmith for things they had forgotten or had used up when they supplied the wagons. He sat on the wagon enjoying the sun, his horses stood hipshot dozing in the day's warmth. He was waiting for the women and three boys to finish their personal shopping when one of the men stepped across the street towards the wagon. He had almost reached the wagon when Moria and Isobel with the children behind them came out of the General Store. Philip was crying and screaming at the top of his lungs as Isobel lifted him into the wagon. Mark and Stephen looked embarrassed at the commotion and noise Philip was causing.

The man suddenly turned and walked down the street a few doors to a saloon. When everyone was in the wagon Gavin moved the team out into the main stream of traffic and started the trip back to camp.

The man who only a short time before had shown such interest in the travelers went into the saloon downed two glasses of rot gut whiskey quickly and returned to his waiting companions, his father, brothers and sister.

"Why didn't you talk to him, find out how many men there are and where they are going. We already seen the horse and cattle herds. Why didn't you find out more huh?" Asked the large burly man wearing dirty clothes, with a grey scraggly beard streaked with tobacco juice waiting for the younger man to answer him?

I could'a done bettern him" said the dirty straggly haired girl dressed in worn men's clothes. "Sometimes I don't think he's worth shootin."

"I recognized him that's why! We was on the Dunbar ship at the same time I kilt that sailor and he might still remember me. There is still a price on my head for our last bank robbery when my bandana fell off."

"Well that's another stupid thing you did. You are gonna get us all kilt." Said the girl hefting her rifle to her shoulder and stomping off to where their horses were tied.

"We gonna ferget them folks Pa? I got a bad feelin' about them."

"Not on your life, they's well fixed, good gear, clothes and two purty women. We will just pick a good place to stop them, take'em off guard and relieve them of their burdensome belongings."

Once on the trail back to camp the three boys fell asleep on the grain sacks, Isobel and Moria were reading newspapers they bought. Gavin could not get the man in town out of his mind. It was almost as if the man recognized him but Gavin could not remember where. He was certain it had not been a pleasant encounter. They returned to camp near sundown as the sun slid westward in a colorful setting of pinks, purple and blues, over the mountains in the distance, and into the Pacific Ocean.

Gavin sat staring into the fire as Moria got their bed rolled out on the floor of one of their wagons. Suddenly it came to him where and why the man in town seemed familiar. The man's name was Zeb Strader and he had been a deck hand on one of the Dunbar ships when Gavin was a sailor. He had only been on the ship a short time when he knifed a sailor, one of the other deck hands and then jumped ship. There had been bad blood between the two men while the ship was still at sea. After the knifing and Strader jumped ship the other man recovered and Gavin had forgotten the incident. How could he have forgotten the weasel faced coward? Although the man now wore an ill kept beard and wore dirty worn clothes it was Zeb Strader alright. Now Strader was in the area, it would pay to be aware of who was around. Gavin already knew the man was dangerous and the outfit he was with looked no better.

Moria and Gavin had just finished the last of the coffee when Gideon and Isobel began to argue. Before long Mark, Steven and Philip came to the fire with their blankets. "We are going to sleep out here stated Mark as he helped Philip unroll his blanket.

"Wait a minute said Gavin as he went to the wagon and returned with a rubber ground sheet. This will keep the damp and cold out, along towards morning it gets mighty chilly the higher we get in the mountains." This ritual was repeated many times before the group reached the ranch and their new home. The children would rather sleep on the cold ground than listen to the bickering of their parents.

The herds and wagons were four days out of Stockton when five riders appeared on the trail. They sat their horses side by side with long guns laid across their saddles. The burly man Gavin had seen in town stepped his horse out in front of the other riders and stopped in front of Gavin's wagon. The two MacDougall outriders Pickett and Jackson with the horse herd that was following the family rode up alongside the wagon, wondering why Gavin had stopped, they also did not see the army scout that rode ahead to scout camp sites and water. They were soldiers and gave the outlaw boss a good looking over as another of their riders came along side of Gideon's wagon.

"Bet'cha wondering why we stopped you?" asked the dirty clothed tobacco stained bearded older man in a factious attempt at humor. He was Buck Strader head of the outlaw family of three sons Luke, Jack, Zeb and the girl Zelda.

"You are now on our land and you gotta pay to cross!" Grinned the man showing brown broken teeth.

The hair rose on the back of Gavin's neck as he gave Moria a hand signal to get in the back of the wagon. In a matter of a couple of seconds she disappeared into the interior of the wagon. "I know for a fact this basin is open range. You may be running stock on parts of it but you don't own it and you got no right to stop anyone from crossing," answered Gavin loud and clear. "This your family Zeb Strader? I remember where I saw you. You knifed a man in the back on board a Dunbar ship. Looks like you have taken up robbing travelers. Unless you want more trouble than the five of you can handle you will let us pass without any more of this nonsense. We are not paying you anything. Now get out of our way!"

The girl with the dirty straggly hair rode her horse forward saying, "I want to see what's in them wagons." She ignored the fact that the drivers held rifles on her family. It did not appear to faze her that the five men in front of her held guns.

"No you are not going to look in our wagons!" said Gavin as the girl rode alongside the wagon.

"Mister you men aint gonna shoot a girl" she said with a smirk as she jerked loose the rope to untie the canvas covering the wagon.

"The men might not but I sure will" said Moria suddenly jerking the canvas up high enough to move her head and shoulders out with a rifle a scant four feet from the girl. "Now get back there with your outlaw friends, NOW! The sullen girl Zelda turned and rode back to her father.

Riding silently up behind the outlaws Clay Daniels said "sit tight men this robbery attempt is a game changer."

At this change of events all guns still pointed towards the remaining outlaws. Clay Daniels the army scout had ridden a mile or so ahead of the wagons until he found water and camp site. He had signed on with the MacDougall's as scout. He was on his way to scout for the army at Fort Halleck up north of the Copper River and had brought two other soldiers Pickett and Jackson who had signed on as horse wranglers and were being transferred to the same Fort. Pickett, an out rider for the wagons, rode to the outlaws and relieved them of their rifles as Gavin told them to drop their gun belts. At the same time Gideon and two more riders appeared alongside Gavin.

Clay Daniels demanded they dismount and stand aside. All the bluster had gone out of the outlaw gang. Another outrider, a soldier named Jackson began to unsaddle the outlaw's horses and throw the saddles into a deep arroyo.

"Now all of you remove your boots" demanded Gavin.

"You aint gonna take our horses and our boots are ya?" asked the girl. When told yes they most certainly were Gavin's men heard cussing from the girl that would shame a sailor. She kept this up until finally Moria climbed from the wagon and walking up to the girl said "Shut your filthy mouth before I shoot you myself." The outlaw girl shut up and sat with her eyes down cast not moving not talking.

Putting his family in danger angered Gavin. Pointing his finger at Buck Strader while struggling to control that anger Gavin said, "Strader you come near me or mine again and I will kill you as quick as any lobo wolf out there."

Pickett stacked all the boots and guns on the back of the camp wagon carrying the workers bed rolls and tools as it passed. Jackson held a gun on the outlaws until the last of the cattle herd passed. With a wave of his hat he raced to take up his place in line.

The Strader's stood in the dust cloud watching their hopes of plunder disappear down the trail. "Well don't jest stand there git after them horses" old Buck Strader yelled at his eldest son Luke an overweight blob of humanity that had to think before he could even spit.

"Paw we can't track our horses after all them wagons and cows been down that trail we gott'a wait 'til morning and try to find our boots then our horses whined the girl." The gang followed the cattle looking for their horse tracks until dark then they stopped for a cold night. Their gear was in an arroyo several miles back. They built a fire but had no means to hunt. They spent most of the night crabbing and blaming one another for their predicament. It took the outlaw gang two full days after retrieving their boots to catch a horse and hunt the rest of the horses and go back for their saddles and gear. By then they had given up all hopes of stopping wagons again. Just too much work.

---◆---

7

MARK

From the time we reached the western edge of the Utah Territory I knew I would never leave this country even if everyone else in my family did. I felt free here in the mountains. My mother and father had argued and fought all the way from San Francisco. I often spent my time with uncle Gavin and aunt Moria. I knew I would never be happy away from the ranch and the land and these mountains. I lived for when I could learn to ride.

I was built more like Uncle Gavin and when I tired of listening to my parents bicker I would ride with one of the other men driving the wagons or walk. I would gather leaves and plants and make mental notes of what I saw and ask the men who knew about such things about them. Cricket had grown up here and he appeared to me to know everything. We became fast friends although he was a lot older than I was. I had a restless energy and could not remain idle for long. I gathered arm loads of firewood for the cook fire just so I could sit on the wagon tongue and listen to him tell stories while he peeled vegetables or prepared the evening meal. I did not want to intrude, I wanted to help and I had and insatiable appetite for knowledge of this country and the way of ranch life.

I never tired of the stories Cricket or the other wagon drivers told of life in the mountains, where they grew up, and stories of their families, they just seemed to have had exciting lives. I wanted to ride the horses but mother would not let me. Uncle Gavin said that when we reached the ranch Tater Fletcher would choose a suitable horse and teach me to ride. And so I waited and dreamed.

Aunt Moria had a pair of beautiful black horses that she and Uncle Gavin rode but they were not for beginners. At this time I was very happy being where I was and doing what I was doing. I was on the wagon behind my aunt and uncle and I knew I would always be safe with them. Stephen and Philip did not like life on the trail. Stephen seldom walked and Philip cried much of the time. They wanted to go back home, I knew I never wanted to leave these mountains.

I truly felt I was at home at last. I had never thought about what kind of house we would have and so it was a great surprise to see the Heritage tucked into a valley with a large lake in front. We would share the house with Uncle Gavin and Aunt Moria. It was like two houses built into one.

What I was happy to see was the corral with horses. I didn't know how to ride but one of the men hired to drive the horse herd also promised to teach me to ride. I could hardly wait. I had the promise of two teachers. I could visualize myself flying over the prairie on a horse.

———◆———

8

STEPHEN

I hated the idea of going off into the wilderness I begged mother and father to let me remain in San Francisco with Aunt Fiona, although I had not asked her permission. Father said no and became abusive in forcing me to go with them. I could see no reason for going into the mountains to live in a house no one had seen for years especially when we had a very nice home in San Francisco. I was the second son and while Father tried to make Mark do as he wanted and stop spending so much time with the work men and riders I was left to my own devises and I learned quickly how to be deceptive and cunning. I had known about my father and other women from listening to my parents quarrel. I was losing regard for my father and felt I had to protect my mother.

I was condescending towards Philip and I made certain he got into trouble at every chance I got. I never missed an opportunity to disparage my brothers. However it was much harder to do with Mark. He was always out with the working men or riding a horse. I did not like the horses or the cattle. I would leave the ranch as soon as I could. I would never be satisfied buried here in these lonesome mountains.

◆

9

THE HERITAGE AT LAST

The men Gavin hired to drive the cattle would remain to work the ranch. With them came the work crew Moria's parents sent to finish the house. When we were near the headquarters of the ranch Gavin and Moria turned off the trail and rode up the side of the mountain. When they reached the summit they looked down into the valley below. From the mountain high view Moria saw her new home below, the house started by Gavin's parents. Moria's heart soared when she saw her new home for the first time. Bright sun shine highlighted the house into a serene beautiful picture.

The house faced the mountains to the west. A huge two and one half story red brick fronted structure greeted the new families. Six tall columns marched across the front of the house like sentries. A wide porch reached from side to side of the house and Moria could imagine sitting on this porch rocking a baby while at least one other child played near her chair. A great double front door entered the house where the wide hall ran from front to back of the house. Tall windows graced the front of the house. A veranda known to sailor's families as a widow's walk formed a circle completely around the second story of the house. The unfinished half circle drive to the front door made an imposing entrance to the front of the house. Unseen in the back an enclosed patio had an entrance into the wide hall.

A short distance from the drive a large barn with an attached corral held a herd of horses. Another much larger corral to the southwest of the drive was where the cattle were being driven. A cook shack and new bunk house had been built northwest of the main house. Two smaller houses were built north of the main house for the house servants and where the foreman's family would live. A beautiful blue lake was located between the mountains and the home. The workmen were building another cabin where the new ranch hands would live. They watched the herdsmen drive the red cattle into one of the large corrals.

There was busy activity everywhere from the workmen at the house to the men working the horses and separating the cattle. Moria held her breath as she looked down upon her new home. Never in her wildest dreams could she have imagined so much beauty could be found in one valley.

With tears in her eyes Moria said, "Gavin it is beautiful, I never dreamed there was so much beautiful country between here and San Francisco. The house is magnificent it will be the beginning of our children's heritage. It is so large that Gideon and Isobel can live in one side and we can live in the other." Gavin's heart soared when he realized his wife was happy.

◆

High above Gavin and Moria a family of mountain lions lay sunning on a ledge watching the activity below. The big cats were nocturnal but this cat was very interested in the cattle and horse herd that moved into the valley. This female was larger than the average female mountain lion, and her cubs were young but large. They still carried the spots which they would lose at about six months of age but they would remain with their mother for as long as two years. The big cats were known by several names, mountain lion, catamount, puma, cougar and panther however most mountain men and miners referred to it as painter. Their cries at night sent fear into the hearts of men and animals alike. Mountain lions were secretive creatures, solitary, nocturnal, they hunted by stalking, rushing or pouncing from trees and overhanging rocks. Like all big cats they killed by biting the neck of their prey. They were grey to tawny from under the chin down the length of the belly. The big cats seldom had any markings other than the black tip on the tail. The cat high on the mountain had a black splotch on the side of her face which she had passed along to each of her female cubs, never the males.

The average mountain lion was approximately forty-two to sixty inches long head and body with a twenty-four to thirty-six inch long tail. The lion high up the mountain was several inches longer and many pounds heavier. The linage of this lion had long been larger for generations.

◆

As their wagon topped the ridge that was the western entrance to the valley Isobel and Gideon first saw their new home. Both were silent for a long time watching the goings on in the valley below. They did not share their thoughts.

Isobel saw a great hulking monstrosity of a house with its back to the hills to the east. There were scattered buildings and pens in front of the house, where she thought they should have been behind the house or located down the valley from the house. She imagined there would be dust from the working of the animals. She had been told the house had been built for two families but she would have never dreamed it would take on a gothic look from this distance. She found the tall columns across the front almost a barrier to the entrance. She did not dare express her disappointment at her new home it would start a fight since she had nagged Gideon to come out here. She began to believe she would live to regret this move.

As he looked down into the valley at the home his parents had begun to build what Gideon saw was what he perceived as a prison. The huge brick house looked more like a jail to him than a home. He would make do as long as there was a room in which he could make into an office to seclude himself in his work.

Gideon and Isobel had gotten to know Moria while they were preparing to leave San Francisco and they found her to be a pleasant happy girl who was anxious to start this new adventure. Isobel had many doubts. It was soon apparent that Moria was very happy to have company and they became friends right away. Isobel began to view the move through Moria's eyes and see things in a better light, but she still could not begin to shake the feeling she had made a mistake coming out to this wild country.

The men of the ranch were helping to unload Gideon and Isobel's wagon. Riders came into the ranch yard and dismounted. As Gavin and Gideon approached the men walking towards them one held out his hand to them and suddenly they recognized the man as the son of their father's friend, Tater Fletcher. He had come to the ranch as a child with his father when Hamish began to build the Heritage and stayed on to become ranch foreman. Only a year older than Gavin they remembered his father teaching them to ride and then they returned to San Francisco. Their new life would be easier with the help of Tater. After talking to Gavin and Gideon Tater walked over to where the men were still unloading supplies.

As Moria and Isobel came out of the house Tater removed his hat and spoke to Moria, "Ma'am some of the boys got together and bought some laying hens and a milk cow when we found there was young'uns comin' to live here. And well we wondered that since there would be eggs, milk, flour and sugar maybe we could get you to make us some donuts sometime, we aint had any good ones since Mrs. MacDougall passed away."

The women looked at one another and began laughing, they had just mentioned that they would need hens and a cow to make good meals. "We will see to it there are donuts often for the men, our own families are fond of the fried treats," promised Moria.

10

GAVIN

My first view of our new home was overwhelming. I knew Da had a special home built but I had forgotten how grand and imposing the house was intended to be. I had never been able to visualize what the Heritage was supposed to look like. There were two and one-half stories built on either side of the main entrance to a long hall that went back to the kitchen and a back entrance that opened onto an enclosed patio. There were six tall pillars that reached to the second floor of the house. A grand stair case entered the hall from each side with a landing on the second floor. A wide half circle drive came past the front entrance and ended on the north side of the house at an elaborate hitch rail near a set of steps up onto the wide porch.

The house was really two homes in one. Moria kept saying how beautiful the house was. The sun was shining brightly in our valley and I was so glad my beautiful wife had demanded to come with me.

Right away we knew we would be happy here and could start our family. Isobel and Gideon said very little about their new home so I do not know how they felt about the move to the ranch. Both of them were given to bouts of moodiness and anger. Moria had a calming effect on their household.

11

PHILIP

I was six years old when we got to the ranch. I didn't like the mountains and the ranch. There was not any neighbors and the people on the ranch worked for my Dad and Uncle Gavin. My birthday happened on the trail not that anyone noticed. My mother and father were not speaking. Aunt Moria made us an apple dumpling for desert. Uncle Gavin and Aunt Moria gave me a new pair of boots.

Mark always called me the baby and I hated him for it. I had a lisp from birth and couldn't talk plain and my brothers teased me. I wished I didn't have any brothers and that Uncle Gavin and Aunt Moria were my parents, and I could have anything I wanted.

◆

12

ISOBEL

I was glad Moria was here. She and Gavin seemed to be a settling influence on Gideon. I hated the house on sight but I began to change my mind as Moria pointed out small nuances that the house had. Her own home in San Francisco had been a large beautiful house. I was becoming pleased with the house once we were settled, it was nestled in a valley with a river that ran down from the mountains and formed a beautiful lake I could view from the house. When the sun flooded the valley I had to admit it was beautiful. Gavin and Moria gave us the finished side of the house and they stayed in their wagon until the workmen her father hired finished their side of the house and had it ready.

---◆---

Five years had passed since our two families left San Francisco and come to the valley. The house known as the Heritage was finished. The cattle herd had produced cattle other ranchers were clamoring to own. Through careful breeding the ranch now produced horses that were known for speed, beauty and stamina.

To all outside appearance the families at the Heritage were doing well and happy. However I knew Moria was unhappy that she had no children. She was very good with my children but I knew she yearned for children of her own. Gideon and I now had five children two little girls were born since coming to the valley. Moria came across the hall this morning to ask me if I wanted to go riding. As she approached our door she heard us quarrelling. She was about to leave when Arabella and Lorelei went running out the door, fleeing from the anger inside their home. Before Moria could stop her Arabella called to me that Aunt Moria was there.

Embarrassed Moria asked if I would like to go riding. We met later when our horses were brought to the house. It took me several minutes to get myself under control as Moria waited until I came out. I am sure Moria could tell I was angry but said nothing. We rode silently into the north end of the valley. We rode the next hour in silence, reaching the small pristine mountain lake we both loved. We tied our horses and taking our canteens to a log to sit and listen to the birds and insects, and watch for the deer, and perhaps the wild horses.

I was nervous and fidgeting and finally I could hold my frustration in no longer and I began to talk to Moria, she was my very best friend and had a right to know why I was so upset. "I know you had to hear Gideon and me arguing this morning. He wants to send Mark and Stephen to apprentice in San Francisco. Mark does not want to be a business man he loves working the ranch with Gavin. Mark and Gideon could never work together like that. Someone will have to take over running the ranch someday and I think if Gavin believes Mark is capable then he should have the chance. Gavin has told Mark he has an unusual feeling for the cattle and horses. Stephen wants to go east to Philadelphia to school to become a lawyer. Both boys want something worthwhile and I am going to fight for them to get a chance to do what they want their future to be."

Although she had no children Moria could understand how I felt about the future of my sons. What mother did not want her children to be happy and work towards something they desired?

We sat for some time in silence. At last I was able to speak again, "Gideon returned to San Francisco this morning. I want to take the boys and go to him to plead their cause before it is too late. It will take about two years but once he makes arrangement for his sons there will be no turning back. Moria, would you look after Philip, Arabella and Lorelei for me? Juanita will do the work but I would feel better if I knew you were in charge. I hate to ask but…

"Of course I will be happy to look after the children. You know I love your children and I promise to care for them as if they were my own."

"Then I will take the two older boys and leave tomorrow. Perhaps I can take them to the Opera while we are in San Francisco. I have to make Gideon see that what they want is important to their future."

———◆———

As soon as the women returned to the ranch Isobel began to pack clothing and make plans to take Mark and Stephen to meet the stage at Red Lodge early the following morning. Philip set up such a howl when he learned he was being left at the ranch that Isobel finally gave in and agreed to take him also.

When they arrived in San Francisco Isobel went immediately to the home she inherited from her parents. She was surprised to find the house was still closed up as she had left it when they had all returned for old Mr. MacDougall's funeral. Sheets covered the furniture on all levels. The only rooms being lived in were the servant's quarters. Stunned she sat down in a chair by the kitchen fireplace. An ominous feeling hung in the air. Mr. and Mrs. Willard returned soon after Isobel arrived surprised to find Isobel and her sons waiting. They stated they had no idea where Gideon was staying, they had not seen him since the family left after the elder MacDougall's funeral.

Attempting to keep her temper in check Isobel instructed Mrs. Willard to prepare the sitting room, dining room and bedrooms for her stay. She went to the master bed room where she found the room as she had left it. Where was Gideon staying? She called Willard and asked him to send messengers to the large hotels to find Gideon. In the next two hours messengers arrived at the house with the same message. Mr. MacDougall could not be found. It was seven-thirty that evening when the last messenger arrived and he knew where Gideon was living. He was at the Montoya-Luna hacienda. Hiding a smug reptilian smile the messenger stated he was told Gideon lived there with a Spanish woman named Alana Maria Montoya-Luna at her father's in town compound one of two located outside of San Francisco. The larger of the two was located many miles east of San Francisco.

For some time Isobel had the feeling Gideon was unfaithful. His actions had become surreptitious, hard to pin down. She had heard the whispers of the ranch hands and the women in the house. There were rumors that he had made advances towards some of the girls on the ranch. He had long lost his appeal for Isobel. With the birth of Lorelei they had moved into separate bedrooms, after all Isobel was now almost forty years old and had not planned on Lorelei. She would not stand for this latest rumor. She would start by taking the three boys to the Opera. Her family still had a private box and tonight she would use it.

She called Willard to see to the boys dress clothes and to bring the barouche around an hour before the Opera started. They ate a light supper and were dressed and waiting when their carriage came to the front steps. As they rode through the evening the sky had turned to the many colors of sunset far out over the ocean, from a blazing pink shade all the way to turquoise on a blanket of stars. As their carriage approached the Opera house the whole building was aglow in golden lights. It was a great joy to see the bright lights reflected in her son's eyes. The boys had never seen anything like this before.

Everywhere they looked people were dressed in their most elegant clothes. Women sparkled in vibrant colored gowns adorned with expensive jewelry. The gentlemen wore perfectly tailored tuxedos wearing tall top hats and white gloves. The children stood in awe as Willard handed their mother from the carriage. Entering the great Opera House under the brilliant lights they stepped inside and were greeted by a staircase with elegant railings and gold statuary set in strategically placed balconies with elaborate carvings that reflected the light from crystal chandeliers. The Opera house glowed with reflections of the gas lights bouncing from every surface from the floor to the high vaulted ceilings. Deep scarlet curtains framed each box of seats.

Isobel had long wanted an evening such as this. She had envisioned arriving on the arm of Gideon and being the recipient of envying glances. Gideon was a most handsome man and while Isobel's ardor had cooled immensely she would have enjoyed the attention their arrival brought. Tonight she would have to be satisfied with the company of her sons. Mark was fifteen and although rather somber was growing into a handsome young man. Stephen at thirteen was still more like a gangly colt than a racehorse. Philip at eleven had the habit of staring most of the time with his mouth open. Isobel had to more than once discreetly admonish him to close his mouth. For this evening she was certain nothing could cause her irritation not even the absence of Gideon. She seated the two younger boys in front of herself and Mark.

Isobel removed her opera glass from its velvet case and began to discreetly scan the lower level for old friends from the past. Her social life had come to a halt since she had gone to live at the Broken Anchor in the house called the Heritage. Red Lodge had a theater where traveling players put on shows but it was very primitive and incomparable to the San Francisco Opera House.

Scanning the crowd Isobel saw two of her old beaus. One was seated with a nemesis from her past. At last the curtain opened to thunderous applause and the house lights dimmed. During the first act the four people in the box hardly moved. No one uttered a word, they were transfixed with the play.

When the lights come on again the boys began to discuss the play among themselves while Isobel continued to scan the audience below and in the balcony to her left. Suddenly she sat up nearly rising from her seat as her opera glass settled on a couple near the front only four rows from the stage. It was Gideon with a beautiful small, slim, elegantly dressed woman and a little boy. The woman wore a mantilla and her face was partially hidden from view. The position of Isobel's box seat offered a clear view of the faces of the lower level. There was no mistaking Gideon and when he stood so did the woman and child with him. This was no coincidence the woman was with Gideon and they were going into the open hall.

Isobel could not remember the rest of the evening. However during the last act she slipped out of the box and returned to the hall where she made discreet inquiries of where Mr. MacDougall usually ate his late supper. She was directed to the Pacific Palace Hotel where she was told Mr. MacDougall had a suite of rooms.

When the opera was over and Isobel and her sons were in their carriage instead of going home she directed Willard to drive them to the Pacific Palace Hotel. The mater`de directed Isobel towards the dining room where Gideon and the Spanish woman, and Isobel was certain she was Spanish or Mexican, were seated with a child. Isobel had no dinner reservations so she simply led her sons to their fathers table. Philip upon seeing his father ran to him calling "Papa, Papa." Mark and Stephen held back feeling the anger in their mother. Stunned Gideon looked from Isobel to his sons and to the woman at his side.

"Aren't you going to introduce us to your "friend" Isobel whispered facetiously? Attempting to keep the interruption to a minimum Gideon made perfunctory introductions saying the Spanish lady was Alana Maria Montoya-Luna and the child was Mateo Montoya-Luna.

So there was more than the Montoya-Luna family being business partners of Gideon he was involved with Alana Maria. White hot anger and a look of hate enveloped Isobel however she did not intend to humiliate her sons. She turned on her heel saying "come children it's time to go home." It was a cold silent ride back to the house.

———————◆———————

Mark did not sleep at all and during the night he could hear his mother pacing in her room where she vacillated between anger and tears. He knew the meeting with his father after the opera had been unexpected and the anger from his mother was most palatable. There would be fireworks when his father came to the ranch again. His mother could not, would not let this discretion pass. He knew there would be dire circumstances.

The next morning Isobel told the boys to pack their belongings and she left the house. She was gone for some three hours. When she returned she looked tired and older to Mark as he watched his mother go about the house as if in a trance. Shortly before leaving to meet the stage coach north the family lawyer arrived at the house where he and Isobel remained sequestered behind closed doors. The lawyer a middle aged man, his bearing straight and dignified looked very serious as he followed Isobel into the library. Emerging from the room and looking more serious if possible the lawyer took his leave. When the lawyer left Isobel looked relieved as she held a sheath of papers in her hand. For years there had been rumors of Gideon's infidelity and affairs but he had not been as blatant as to bring his mistress out in public. It was time for revenge and she knew how to hurt Gideon in the worst way. In her hand were papers that would bring him to his knees. With the complete filing of the papers in court Gideon would be all but bankrupt. Once she set in motion the results of her visit with her lawyer there would be no going back to an unendurable marriage for Gideon and herself. She had just sent her lawyer to begin that road of no return.

Isobel hardly spoke from the time the stage left San Francisco until they reached Red Lodge. The stage stops and stage changes were as though she and the boys were strangers. No one talked they just stared out the windows of the coaches as days passed into night and slept when they could. They had left their carriage and team at the livery stable in Red Lodge where they arrived in the late hours of the evening. Waking the boys Isobel directed the livery to ready their carriage to leave and to find a driver. Mark was surprised they did not stay the rest of the night at Red Lodge and travel on to the ranch the next day, as the family had always done before. It had been a long hard trip from San Francisco to Red Lodge spending several days by stage coach and they were all tired. More disturbing was the fact that Isobel seldom spoke. Mark had never seen her like this. When a coach driver could not be found on such short notice Isobel instructed Mark to take the reins. As they drove toward the ranch an ominous gloom settled over the family.

Isobel had closed accounts of her family's holdings that Gideon had managed. This single action would greatly diminish his control of her money. She and her lawyer began a long term effort for revenge. She told no one else of her actions or plans not even her best friend Moria. Slowly with the help of her lawyer in San Francisco she diverted her holdings into an untraceable account. Gideon would find his power and a large part of his income no longer existed. Her only thought these days were to ruin Gideon, she fed on the thoughts of revenge.

◆

13

GIDEON

By the time our two families had been on the ranch more than five years the situation between Isobel and myself had become desperate. I entered into a business deal with Don Carlos Montoya-Luna in which I loaned him money to retain a portion of his Spanish land grant that he had borrowed against to maintain a lavish life style. His sons and grandsons spent lavishly on beautiful clothes and gambling. Then I met his daughter Alana Maria Montoya-Luna. Of all the women I had ever known including Isobel, Alana was the only woman I ever truly loved. I intended that someday I would marry her. I was to learn she felt the same for me. Dreaming of Alana and my business was what sustained me those years. I had at one point after Isobel lost a baby asked her if she wanted a divorce. Her answer was never, I hated the fighting between us that sent our sons scurrying away from us like frightened kittens.

The year Mark turned fifteen and Stephen was going on fourteen I believed they should begin schooling to come into business with me. Mark rebelled saying he wanted to become a rancher. I dreamed my sons would be business men and I was not going to give up my dream. Ranching was something I had given into to appease my father and Gavin and I listened to Isobel. I was aware that she wanted me out of San Francisco and away from society where temptations in the form of beautiful women were plentiful. I believe she encouraged Mark to go against my wishes.

I resented the fact that Mark had become a younger version of Gavin than he had of me. I often saw them riding together with the ranch foreman Tater Fletcher. Gavin and Mark learned to ride the ranch horses when we got to the ranch and perhaps that was why they spent time together. Mark had no interest when I tried to explain business to him. He would rather rope and ride in the dust than to have a well-meaning job.

I had taken Alana and our son Mateo to the opera. She was spending a few weeks at the Montoya-Luna compound in San Francisco and would return to the hacienda far south east of San Francisco very soon. It was time for our son who was two years younger than Philip to be introduced to life outside the hacienda. After the opera we went back to our hotel and were seated in the dining room of the Pacific Palace when suddenly I heard a child crying out "Papa, Papa" and my son Philip ran to me. Isobel, Mark and Stephen stood looking at me and Alana and Mateo. I believe this was the only time in my life that I was speechless. I was so sorry this had happened to all my sons and Alana. Isobel looked smug, her eyes were fierce and cold as obsidian, hate fairly spewed from them, she had finally caught me.

Isobel said "aren't you going to introduce your friend?" However she turned trailed by my sons and left the dining room. She had ruined this special outing for me and embarrassed Alana and the children. In my mind I knew Isobel and this was not the end of this disaster. Isobel was a formidable enemy and that was how she saw me now, I was certain of it. But I had no idea to what length she would go to when she set out to ruin me, I was certain of that.

———◆———

14

STEPHEN

My brother Mark loved the ranch, I hated it. Our brother Philip was a pest that followed me everywhere I went. Sometimes I would pinch him just so he would go tell Mother and I could get away from him. I spent a lot of time with the ranch children away from my house. I was the owner's son and I would intimidate them any time I wanted to.

As I grew older I maintained the round face and pudgy body I hated. I would like to have been tall and lean like my brother Mark but I would not get in the dirt with the cattle and work like Mark did. I was positive I would outgrow the baby fat, as my mother called my over-weigh, as I grew older. Mark had grown from a more bulky shape like Uncle Gavin to tall and lean.

I had a knack for being able to watch people without being seen. We had been at the ranch only a few weeks when I watched my father with the wife of one of the cowboys. He was kissing her and she fought him off. The girl ran from the barn and my father laughing left the barn also, passing within mere feet of where I stood. My father and mother fought all the time we were on the trail. I realized I could get what I wanted by going first to one parent then the other and over the years I became very good at it. But I was afraid for my future, my father was adamant that Mark and I would become business men like him.

I hated living on the ranch but I hated more thinking of going to live with my father and learning his business. He was not an easy person to know or be with like uncle Gavin. I liked uncle Gavin and aunt Moria but they talked all the time about the ranch, the cattle and the horses.

I was not at all surprised to find my father with a beautiful woman at the opera, but the kid I hated on sight. It should have been my family sitting there for an evening out. From that time on I began to scheme and plan on how to get even with my father. I had secrets and was suspicious of everyone and when I realized someone had made a fool of me I could reap revenge on that person relentlessly. My enemies told stories and lies but I always got even. My down fall was my temper and I never missed a chance to disparage my enemies. I spent a great deal of time doing skullduggery in an attempt to enhance my wellbeing. All this I learned at an early age.

I wanted to be a lawyer. When we saw my father and that woman in San Francisco I knew I would never go live with him. I would run off to sea first. When I saw my father at dinner with that woman and kid I began to really hate him.

Mother changed, she was preoccupied all the time and she was angry almost all the time unless she was crying. I wished I was old enough to leave home and live by myself.

I did not have the dark good looks of my brother Mark nor his build. I dwelled on the fact that I was shorter in stature and was not as strong as Mark. He had worked on the ranch and become whitleather tough. I did however have the knack of talking to anyone. Where he was the silent type I was out going and would always be in the center of a gathering. I seemed to always find myself surrounded by pretty girls while Mark was a loner.

◆

15

MARK

It was sometime later when my father came to the ranch to demand that Stephen and I return to San Francisco with him so that we might go into his business with him. I was called into his ranch office. He began by saying "you are going to come into the business with me." He had no interest in my thoughts or what I wanted to do the rest of my life.

At fifteen I had grown to be almost as tall as my father. I had my mother's dark hair that I kept cut rather short because it was curly and I did not want the other cowboys to nick name me 'Curley.' Working with my uncle Gavin I had grown very strong. I still preferred the quiet of working with him and our foreman Tater Fletcher to the rowdy cowboys and the bunk house revelry. I guess I was considered a serious person but I thought a lot about the ranch and kept most of those thoughts to myself.

On one of his rare visits to the ranch I was called into his office. "Prepare yourself to come to San Francisco when school is out. You will take some business classes then begin work with me. That is all. You may go," said Gideon angrily dismissing his eldest son. I got sick to my stomach thinking about maybe having to go live in town. I did not know if my father had made an idle threat but just the idea of leaving the ranch was a sickening thought.

"Father I do not want to go into business I want to stay on the ranch and someday manage the Broken Anchor..."

"Absolutely not, my sons are not going to be just cowboys, it is out of the question. You will become business men and someday take over my business enterprise."

"No I will not leave the ranch!" I spoke in anger but I meant every word. I would never leave the ranch or these mountains.

"You will do as I say or there will be no ranch for you to manage!" My father was fierce when he became angry.

I went to tell my mother that I would hire on with one of the other ranches before I would go back to San Francisco. She told me not to do anything until she had a chance to talk to my father. Later mother took Stephen, Philip and myself to San Francisco to plead with father to allow us our choice of life's work. That never happened, she did not get the opportunity to talk to him.

Now my days were filled with fear of having to leave the ranch and life I loved so much. Our life settled back into the old routine after my father returned to San Francisco but his threat was never far from my thoughts. Often at night I saddled my favorite horse and rode in the valley toward the mountains trying to figure out in my mind the fighting between my parents. After father left life on the ranch continued as before but there was a tension in the air as though waiting for something to happen, it seemed as though there was a thunder storm building up.

———◆———

The thoughts were never far from my mind that I might have to leave the Broken Anchor. Our life continued to be involved in the community social life that was centered on the school where there were picnics, holiday social gatherings in the summer, even wedding receptions.

The school was located about five miles from the ranch house. Our teacher lived in a little house next door to the school house on one side and an elderly couple that were care takers lived in a house on the other. This was my last year to go to school. Next year Stephen would drive the buckboard for himself, Philip, Arabella and Lorelie and the ranch kids if there wasn't a ranch hand to drive. We always had a wagon load of kids from the ranch that went to school. It was aunt Moria who demanded the ranch children go to school at least through the eighth grade. I liked it when Cricket drove, he knew almost as much about ranching as Tater

Fletcher. I wanted to be a rancher like Uncle Gavin and he said it was important to learn all I could in school. I had stayed in school until the teacher said she could not teach me anything else. I had a knack for numbers that Uncle Gavin and I sparred with all the time.

Then we had the explosive event after the opera.

When we left San Francisco I knew our lives would never be the same. I had never seen my mother so angry. She became a cold non communicative person. She never seemed to hear or comprehend when we talked to her.

As time passed mother became even more distant, cold and short tempered. She ate little and slept what seemed to me not at all. We would find her pacing in the hall between our part of the house and uncle Gavin and aunt Moria's living quarters. Then she began walking to the lake late at night. I was afraid she would be killed by the mountain lions that roam the ranch but she appeared not to hear anything we had to say.

My father did not come to the ranch again for a long time but I never knew where he was.

———◆———

When we arrived back at the ranch from San Francisco Mother went straight away to her rooms. All the way home she read and re-read the papers. She constantly went over the papers the lawyer had given her. The next morning I ran to the barn to check on my horse. Stephen followed. It soon became apparent to Gavin that Mark had something on his mind, and when Stephen returned to the house Mark asked Gavin if he could talk to him.

Mother took her meals in her room. She had little time for her children. She was on a mission and she would let nothing or no one stop her. She could think of nothing but revenge for the humiliation she had suffered by Gideon and his Mexican woman. Mother now refused to acknowledge the woman was Spanish.

Gavin had ridden in from several days on the north range and was tired as he led Mark to one of the large cottonwood trees located farthest from the house. Mark watched the only man he really loved and trusted walk ahead of him to the trees where he and his uncle Gavin had spent many hours talking, where he learned of nature, cattle, ropes, horses, all the things that a rancher needed to know. Gavin wore chaps and a well-worn buckskin vest with deep pockets that held several Winchester rifle shells. A dark blue bandana fell in the shape of a triangle from his thick neck. When they were seated the events of the past few days fairly spewed from Mark. When he finally completed his story he sat slumped shouldered with his chin resting on his chest, trying hard to hide the tears from his uncle.

The pain in Mark's voice seemed to come from a much older person than the fifteen year old. Gavin chose his words carefully, "Mark your father has always had an eye for the ladies even when he was a young man he was very popular with women. Your mother has a volatile temper and the two of them are like mixing oil and water. I believe they love you children more than anything on earth and their quarrels do not have anything to do with how or why they fight, if it wasn't one thing it would be another. And nothing you did caused them to fight, or for your Da to be unfaithful. Your job in life is to become the best kind of man you can be. I believe your Da is wrong, his family should come first and I will talk to Isobel about your learning the ranching business and management if that is what you want. You are already a more than fair drover and a very good horse wrangler." As Gavin talked his Scottish brogue became more pronounced. He was angry at the two people who made their child so unhappy and afraid. Their selfishness was unforgiveable.

Mark had one more question. "Uncle when we were standing at the table where my father sat with that woman and the red headed boy some people at the nearby table said, "that's his other family. Can he have two families and would they ever try to take the ranch away from us?"

"No Mark he cannot legally have two families and unless Gideon knows something I don't they would not have a claim to the ranch. As long as I am alive it will not happen. Mark, Tater wanted a volunteer to ride out and check the cattle and range at Gotome Canyon. I'll be gone a couple of days and we will work on this when I come back."

"Uncle Gavin could I come… could I go with you, I need to think."

"That would suit me fine. As you go to the house to change clothes ask Anna to pack us some grub for a couple of days. I'll saddle the horses."

Mark rode silently for the first two or three hours but the closer they got to Gotome Canyon the more alert he became. He broke the silence by saying, "uncle Gavin this canyon is one of my favorite places. I would never want anyone else to own it. I think it is beautiful."

"Actually Mark only the first few miles of the canyon is ours the rest of the canyon is part of the open range. I don't know if the Marsh brothers used the canyon for grazing but our Highland cattle prefer the canyon to some of our range to the west. Mule Creek a branch of the Copper River, runs through the east end. I thought we would camp at the creek tonight and check the cattle tomorrow. It will be dark by the time we get through the canyon." Mark nodded his understanding as they kicked their horses into a long lope.

Later when they had made camp and finished eating their supper Gavin began to talk as they sat finishing the good Arbuckles coffee Anna had packed for them. Mark had questions that had been nagging him and he wanted to talk. Although he was in a place he loved he could not shake the fear of having to leave the ranch that never left him. "Uncle Gavin why haven't we I mean the Broken Anchor bought the canyon? I think it is the best place around."

"Mark, your Da and I own the Broken Anchor and as partners we have to agree as to what is best for the ranch. We just could not agree on the canyon. There were more important things to worry about so I never pushed him on that. It was more important to me to bring in better breeding stock of horses and cattle than where they grazed. Someday if you become manager of the ranch you might want to buy up this area of two or three thousand acres that includes the canyon."

"Yes... yes Uncle Gavin I will!" That night began the dream Mark dreamed each night and that was of riding and owning the canyon and managing the Broken Anchor.

As they rode out the next morning Mark was in a talkative mood and had more questions for Gavin. Just the thought that perhaps someday he would be manager of the ranch had lightened his thoughts.

"Uncle Gavin do you know why the canyon is called Gotome? What does it mean?"

"Gotome is a rough translation of a Paiute Indian name and it has to do with the stone pillar called an obelisk located high up on the top of the canyon rim about half way through the canyon. The Paiute lived here for as long as they have been in this area. The first American traders were the ones to name the canyon I don't think they could remember or pronounce the Indian name. The Indians tell the story that says the spring army campaign was led by Major Wm. F. Conrad at Big Thunder Mountain. Their quarry was the Indian tribe living in Gotome Canyon. Gotome was a loosely Americanized name of a fifteen mile canyon in the Big Thunder Mountains. Major Conrad considered this patrol to remove the Indians from the canyon a disciplinary action by his commander."

"The Indians were considered hostile because they had not come voluntarily to the reservation, but they also had little contact with the outside world. The cave pocked walls of the canyon rose to one hundred fifty feet in some places with the widest part of the canyon being five or six miles wide. The tribe was led by a venerable chief, Black Wolf, a fierce old man who held his people together with an iron hand."

"It was dawn when the army reached the stronghold and there was no give in Major Conrad, he believed this campaign would be his return to what he called civilization. He hated the west, the Indians and most of all the long rides that most of the time ended in the long ride back to Fort Ruby with nothing to show for it. What he wanted was a post in Washington where decisions were being made. He found the elusive Indian battles frustrating."

"Soldiers stationed at the top of the canyon were instructed to kill any Indians that attempted to escape. By the time the sun had risen high enough to reach the floor of the canyon Major Conrad was certain the whole tribe had been wiped out the village burned. Retreat had been called and the unit was returning back up the canyon. All in the village were dead all but five. Five young boys had gone fishing early before the sun had begun its climb over the distant mountain to the east. When the massacre began they hid along the river bank, when the firing stopped and the canyon became quiet they returned to their village only to find that all were dead." The oldest of the boys directed the others to gather anything they could use and they moved higher into the Big Thunder Mountains where the boys lived and hid out for several years.

The Indian story continues that not far from the village to the north of the canyon the leader of the wolf pack a huge grey male had left the den when the shooting began, and now he sat at the rim of the canyon and watched the scene below; the soldiers leaving, the dead Indians and the young boys that were quietly returning to their village. As the story goes for an unknown reason he did not attack, instead he returned to his den."

"For the next several years the offspring of the big grey wolf and the Indian boys lived north of the Gotome Canyon in a standoff. The wolf allowed the boys to take portions of his kill of deer, sheep and goats. The boys did not attempt to locate the wolf den nor to harm him. They watched as the large male and his mate brought their pups to the area where the boys lived. Then one day the boys were joined by more Paiute that were displaced. There must be twenty five or thirty Indians that lived there now. Black Wolf died in the raid and the leader became Broken Thumb. I met him, several times in fact when I first came out here. He was an honorable man. The chief now is Tall Bear, he is a famous tracker the Army has asked for his help many times. They make contact through the Sheriff at Red Lodge. I have never before told anyone about the Indians that live here. If the word got out they would be forced to go to a reservation. I believe they butcher a cow now and then but also they keep the wolves and the mountain lions out of the canyon, so I think it is a fair trade off."

Mark rode in silence thinking of all that his uncle told him and of the future of the ranch and of his future. It would depend on what his parents did.

———————◆———————

16

PHILIP

When I saw that kid having dinner with my father I wanted to punch him in the nose! I don't know everything that happened but our mother became angry and nothing was the same ever again.

By now I didn't mind living at the ranch. There were other kids. I got almost everything I wanted if I cried or nagged mother. I did not like my brothers Mark and Stephen or my sisters. I wished I was an only child.

I was an enigma, a total puzzlement to my parents. There were times I would find them staring at me as if they had never seen me before. I had a habit of woolgathering and would forget what I was told to do or where I should be going. I knew I could take what I wanted from the other children on the ranch by threats of their father losing his job. I was pretty safe since none of them dared tell on me. I was condescending to almost all the workers. Had I been discovered I would have gotten absolution from mother. It seemed in her eyes I could do no wrong. Mark accused me of skullduggery but he could find no one to witness against me.

We got a baby sister in the fall after we got to the ranch. Now I didn't have to be the baby and two years later there was another baby girl. I disliked her on sight she was my opposite, happy laughing, content to be alone. Mark still called me the baby. I hated him and the name.

Steven and I were at a stalemate, and as we grew we each disliked the other even more.

17

GAVIN

Gideon was gone from the ranch almost all the time now. He and I each had independent investments and holdings before the ranch. Moria's parents had given her a percentage of her families shipping business and since I had not taken a wage all the years I was at sea my wife and I were joint owners in a large shipping company.

Once we reached the ranch Moria and I both fell in love with the wild range and beautiful mountains. We often rode into the mountains for a few days to camp. More often than not Mark went with us. His love of the ranch was equal to ours. He had a real honest feeling for the land and animals and he learned how to work and manage the ranch from the ranch foreman Tater Fletcher. Then the day came when Gideon came to the ranch to make demands of Isobel concerning their sons.

I was to learn much later that Gideon was demanding his two older sons come to San Francisco to train to become business men in his company. Isobel would have none of it, she left her two daughters in Moria's care and took the three boys to San Francisco to persuade Gideon to allow them to do what they desired. Mark was desperate to go into ranching while Stephan wanted to become apprenticed to a lawyer. Philip had not decided what he wanted but then he was too young to be certain and had time enough to decide. As I understand it Isobel found the house in San Francisco just as it was left after Da's funeral a few years after we went out to the ranch. Gideon was not living there, as we all believed he did.

While in San Francisco she discovered Gideon, his mistress and their son at the Pacific Palace. Realizing she had been betrayed once again she began a plan of revenge that not only tore her family apart but nearly cost us the ranch when Gideon cut off all funds to the ranch operation even my share. At this time he had almost total control of the ranch finances.

Moria suggested she and I borrow against our shipping enterprise to pay riders wages and ranch supplies until Gideon was held responsible. I believed that once he realized he could not make Isobel come around to his way by withholding money from the ranch and with his run in with Mark that did not go well he would release the ranch funds. Mark threatened to take Gideon's management of the ranch away from him and with our shares and Isobel's help he could have done that. What Gideon had not counted on was Mark and Isobel had bought up some of the border ranches and their percentage in the ranch had raised significantly.

Gideon lost his family in the Utah territory. He was out numbered because of his outrageous behavior with his family.

————◆————

18

ISOBEL

Three months after his discovery in San Francisco Gideon arrived at the ranch, going immediately to the ranch office he summoned me. Upon entering the office I knew my efforts had been successful. Gideon was livid. "How could you be so stupid as to close accounts that were highly profitable and divert funds into such inconsequential accounts?"

I had held my breath until my chest hurt, calming down I let my breath out quietly. I could not allow myself to lose control. The dummy accounts were successful and he still knew nothing of the large general account, the account that would undermine his business. I remained silent as he paced back and forth across the office.

"This ignorant move of yours will cost us millions of dollars, Gideon continued to rave."

Finally I could stay silent no longer, "Do you really think I am so stupid as to continue to finance your peccadillo with that Mexican whore?" I said as controlled as possible. "You did not have my son's interest when you refused to allow them to choose their own path in life. Well now you can go back to your harlot I do not care any longer. I intend to see that Mark and Stephen do what they want to make their way in life. Mark will continue to learn ranching from Gavin, yes the sailor Gavin, the man you believed inferior to you because he chose the sea instead of business and politics. Well did you know Gavin and Moria are silent owners in one of the largest shipping companies on the west coast? All the years Gavin was at sea he never took a wage, he put his money back in the shipping company, I asked smugly." I finally knew something he did not know.

"He has spent his time since coming here learning the ranching business from his foreman and his neighbors. The holdings of the ranch has increased substantially through his careful planning with the cattle, horses and land, you didn't know that did you? No, you were too busy romancing that Mexican and what has it gotten you besides a philandering reputation? Even the people you once worked with doubt you, they are skeptical of your ability. This conversation is over! Over!" I shouted at him! My anger finally spilling forth in a venomous action, exiting the room and slamming the heavy oak door. I knew Gideon was being obstinate when refusing to change his course of action despite the ruinous outcome, and that was what I now lived for. I wanted to hurt him like he had hurt me and I could do it by taking away some of his important business accounts by ruining his reputation as a business man.

19

GIDEON

Within a few weeks I realized Isobel's goal was to ruin me and the business name of Gideon MacDougall. Accounts in her name, business ventures she was financing, business associates and accessibility were all closed to me. I went out to the ranch to attempt to persuade her to put back into the family name the accounts. She was beyond reason. Without her money I was facing complete ruin.

I returned to San Francisco and began work to rebuild my reputation and my business. It was like starting over, it would take time and hard work. Some of my most prosperous accounts would never be recovered.

With the latest events any thought of my sons going into business with me was over. I had alienated my family. Perhaps Philip could be persuaded to come with me, but not if Isobel had any say in the matter.

As I contacted old and new clients I realized just how well Isobel had planned my downfall. She and her lawyer had done their work very well. I found many doors closed to me where once I had been given access. Even old friends shunned me and for a time I did not know why. But soon everyone knew of our quarrel she made certain of that. Slowly I began to regain the ground I had lost. I began to obtain new clients and contracts. One of the most lucrative was the Walcott Mining Enterprise. I also had an appointment with Mountain Coastal Railroad. With these two contracts alone I was on my way to recovery.

Through rumors and business associates I learned that Isobel was becoming a very wealthy woman. She remained at the ranch and no one in San Francisco had seen her since the opera incident.

I did not look forward to any meetings with my wife. If only she would agree to a divorce we could end the hostilities and go on with our lives. I was certain she would not agree at least not now, her main goal was to ruin me and she would accomplish this or die trying.

———◆———

20

THE APPALOOSA

Standing at the window on their side of the house Moria was thinking of the time she had spent at the ranch. The days and weeks turned into months and months were becoming years. Isobel and I continued to be fast friends and rode often to our favorite lake in the foothills of the Medera Mountains, where there was a beautiful lake at the end of the waterfall. The lake where the wild horse herd drank was of a rare pristine beauty. It was a most fascinating place.

The only sadness on the part of mine and Gavin's horizon was the fact we had no children. I was desperate to have babies. I enjoyed Isobel's children and spent as much time as I could with them. I day dreamed of how I would write to my parents telling them they were going to be grandparents.

◆

The big cat was returning to her den from her tree where she marked her territory. She had stretched even higher as she left claw marks on fresh bark. Low growls emanated from deep in her chest when she first saw the riders. Her yellow eyes glowed ominously, she hated the humans.

The generations of mountain lions continued and the latest matriarch watched the two women riders invade her territory again, they came often to the lake. The lion always became agitated when humans came into her territory or close to her den. She had been shot when she ventured too close to the ranch and carried that bullet in her hind leg. Like her ancestors before her she was an enormously large cat and she still patrolled what she perceived to be her territory and that included the ranch valley. Often at night those at the ranch could hear her screams high on the mountain. At those times the night guard was more alert. The horses in the corrals became restless and gathered closer to the ranch for security.

The ranch hands called her the ghost cat. Every one of them at one time or another had her in their gun sights and she seemed to melt into the rocks, timber or even into the side of the mountain. Some of the men believed the Indian stories that had been told for years, this line of cats were shape shifters, animals that could change into another thing or being. A shape shifter was believed to be a creature of mythology, a wide belief of several cultures to be witchcraft. Shape shifters or as the Native Americans referred to them as Skin Walkers because it was believed they literally took over the skin of an animal and became as that animal with all its cunning and powers by magic. The term shape shifter struck fear into the hearts of the southwestern tribes. This cat was extremely elusive and intelligent.

Today the matriarch who had given her leadership to her daughter could not get comfortable the bullet in her leg hurt more than usual, it had become difficult for her to bring down large game animals. She could no longer run as fast or as far nor leap as high as she once did. Her tawny eyes flashed with irritation as she too watched the riders, a low menacing growl came from deep in her throat. She stalked the riders keeping inside the tree line on the side of the mountain until she came to a split in the rock and a century's old pile up of scree blocked her way. She climbed up the mountain until she could go around the loose scree and continue to follow the women. Silently the big cat watched as the women tied their horses and went to sit beside the lake. The cat's long tail whipped back and forth as she watched the women, the yellow eyes never leaving their movements.

---◆---

The women sat in a favorite spot near the lake on a fallen log. They were waiting for the wild horse herd to come to water. One of the riders told Gavin the herd was on its way north. Both women were sitting quiet. Isobel worrying about the future of her sons. Moria thinking of things in general, wondering why she has not had children, enjoying the wild life and the day. The women sat quietly each in their own thoughts. Isobel worrying how to get Gideon to change his mind and allow the boys to choose their own future. Perhaps if she could talk Gavin into talking to him in behalf of her sons he would change his mind. However Gavin was always reluctant to interfere in their family problems. So worried was she that she was scarcely aware of her surroundings.

Moria loved this spot on the ranch. It was somewhat isolated but always teeming with wild life. Deer had come to drink on the other side of the lake that was fed by a small waterfall on their left from the mountains. Watching closely she saw birds come to the muddy shore then fly off, always in the same direction. They were swallows building mud nests somewhere.

Watching closely she saw bees come to the water on this side of the lake in front of her. Careful not to cause them to change their route she watched as they returned time and again to an old dead tree a few hundred feet from where they sat. She realized they were honey bees and the tree was probably full of honey. She made a mental note to tell Beekeeper of her find. Some of the folks on the ranch preferred honey to sugar and a find this large if she was right could yield several quarts of honey.

When he came to the ranch looking for work he told Gavin he was excommunicated from the Mormon Church. He told Gavin why to which Gavin replied that was not the affair of the ranch. He would be judged by his work and the treatment towards others. Period.

With that said Gavin assigned two boys to help him set up hives in the alfalfa fields and to prepare a room for the harvest of the honey at the edge of the alfalfa field. No one knew what the little one room shack had been used for, it had a hard packed dirt floor and was weather tight. Tater said it was there when he was a boy. The boys expressed concern that they were going to work for a crotchety old man, however this being their first paying job they decided to try. What they discovered was a very humble placid man who could work among the bees and not get stung. He went out of his way to avoid any type of fracas. Gavin found him to be astute when judging people. He was a friend of Moria who used copious amounts of honey in baking. She spoke highly of his work and demeanor.

Beekeeper was the only name he had ever used. Gavin suspected there was a longer story but as he and Tater agreed more than a few people who moved from one place to another used their nick names or a name that designated their work. And with that the man came to work at the Broken Anchor keeping the ranch in honey. A small building near the field suited Beekeeper well to harvest the honey. He could almost always be found working with or near the bees.

A large new shinny laundry tub sat on a table with a frame of heavy woven wire that held the honey combs above and the honey ran into the tub. The honey was then strained a couple of times before being poured into quart jars and stored in a cave in back of the big house. With the fruit jams the women prepared in summer and the honey there was always a wide choice for hot biscuits, pancakes or light bread. The honey comb beeswax when prepared was in demand for use on the ranch. The women made candles from the wax and it was used to water proof saddles and all leather.

Suddenly a small herd of horses broke into the clearing. The big grey stallion that led the herd veered away to the right of where the women sat. Both women ran to their horses that had begun to call and pull at their leads. The stallion stopped came back several yards and began calling to the two mares tied to trees. The women calmed their horses and waited for the herd to move on. Moria watched fascinated as the horses lined up along the bank of the lake to drink. She recognized four of the Broken Anchor ranch mares. This was one of two stallions that stole mares from the surrounding ranches. While drinking the stallion showed inbred altruistic traits that kept him on alert. He was constantly watching the surrounding lake, his mares, and deer never letting his guard down. He led the herd around the back side of the lake and disappeared into the mountains. One horse that caught her attention was a strangely colored horse. She had never seen coloring like it. The horse was medium height compared to the other young horses. The front half of the horse was a red brown color, a chocolate color, while the back end of the horse was white splashed and spotted. The horse was stocky build and extremely alert. From where she was she could not tell if the horse was a mare or stallion but it was young. Moria could hardly wait to tell Gavin of the horse she had seen.

Calling to Isobel Moria told her she recognized the mares. The women hurried back to the ranch to report to Gavin and Mark that the wild horse herd had returned to the valley. As the two women were returning to the ranch house Moria could not get the chocolate colored horse out of her mind. She had no idea what breed of horse she had seen but she knew it was special. A few miles from the house Moria said to Isobel, "I am going to ride towards the north east range to find Gavin and tell him of the strange horse we saw."

"Moria I am so tired I will return to the ranch. Be careful don't ride alone for too far and I'll see you later."

Moria waved goodbye and turned her horse to the north east. She found the men working about five miles from the ranch road. Gavin and Tater Fletcher were cleaning out a water hole and were happy for the work interruption. However Gavin was concerned that she was riding alone. "Moria is everything alright at the house? Why are you riding alone?"

"Isobel and I rode up in the Madera's this morning and a wild horse herd came through. Gavin I couldn't wait to tell you of the horses. Some of the mares from the ranch are with them." At this news Tater stopped digging. "Boss we might get our mares back and pick up a few others. There's usually a few good horses in the wild herd."

"There was a strange horse in the herd, a young horse with them."

"What do you mean strange" asked Gavin?

"It was a strong stocky looking horse, young with several other young horses that trailed the main herd, but it was the coloring that was so strange. The front, oh I'd say two-thirds of the horse was reddish brown like chocolate candy but its lower back and hips were white splotched or dappled."

Tater dropped his shovel and ran to where the couple sat on the ground. "Moria are you saying there is an Appaloosa horse in the herd? He asked excitedly."

"I don't know what an Appaloosa is but this one horse was colored different than any horse I ever saw."

"Moria from your description I think it's an Appaloosa horse, an

Indian tribe up in the Montana territory bred the horses for speed, endurance and color. The Indian tribe was the Nez Pierce and the army tried to destroy these horses when they drove the Indians to the reservation. Chief Joseph took some of his people and tried to get to Canada. This horse you saw has to be from a survivor of the slaughter or from some that got missed. The Nez Pierce were careful with their breeding stock and they didn't trade horses, preferring to raise their own. Some could have been stolen by other tribes."

"Tater are you saying this horse Moria saw is special?"

"Yes I believe it is."

"Things are slow at the ranch right now let's head for home and get things ready for a wild horse round up. I'll send one of the men to see if he can tell us where the horses are. I would sure like to get our mares back."

Reaching the ranch Tater stopped one of the ranch children and asked if he knew where Beekeeper was. The child replied that he was in the honey shack. Knocking on the door as he stepped into the room Tater found Beekeeper straining honey from one of the many hives he kept in the alfalfa hay fields.

"Beekeeper Mrs. MacDougall thinks there is a honey tree over at Wild Horse Falls. The two MacDougall ladies were there this morning and she watched bees going to water. Take a couple of the teenage boys and any rider that is not busy and check the tree out. She said the honey tree is on the west side of the lake, she said it stands alone."

Beekeeper was excited to think he had another source of honey and perhaps he could lure the bees into his newly made hive. He gathered large spoons, a clean tub, a hand saw and a hatchet and an ax and headed for his wagon. He told a couple of the teenagers to get the two man saw from the tool room. Tater had sent a couple of the twelve year olds and one of the cowboys that had a sprained ankle to help gather the honey.

Beekeeper soon spotted the tree and Moria was right it was a honey tree. With the help of the boys they cut the tree down and Beekeeper smoked the bees out and into a new hive. The hive full of bees was covered to darken the hive as the men set to work harvesting the honey.

One of the boys spotted two small bear cubs at the edge of the tree line. The cowboy told all of them to watch closely as the mother might return. The men cut the tree open and scooped the honey into the tub. When the honey was harvested the men loaded the wagon to return to the ranch. One of the boys wanted to capture a cub and take it home. Beekeeper listened for a while before saying "you whippersnappers have had no truck with bear cubs or their mama. You would find your hands full with the cub alone and if that mama bear is within distance of those cubs she will most certainly come after them." With that bit of advice he turned his attention back to the drive home with their loot. The boys looked longingly at the cubs. They drove back to the trail and stopped, watching to see what the cubs did. It only took a few minutes for the cubs to approach the tree. Back on the trail one of the boys spotted the mother bear approaching from the side of the mountain going towards the cubs.

When they reached the house Beekeeper dismissed his helpers after they unloaded the wagon and put the horse out to pasture. He took a jar of the honey he had left earlier to strain to the house. Moria was in the kitchen preparing supper, she and Anna were glad to get the jar of sweet golden honey promising johnnycakes for breakfast.

———◆———

Two days later the scout returned with word that the wild horses were making their way back south. Gavin took Tater, Mark and seven men who would act as relay riders. Once the herd was started toward the canyon in the foothills of the Madera Mountains, where south of the lake there was a blind canyon that could be closed off once the herd was driven into it. The men would use the same prey tactics that large cats and wolves used to run prey to ground. They would ride the herd by relay. It would tire the wild horses out but the relay riders could keep the herd on course to the canyon. The wild horses seldom ventured from the safety of the mountains and the canyon was out on the plains. The sides of the canyon was too steep for the horses to climb out. It was a natural trap that had a lake at one end and grazing for a fairly large number of horses.

For the next several days the riders flanked the herd but at a distance so not to spook them. Finally they headed for the lake and the riders closed in driving the herd hard towards the blind canyon. Too late the herd turned into the canyon and the brush covered opening was closed. The stallion that led the herd screamed and rushed the gates but to no avail. For two days the stallion raged until worn out he began to settle down standing off to one side hipshot with his head down. No one believed all the fight was gone but at least for the time being he settled down. The men rode the top of the canyon rim getting the horses used to the riders.

The young stallions kept to themselves at the far end of the canyon. Gavin and Tater stopped above the young horses. There in the middle of the herd was the horse Moria told them about. Gavin could see that Tater was excited by the young horse and said, "Tater I think that chocolate horse has his eye on you, I'll bet he is planning on making you work for him."

"He's a beauty boss, he'll be some horse when he comes around."

"You have been talking about starting your own herd over on the place your dad started had you thought about your horses?"

"Oh yes, I think there is a future in the mustangs and the spotted or painted horses."

"Tell you what, let's get started riding closer to the herd so we can get to the point where we can ride through the herd and see if any other ranches has horses in there. We will get our mares back along with a few mustangs and that chocolate horse and the other paint horses are yours. Looks like there are eight or ten. We can keep them penned here after we separate the horses. We will turn the ones we don't want loose and return the other horses to their owners. I saw at least three of Johnson's mares and a Baker mare with the spyglass. Once we get all those mares out and turn the others out you can start to gentle your horses."

Tater could not believe his ears. Gavin was giving him a chance to start his own herd, and with a magnificent animal like the Appaloosa.

As the grazing in the canyon diminished Gavin had hay brought to the horses.

A few days later Moria, Isobel and Philip rode out to the canyon where the men had separated the herd. They had returned the horses to the ranch owners and Philip had been at the Johnson ranch when Mark and Tater had returned their horses to them. Word had gotten around about the chocolate horse and Philip wanted to see it for himself.

As they rode up to the canyon corral gates Gavin came to meet them. "You are just in time to watch Tater ride his stallion. That appaloosa horse is gonna take some tamein' but Tater says he will be worth it." For the next thirty minutes Tater and the appaloosa tested one another until finding a give attitude with the horse Tater quit for the day and turned the horse loose.

Watching the horse return to the herd Philip expressed his appreciation for the horse saying to Gavin, "When Tater gets that horse broke I want him."

"That's not possible" said Gavin, that horse and all the paint or pinto horses belong to Tater!"

"Are you crazy they were caught on our land so they belong to us not one of the cowboys," answered an angry Philip, his dark eyes flashing hatred at Tater and Gavin.

"The horses belong to Tater because I gave them to him, and he is not just a cowboy, we could never have built this ranch into what it has become had it not been for Tater. He wants to start his own place and these horses will give him a start. If he does as well for himself as he has for us he will have a good ranch in no time. He will turn over more responsibility to Mark soon and spend more time at his own place, helping us when we need him."

"But I want that strangely marked horse," said Philip pouting.

"Sorry Philip but you will have to choose another from the herd and you will have to help train the horse not just ride it."

"Mother," wailed Philip.

Moria was embarrassed at the way Philip was acting, like a petulant child, not even his sisters when they were babies had ever wailed or acted like he was doing now.

Without looking at Isobel Gavin said angrily "The matter is closed I have given my word and that's settled."

Philip mounted his horse and jerking on the reins that made Moria grind her teeth, dug spurs into his horse and raced towards the Johnson ranch to the west.

Moria could have sworn Philip was present when she told Isobel of Gavin giving the Appaloosa and the paint horses to Tater. Philip had always been selfish but this was a new low even for him.

As the sun began to slide down behind the mountains to the west the two women returned to the ranch house.

———◆———

Silently the big cat watched her prey leaving the valley going quickly back the direction they had come. She continued to watch the horses as they milled around. As the horse herd continued to nervously circle the enclosed corral the big cat returned to her den and her hungry cubs. She would have to wait patiently for another opportunity. She would wait until the horses were alone and there were no guards riding the rim of the canyon. She would have a long wait. Tater posted a night rider above the canyon just to be certain the big cat did not make a meal of one of his horses.

◆

A few days later the men had turned the unwanted horses back into the mountains. There were several mares with foals that showed signs of making good ranch horses when they were old enough to break. The old stallion had been taken by one of the ranches. Most of the ranches looked to the wild herd to replace their ranch horses. Moria thought to herself she would watch the herd. Gavin and Mark believed the new herd stallion would be a big line back dun stallion that had begun to challenge the previous leader.

◆

21

YOUNG CALEB G. MARSH

Young Caleb G. Marsh sat at the table in the tumble down line shack on the Marsh Double M ranch, nursing a hangover. Although referred to as young Caleb he was only a couple of years younger than Gideon MacDougall. He had spent the last few days at Fort Halleck. Sometimes he thought he had gambling fever as bad as his dad old Caleb and his luck was just as elusive. He had driven some twenty head of cattle to the fort to sell. Demanding top dollar for poor grade cattle had proved his undoing. He had to settle for much less and he needed the money to pay off the loan he had at the bank at Elko. He had hoped the cattle would pay off the loan and have enough left that he could gamble a little, maybe even make enough to do some fixing up around the place.

The night after the sale of the cattle found young Caleb at the gambling table. By the time the game was over he had lost every penny he had sold the cattle for. He was on the way home and had stayed the night in the old line shack sick with a drunken hangover. He could not recall the last few days. He had gotten into a fight and spent one night in jail. He woke up a day later behind the livery barn. He could not remember why he went to the livery in the late hours. The stable owner said he was trying to leave without paying his bill. He did not remember any of it.

In desperation the homeless young woman, young Caleb's mother, had married old Caleb Marsh after knowing him only a few weeks. When they reached the ranch she realized she had made a very bad bargain in this marriage. She had heard one of the other girls at the saloon where she worked refer to Caleb as Shanty Irish, a term she had never heard before. One of the girls tried to explain to her the difference between Shanty Irish and Curtain Irish the description made her ill. Caleb was definitely Shanty Irish with his filthy, dirty habits, and no manners. Then she realized she was with child and had no place to go. The Marsh brothers were piggish Neanderthals, crude and primitive. Their houses were no more than tumble down shacks. Doors hung on broken leather hinges. Windows were covered with oiled paper where the glass had been broken and never replaced. Boards on the steps were broken or missing.

Inside the kitchen dirty dishes stacked in the area that passed for a sink, and on the floor crawling with flies and tiny white things that she was not going to look at too closely. A half dozen mice scurried away. A small bowl of honey on the table had flies stuck in it or dead layering the top.

Two children later Caleb gambled away the ranch and they moved in with the older brother Daniel, now she had two filthy men to live with. Old Daniels home was even worse than Caleb's if possible, she packed up and left. Even alone with two children she didn't think things could be as bad as her life on the ranch.

Young Caleb had been five years old when his father gambled and lost his half of the ranch with all the thousands of acres and the family had to move across the Copper River to live with his uncle Daniel Marsh. His mother overworked and disgusted had taken him and his sister to Denver Colorado and never returned.

By the time Caleb G. was thirteen his mother could no longer handle him and sent him back to the ranch to live with his uncle Daniel. His father had become a hopeless drunk besides being a consummate gambler. Young Caleb had felt nothing when his father's body had been returned to the ranch after being killed during a gambling fight. His uncle Daniel had never married so naturally when old Daniel passed away the ranch was left to him. The ranch had not prospered as well as he had planned. Had his father not been so foolish he would be the owner of a ranch of more than twenty thousand acres. At the time of his father's death Caleb was well aware of old Hamish sons and how well their ranch was doing however the men from the two ranches avoided one another.

Always alone Caleb G. like his father and uncle frequented the gambling tables the MacDougall's did not. Gideon spent his time in San Francisco, Gavin worked the ranch. Old Daniel had continued to run cattle on the south side of the Copper River on the MacDougall land. Gavin and Mark MacDougall had been with Tater Fletcher the day they came to the Double M ranch to tell him to move his herd back across the river. It had angered old Daniel that the MacDougall's had prospered and he passed that anger on to young Caleb. Daniel Marsh had seen the house old Hamish had started to build and it made his home look like the hovel it was. He gambled hoping to make enough money to build a new house. He knew no woman would live with him in his present home. He needed a woman to help work the ranch, to help fix up the cabin. The cabin was old, falling down, it consisted of three rooms. He always intended to build on at least two more rooms but just didn't seem to have the time.

Over the years Caleb G. had skirted the Madera Mountains and rode across the Broken Anchor to spy on the MacDougall ranch house they called the Heritage. He had spent several days at a time watching the ranch from high on the mountain. When the two brothers came there with their families they had brought in a different breed of cattle. The red, long haired Scottish Highland cattle had spread out across the range mixing with the other cattle. The next year's calf crop had appeared to be mostly from the red highland bulls. Gavin MacDougall had brought in some blooded horses from the east and when crossed with the mustangs had gotten a good ranch horse.

Old Caleb and Daniel had always relied on their riders to catch the mustangs but they had never practiced selective breeding to build their herd. Some men had all the luck. They believed they were as smart as Gavin MacDougall, it looked like the Broken Anchor was just plain lucky. He had also seen the wild horse herd and intended to drive them across the Copper River onto his ranch. He had seen the Broken Anchor mares and intended to catch them, rebrand them and add them to his herd after all the Broken Anchor had more horses than he had. That was the way of luck some had it all.

As he sat in the line shack he recalled to himself what he remembered had been talked about at Ft. Halleck and how some felt about the big ranches. There was open range to the north east of the Broken Anchor, he knew that it would be used by the MacDougall's to expand but what if someone beat them to it?

It had taken time but he had sent word along the immigrant trail of free land north of the Big Thunder Mountains. Then two families had settled, the Preston's and the McGill's. What he had not planned for was the fact the new comers were sheep men. Between the two families there were more than thirty-five hundred head of sheep. McGill had known of Basque herders that were looking for work and hired them. Within a short time more shepherds from the Basque region located between Spain and France had arrived. The ranch owner provided each shepherd bedding and cook gear, a packhorse and one or two black and white herding dogs. That was all it took for each herder to herd from five hundred to a thousand or more sheep. A rider from the ranch took supplies to the shepherd about every two weeks. The sheep ranches prospered then some of the cattle ranchers got word of the sheep. Those ranchers were ready to do something about the sheep men. The majority of the cattlemen believed there was no room for sheep in cattle country. There were enough hot heads that objected to sheep to cause trouble.

Gavin and Mark had driven into Red Lodge for supplies and stopped to eat at the Big Dipper Café. As they entered they saw several of their neighbors seated at a table in the corner. They spoke to the men but since the table appeared to be full Gavin and Mark sat down at the long table against the back wall. When they finished eating and the table had been cleared the five men from the corner table joined them. Tom Baker of the Half-Moon, Bill Johnston of the Bar J, Dave Tucker of the triple 888, Will Norton of the Box N, Bill Myers of the Slash M all sat down across from Gavin and Mark. Everyone ordered coffee and finally Johnston asked the question the other men had wanted to ask.

"MacDougall what are you gonna do about these sheep men that are here?"

"Bill I don't intend to do anything. To my knowledge there is not one sheep on our range and our men are very good at knowing what goes on at the Broken Anchor.

Johnson asked Gavin if he had heard that sheep men had settled northeast of the Broken Anchor. "Have you met the sheep men McGill and Preston? They are just north east of your place."

Patiently taking a sip of coffee and setting his cup down Gavin quietly answered both questions. "Yes I've met both men when they came to the ranch to buy herding dogs from Nacho. He is one of our riders that raises black and white herding dogs. When McGill and Preston first came here they bought a whole litter of weaned pups. Several families on the Broken Anchor has a dog and some of our twenty riders take the dogs with them on herding drives to move the cattle."

"They appeared to be solid men and I found nothing to dislike in either man. My Da came from the sheep herding country of Scotland and I don't intend to do anything about them if they stay on their side of the river."

Johnston rose from his chair, with both palms on the table, his voiced raised in anger "you don't know what you're saying, sheep ruin the grazing for cattle, and cattle won't drink where sheep drink!"

Gavin looked Johnston square in the eye when he spoke, "the grazing comes back with the next season, sheep in fact eat what cattle leave and as far as water is concerned our cattle don't even know that sheep drank upstream from them. We all settled here in this western end of the Utah Territory for the same reason to make a living and raise a family. We are now a state, the young state of Nevada and what we have to do is make the state grow and become productive. I think there is room for cattle and sheep," answered Gavin with finality.

"You are a fool MacDougall, the other big ranchers won't stand for sheep coming in here" replied an angry Johnston. As for me and mine I intend to fight to keep'em out. There's no place for sheep in Nevada!" With that said Johnson left the table and angrily stalked from the café. He could not understand Gavin's amicable acceptance of sheep men. Dave Tucker and Bill Meyer followed.

"Where does that leave the small ranchers asked Tom Baker of the Half Moon? You big ranchers got more water and grazing land than some of us have."

"That's a good question answered Gavin, if they have to share water with the big ranches then they will go along with the big ranches. They can't afford fighting over water. If they don't depend on any of the big ranches then it's hard to say, depends on how they feel about sheep." After talking to the ranchers at the café and Johnson getting mad and stomping out the men all finished their coffee and left the café. Johnson was standing across the street, his face red with anger.

Mark said "watch your back uncle," as he untied their team from the hitch rail.

"Always do Mark, now let's get these supplies back to the ranch."

On the ride home Mark said very little until they were about halfway back to the Broken Anchor, "Uncle Gavin will the sheep ruin the small ranchers? Do you think there will be some kind of war, Johnston was mad."

"Mark there is enough land here for everyone and the ones that want to work can make a good life. It appears the ones doing the most squawking are the ones that do the least amount of work. Remember when we delivered those horses to the Bar J last year? There wasn't a building, fence or corral on the place that didn't need fixing. When we got there at midafternoon Johnston was in the house, in which the door swung on broken leather hinges, and came out without his boots on. Most likely he had been asleep, yet he whines about not having what others have. His ranch was started by his Da and over the years Bill Johnston has had to sell off the land bit and parcel to feed the ranch. His men won't stay with him, most of them are drifters, they work long enough to get a grub stake and move on. He may talk a fight but I don't think he would want to work to keep it going. All this talk about sheep...I don't know. The triple Eight and the Box N are north of the Humboldt and I don't see Norton or Tucker joining with Johnston. I am afraid it's a wait and see deal."

———◆———

MORIA IS KILLED

Moria thought about the wild horses constantly. She loved to watch the interaction of the herd stallion and the young challengers. She could match the mares and their foals even the separate family members. Her love of the horses had her spending more time watching the herd. Another herd had moved into the mountains and the two herds were now joined and led by a large grey stallion. They no longer saw the line back dun. He had either been caught or run off by the new stallion. Gavin and Mark had been very interested to hear of the herd. The gray stallion could very well be the off spring of one of the stallions Gavin had brought to the ranch. He had traits that would indicate the stallions sire. After the round up Gavin would send the men out to locate the herd. In the meantime all the ranch hands were to keep a lookout to determine how often the herd went through the valley in the Madera Mountains. Gavin and Mark had discussed capturing more of the herd. Not only would they get their mares back, as the wild stallions were constantly stealing ranch mares, Moria had described several other horses that would be worth catching. The Army was coming to the ranch often to see if the Broken Anchor had any horses for sale. The Army was in desperate need of good broke horses and the Broken Anchor had some of the best wranglers.

After her morning chores were finished Moria went across the great hall to inquire if Isobel wanted to ride out to the lake. "I can't this morning replied Isobel, Lorelei is sick again. She has a fever and I think her throat is sore or she has an earache, this poor child is so sick. One of the things I dislike about living at the ranch is there is no quick availability to a doctor. I have sent one of the cowboys to Red Lodge but Dr. Carter is getting too old to travel far. I pray he will come today. Her fever can get so high. I get so scared when my children are ill."

"Is there anything I can do? I don't know much about sick children but I could do chores or entertain Arabella."

"Juanita took Arabella over to her house to play with her children. I almost wish that Gideon was here but I don't know why. He never seems to be around when we need him and he is useless when he is home said Isobel bitterly. He has other interests that keep him busy. Moria I am glad for your sake Gavin is not like Gideon." Lorelie began to cry again and Moria followed Isobel into the child's room. The child's face was flushed red with fever and Moria went to get another wet wash cloth. Passing the window she saw that Dr. Wilson Carter's rig had pulled up to the hitch rail out front. She hurried to answer the knock at the front door.

Moria led Dr. Carter to the nursery, where he went straight to the sick child, barely acknowledging Isobel. After examining Lorelie Dr. Carter gave Isobel instructions and a medication to help bring the fever down. Dr. Carter picked up his medical bag to leave when Moria invited him to come to the kitchen for a cup of coffee and pie. The doctor looked tired and accepted the offer gratefully. After seeing the doctor to the door Moria was feeling helpless as she returned to the room to stay with Isobel. Sickness in children could turn deadly in such a short time.

Both mother and child were asleep. Moria silently closed the door and returned to her own side of the house. She was restless as she tried to sew, and to read. She went down stairs to the parlor to play the piano but she became even more restless. At last she gave up all indoor activities and dressed to go riding. Going to the barn she asked one of the men to bring in the blue roan gelding. She was going to go to the lake to see if the wild horses had been back. She would ride the gelding in hopes of getting close to the herd. Her Morgan mare was a beacon for the wild stallion and if he decided to take the mare there would be very little Moria could do to stop him. The stallion would ignore the gelding.

Moria allowed the gelding to choose his fast pace swiftly covering the ground to the lake. The wild horses were lined up drinking at the shore of the lake. On a ledge overlooking the valley the old mountain lion was also interested in the horse herd. She was most interested in a late born colt with wobbly legs that was a good prospect for a meal if the herd left the security of the open valley. The cat became silent and fastened her eyes on the blue roan horse and the blond woman rider. The cat's long tail flicked slowly back and forth watching Moria and her horse.

There were four Navajo riders on the Broken Anchor. They all insisted the big cat, that they had all had in their gun sights at one time or another, was a real skin walker, also it was called a Navajo wolf a Yeenaaldiooshii, a witch. They never went into the Medera Mountains alone always two men always watchful. Some of the other ranch hands considered these men to be superstitious or backward people. Gavin always remembered what his father told them, don't discount anything.

Seeing Moria enter the valley the horse herd began to move away. Moria turned off the main trail and followed a game trail up the mountain. The trail was narrow and dangerous in places. Sheer walls came down to the floor of the trail for several feet at a time. By going up the mountain Moria could watch the horses longer. A half mile along the game trail she came to a place where she could see almost all of the valley. Using the long glass given to her as a present from Gavin she was able to count twenty three mares and young stock and the beautiful stallion. So absorbed in watching the herd Moria at first did not notice her horse had become agitated pulling on the reins, tossing his head and stamping his feet.

Suddenly with a high pitched scream the old mountain lion leaped from her ledge onto the horse below. Moria looked up in time to see the cat coming straight at her. The cat landed on the horse's neck digging in with claws and teeth, trying to get teeth into the horse's neck. The horse began to buck and pitch in an attempt to dislodge the cat. Moria found herself being pitched to and fro in an attempt to stay on her horse. Unable to control the injured, scared horse Moria was thrown off. She found herself high in the air before going over the cliff into the rocks below where she lay sprawled unmoving.

Continuing to fight to get the lion off its neck the horse began to whirl around and around. The cat lost its grip with its hind legs yet continued to claw the horse. Great screams of pain and fear came from the horse. The horse continued to whirl in circles and slam the cat into the wall of the mountain until finally the cat lost its grip and fell from the horse. The pounding against the wall had done considerable damage to the cats body, it lay panting as the big horse reared bringing both front feet down on the cats body. Again and again the horse reared striking the cat each time. Finally exhausted the horse stood with its head lowered sides heaving, shaking with fear and fury, blood dripping from a dozen cuts and bites. With its rider gone and still having the smell of the cat in its nostrils and the bloody gore on his legs to his knees, the big horse with broken reins trailing the ground turned back down the trail for home. Blood ran down the neck and front legs of the gelding from the claw and bite marks of the lion mixed with the gore of the dead cat. There was deep cuts along the horse's shoulders, pain and fear overtook the horse and it began to race towards the ranch and security.

Gavin and several men were repairing the corrals when the roan gelding ran into the ranch yard. Fear hit Gavin like a blow from an axe handle, this was the horse Moria rode off on this morning. Seeing blood pooling under the horse the men quickly mounted their saddled horses and rode back in the direction of the lake. Gavin wished Mark was there but he had gone with men to the east range to gather cattle and would be gone for several days.

When they reached the game trail it was easy to see where the horse had gone up and come back down on the trail. They soon found the remains of the dead lion and searching where the fight had taken place they saw the body of Moria in the rocks below. Gavin's heart and breathing stopped when he looked over the edge of the cliff and saw the body of his wife lying several feet below.

"Oh please God no, not my beautiful Moria wailed Gavin as he tried to clamber down to Moria's body. The cliff was too steep, a sheer straight down angle. The men made a sling of their lariats and lowered Gavin to the rocks. Picking up the broken body of his dead wife the men pulled him back up to the trail cradling, Moria in his arms, her long blond hair windblown. Carrying his dead wife it was a solemn group as Gavin and the men returned to the ranch. A rider was sent to find Mark and Tater and relay the bad news. They reached the solemn group on the trail as they return to the ranch.

Moria was buried in the same small cemetery where Gavin's mother and two baby sisters were buried. Gavin inconsolable sat alone in his side of the house talking to no one, he left the food tray untouched. He lit no lamps. He refused to talk to Mark of the operation of the ranch. No one could reach him.

Mark could see that Gavin was not going to be able to go to San Francisco to tell Moria's parents of her death. The day after her funeral he told his uncle goodbye and left the ranch to go tell the parents their only child had been killed. When he reached the Dunbar home he found both parents waiting for him. Offering condolences was of little use to the parents. They wanted to know all the details which Mark supplied since he was one of the men who helped retrieve Moria's body. He told them that if they so wished it her body could be retrieved from the family burial grounds and reinterred near her parents.

The Dunbar's asked Mark for some time before they decided. After the young man left Moria's mother retrieved the box where she had kept all the letters Moria had sent. The parents carefully read each letter beginning with the first week on the trail. After reading again every word their daughter had written they sat holding one another, then silently they each nodded their head, they had made their decision.

Early the next morning Mark returned to the Dunbar home where he was again greeted by both parents. It was Mr. Dunbar that spoke saying "we have determined she was so happy from the day she met Gavin. Her happiness showed in every letter she wrote. She loved the mountains and the ranch and she was as happy as she could be without children. We believe she should remain in the mountains she loved and we believe it would be best to help Gavin heal. We are just sorry we can't be with him at this time."

"Please give him our love and condolence" said Mrs. Dunbar.

"Yes, ma'am I sure will. Please keep in touch with my uncle this is the hardest thing he has ever had to do in his life, Moria was his world."

---◆---

One afternoon several weeks after Moria died Lorelei slipped past her mother and entered the portion of the house that belonged to her aunt and uncle. She saw nothing wrong going into her aunt and uncles side of the house. She had always been allowed to see them at any time. Entering the dimly lit upstairs parlor where the drapes were drawn, she saw her uncle sitting slumped in his chair. He had one of Moria's handkerchief's spread across his knee. As he stared at it he traced the picot or small loops around the edge of the satin square cloth. It was something she has sewn with great care and had given many away as gifts.

Going to him she took his hand and said, "Uncle Gavin I'm sorry Aunt Moria died." With those words the flood of tears began, the tears that would not come before. Lifting the small child onto his lap and holding her close Gavin cried the tears of those who have lost someone precious to them. Lorelie kept patting his hand saying over and over "don't cry Uncle, don't cry Uncle it will be alright." At last the tears stopped and Gavin for an instant thought it might be alright. He knew Moria would not want him to grieve, it was not her way. Leaving his chair and taking the child by the hand they walked down the stairs into the wide hall and out the front door, down the porch steps and into the sunlight.

"Come Lassie lets go look at the new baby foals."

Holding her Uncles hand Loralie asked, "Is it going to be alright Uncle?"

"Aye Lassie it will be alright – someday."

Mark was happy to see his uncle and little sister coming to the corral. Gavin had not been to the barns since Moria died more than six weeks past. His uncle was pale and gaunt but he had come outside and that was a start. Mark just hoped Gavin would not ask about Moria's horse at this time. The horse had to be put down, the severity of its injuries had been extreme. There had been many changes in the weeks since Moria was killed.

There was more unrest between the cattlemen and the sheep men. The ranches that had tried to stay neutral were being fired upon. The Broken Anchor sent their riders out in teams of two or three men.

The ranch prospered, Mark was now the foreman taking over from Tater Fletcher when he retired to his ranch and horses. Gavin found himself pleased the way Tater had brought Mark along running the ranch. Their grazing land holdings had grown by more than six thousand acres. And all of Gotome Canyon was now part of the Broken Anchor. Steven was learning the law at a firm in New York. Gavin felt old, he had no children and he missed Moria so very much. He was thinking very strongly of returning to the sea, but he knew he could never leave Moria.

◆

23

GIDEON

I sat at my large desk in the opulent office I had acquired when my business was doing so well a few short years ago. My new investors appeared to once again find confidence in me as before when I was so well established, so confident and sure of myself. But not my old investors, they avoided me as though I had a plague. Today my mind was not on my usual business. All I could think about was how to force Isobel to give me a divorce. The death of my sister in law had reminded me of how short life was, shorter for some than for others, this was something our Da had often said when we were young.

When Moria died my brother Gavin became a recluse. Moria was a good and faithful wife to my brother as she was a sister to Isobel and myself. I believed that without Gavin's guiding hand the ranch would fail and it would be sold and I would invest the money into business for Gavin and myself, which is how I thought of the family business even the ranch. I did not count on his and Marks knowledge of ranching to continue but they held the ranch together although I had cut off all the funds of my own and Gavin's that I had agreed to invest in the ranch. I wanted no part of ranching and I wanted to break Mark to force him to my way of thinking, I have to admit I was trying to get back at Isobel and at this time I was feeling her revenge. It was time for me to get on with my second family but I doubted Isobel would even think of signing divorce papers. There had to be a way for me to rid myself of Isobel.

24

GAVIN

Mark had grown into a responsible ranch manager and he had a genuine sense for the cattle, horses and management of the land. He had entered into a partnership with a logging company and the Broken Anchor was sending rail cars loaded with timber to Nebraska and Kansas. We no longer had to drive the cattle to market in California or Kansas. We now drove them to the rail head and shipped them to buyers much farther and faster than ever before.

A very young Loralie wanted to go into the convent. She was still a child in my mind, she was barely thirteen. She had always been a very compassionate child. Now she had become insistent in her cause to join the church. Gideon had little real interest in his daughter's futures. He expected them to marry and become the say so of their husbands.

Stephen had gone east to become a lawyer. Philip tried unsuccessfully to follow his brother's footsteps. His time in school at the new University of Nevada that had just opened had been spent at parties and saloons and he was sent home in disgrace. He was apparently destined to fail at every turn. When he returned to the ranch he began to spend his time at Fort Grant or Fort Ruby where he had accumulated gambling debts. He borrowed money from Mark, me and Isobel with the promise to work off the debt. He would not stay with any project long enough to see it finished. The time had passed quickly since the two families had come to the valley. I had talked to Gideon about Philip however Gideon did not appear to have any interest in what Philip did. I was afraid the boy would come to no good.

◆

25

STEPHEN

Soon after mother discovered father's affair with Alana Montoya-Luna I found she was referring to my schooling as becoming a lawyer and she would talk of my going back east to school after I finished with the local school. At her considerable instigation I began classes at New York University and for two years I studied hard and did not return to the ranch even for holidays. I studied law with zeal and tirelessness I had never before applied myself and my time like this before. I was dead serious in becoming a lawyer. Revenge for what my father had tried to do drove me night and day. Finally the day came when I was to be apprenticed to the law firm of Street, Beck and Hamilton. They were one of the most prestigious law firms in New York City. I don't know how Mother pulled it off but I was thrilled to be accepted as a law clerk for the firm. I worked hard and read every law book and law case I could. I made certain I was first in the office in the morning and I stayed late, sometimes near midnight studying law and memorizing cases. I was determined to succeed.

◆

Stephen MacDougall was five minutes late as he followed an elegantly dressed couple into Delmonico's, one of New York's most elite restaurants. Two of his three bosses' Street and Hamilton were both seated. He should have been at the table when they arrived after all he was only a law clerk studying to become a lawyer. There was small talk while waiting for their food. Neither of the two older men ordered alcoholic drinks. He certainly needed one.

The couple Stephen had followed into the restaurant were seated a couple of tables to his right. The girl was the most beautiful woman he had ever seen. Finally he got the nerve to ask Street who the couple were, pretending a slight acquaintance. Street answered they were Aaron and Marta Schultz. They were oblivious to all around them.

Aaron Schultz was a very unimposing individual of medium height slight build, sandy hair that was thinning on top. He wore wire rimmed glasses. Stephen didn't know if he was the young lady's father or not but he was definitely much older than she was.

Watching the couple engage in animated conversation he had to wonder to himself what the beautiful creature could possibly see in the man. Finally curiosity got the better of him and he asked his bosses just who was Aaron Schultz?

Hamilton raised his eyebrows as if to say "you don't know?" "Aaron Schultz is one of this city's largest financiers. He owns railroads, mines, manufacturing steel plant and real estate. The young lady is his wife. Our law firm handles the railroad entities of his empire, in fact we have a contract to take to him. He never discusses business when he is with his wife, he gives her his full attention."

"I have never seen him in the office" answered Stephen.

"And you won't, we go to him he does not come to us!"

The matter of the subject for the meeting at luncheon seemed unimportant, and Stephen did not even think about it, in fact all afternoon he could not get Marta Schultz off his mind. He had never seen a woman like her and he was no stranger to beautiful women.

It was a week later that he was returning to the law offices of Street, Beck and Hamilton after having lunch downtown that he saw Marta Schultz alight from a carriage and go into a dress shop. He waited outside as long as he dared for another glimpse of her. Realizing he would be late returning to work he left. His work had begun to suffer with his obsession of the woman.

Within weeks he was called into the office of senior partner David Street and was shocked at the announcement. Street was a tall well-built man with dark piercing blue eyes that Stephen believed could see into his soul. "Stephen my partners and I had intended to make you an offer of permanent employment with our firm but recently your work has become so inferior that we have doubts of your ability. It will be necessary to let you go to make room for a more capable law student. I am sorry to see you leave as I believed your potential would be an asset to this firm. That is all. Your dismissal will be final as of this hour. You may go."

Stunned at the dismissal Stephen gathered his coat and left the law firm. Angrily he thought to himself Street, Baker and Hamilton was not the only law firm in New York, perhaps one of the most prestigious but he could do better than work with those old men. He went into the first saloon he came to on his way home. It was late and dark when he finally left to go to his apartment. He was unsteady as he hailed a cab. The driver awakened him at his apartment house.

For two days he never left his rooms. How could he have been so stupid as to lose his job? He could imagine his father's glee and the "I told you so" when he heard the news. And his mother would be disappointed after all she had fought to get him the opportunity to become a lawyer. She had called in favors to get him a position with Street, Beck and Hamilton. He decided he would not go home until he was a success. He could not face anyone until he was successful. He would not go home in disgrace.

For the next few weeks he spent his days going from law firm to law firm in search of work, but his mind was filled with Marta Schultz.

The law community at least the honest law firms would not hire him, he had no recommendation and no credentials. Now he could never approach Marta Schultz and he had been working on a plan to meet her. He had followed her to her home at one point and had begun to learn of her movements such as each Wednesday she went to the same dress shop at the same time of day. So besotted was he that all he could think of was seeing her again. He had to meet her to talk to her. He just knew he could impress her if he could only talk to her.

He believed he had kept a discreet distance as he followed her on her usual Wednesday shopping trip. Today he would speak to her, introduce himself and refer to his past employment as if he was still working for the law firm.

He stood next to the building daydreaming of Marta Schultz unaware of the passersby on the sidewalk until two uniformed police officers stepped on either side of him. Startled he looked from one to the other asking, "What is going on?" At that moment a man in a livery uniform stepped up.

"That's the man that has been following Mrs. Schultz on more than one occasion" the man said pointing to Stephen.

Stephen was taken to the local police station and placed in a room with six or eight other men of varying ages, most of them were drunk, ragged and dirty. He certainly did not belong here. Why was he here he had done nothing wrong he kept asking himself? Stephen was mortified and speechless. This was not what he had envisioned at all. How could he ever explain this to his family and certainly not to a perspective employer?

After about thirty minutes an officer took him to another room where two young men he supposed were prisoners also were seated at a table. They were each questioned asked if they knew one another and why they were at the specific location when they were picked up. Finally all three were released being told they were not under arrest. As Stephen waited in line to receive the possessions that had been taken from him when he came into the station, a man in front of him said "we need a lawyer for this type of treatment." Several began to repeat the hue and cry "we want a lawyer."

Suddenly Stephen thought "I am a lawyer!" Well almost anyway, he did not have courtroom experience but he had read courtroom procedure and law cases. Raising his hand he announced, "I am a lawyer!" And so began Stephens practice in criminal law. He managed to write and pass the states examination. He took only cases that were paid in advance and he began to haunt the courtrooms watching practiced lawyers at work. He was a quick learner and soon had a standing list of clients. He opened an office, hired a body guard and became well known for skirting the law and fouling the court system. He was a practicing lawyer and he had the paper work and cases to prove it. There was no doubt that his duty of providing justice was discharged. The trouble with Stephen was that his honey tongued eloquence was merely a top dressing on a scoundrel hypocrisy. He was clever and ingenious but at the same time hot tempered, willful and capricious. He was generous to those who could not harm him and merciless to anyone who could. Above all he was secretive and suspicious, over sensitive to opposition and relentless in revenge. He became a feared opponent and subject to vicious rumors, it was no wonder men told stories of his wickedness without bothering to establish authenticity.

While still in New York his family knew nothing of his life in that city. He took the position of power illegally or by force. He hired thugs to seek information on his opponents with unrelenting zeal. Never relaxing or slacking of his opponents whom he considered enemies. He was not above underhanded trickery to win his cases. He had inherited this trait from his father however he would have never admitted to it. He spent his nights gallivanting from place to place seeking pleasure for his lusty needs, like his father he chased women. This habit did not stop even after he became engaged.

◆

The man that entered Stephen's office looked more like a thug than a representative of a well known railroad tycoon. The man sat down uninvited and began to tell Stephen what his employer required of Stephen. Jason "Jay" Gould, his father in law Daniel Miller and James Fisk were deeply involved in the New York political ring namely Tammany Hall. Gould and Fisk succeeded in getting Boss Tweed elected as director of the Erie Railroad and as the returned favor Tweed saw to it legislation benefited Gould and Fisk. So lawlessly blatant were their dealings they became the characters of newspaper cartoons. Stephen had become one of the same type men, his opponents had grown to despise him learning of his lawless ways often said he would steal the pennies from a dead man's eyes. He was ruthless always. When Gould's man mentioned President Grant's brother in law as one of Jay Gould's affiliates Stephen was sold on the plot.

Gould and Fisk attempted to control the gold market. The gold speculations failure was the main cause of the Black Friday panic on September 24, 1869 when he saw the value of the gold Double Eagle take a nose dive from sixty-two percent to thirty five percent. The money he made in this venture was lost in lawsuits at the age of thirty-three. Although the gold venture failed, newspapers helped build his reputation as an all-powerful man who could drive the stock market at will. He was feared by many for his influence.

Gould's next venture was railroads and by the early 1880s he controlled ten thousand miles of railway, eventually controlling fifteen percent interest in the countries railroad tracks. This was an extremely profitable venture and his power continued to increase. He was a feared man and hired strikebreakers during the Southwest railroad strike. One report said as a quote from Gould "I can hire one half of the working class to kill the other half and then go to work for me." He was ruthless, always.

He gained control of four western railroads including the Union Pacific which completed part of The Transcontinental Railroad. Gould, a man that life demanded keep a finger on the pulse of his many enterprises sent his man to hire Steven to be his eyes and ears on the California holdings. He was well aware of Stephens past transgressions and deemed them useful. He was a man who never did anything without a reason.

If Jay Gould made money then Steven made money. Although the man was known for underhanded business dealings Stephen joined his crew and fit right in.

He told no one of his pending marriage. He at last married Rebecca Horowitz heiress of the great mining empire. He believed he was on the way to becoming one of the richest men in the new state of Nevada. Theirs was not a happy marriage. Rebecca had married against her father's advice and soon realized the degree that Stephen would stoop to get what he wanted and what he wanted was the Horowitz fortune. Rebecca played no part in Stephen's public life and it is doubtful if she played very much of a part in his private life either. Certainly she bore him no children. When he announced to his wife they were going to live in California she balked. She would not leave the security of family to live with the unreliable Stephen in the Wild West. He was given a large severance settlement and sent on his way. Rebecca had the final word, "There's a curse on your family, you spend your lives fighting each other then you die alone. There is a curse on you."

Then he returned to the Broken Anchor and on to San Francisco to flaunt the wealth he had begun to obtain. His return to the ranch for a few days was about all the "rest" he could stand, he had to be where the excitement was. He had forgotten how much he hated cattle and the loneliness he perceived the ranch to be. In San Francisco he stayed at the best hotels, dined at the best restaurants and was seen nightly at some posh gala with a different beautiful woman. It would appear the New York scandal had not reached this far west. He did not contact his father. He had no use for his father, he was now associated with wealthy prominent people.

He could not talk to his mother, she had little to say other than to be angry at Gideon. He was ready to take revenge on his father. The fire of revenge burned deep as he imagined how he would bring his father down. He had become wealthy and when the time was right he would go see his father and remind him of how Gideon had fought to break his sons to his will. Until that time he would practice law and undermine Gideon's wealth with the help of very influential people.

———◆———

26

THE WEDDING

Arabella was preparing for her wedding. Even Lorelie had come home from the convent in the south west territory for the ceremony. She had gone the year before to become a novice at a mission in New Mexico. It would appear that Gideon and Isobel had come to an un-speaking truce concerning the wedding. This was due to Arabella begging and pleading with her mother not to embarrass her with her almost new in-laws. On the surface it appeared all was well.

The wedding would unite two well-known families, the once powerful MacDougal's and the wealthy successful Granville's and take place in San Francisco in the great magnificent cathedral on the cliff that looked out over the ocean. The family gathered at Isobel's home which had been opened and decorated to impress the new in laws. Isobel, Arabella, Philip and Lorelie had arrived in San Francisco weeks ahead of the grand event date.

Gavin and Mark left the ranch a few days before the wedding, they just wanted to see Arabella happily married and return home. Stephen returned from abroad where he had gone for a client. They all had figured this would be a big deal but they had no idea there would be so many people. They were introduced to important politicians, professional men and the elite of San Francisco. The day of the wedding was bright and California sunny.

Mark had met his future brother in law David Granville and was not impressed. He appeared more effeminate than graceful. His appearance was that of a gambler in that he wore showy unnecessary frills and lace shirts. He gravitated to foofaraws and glitz. He was known for his free spending ways, a very real concern for his father Gordon Granville who was considered rather crafty and frugal. His son however was cocky and arrogant, condescending. He was handsome as well as wealthy and came from a family that was a pillar in society but there appeared to be missing that element of the man that instills trust. For his sister's sake he hoped that Isobel had given this wedding much thought he doubted that however, she was so wrapped up in her fairy tale wedding. He mentioned his doubts to Gavin.

"It's not what we want or think that counts here lad, it is what your sister believes and at this time she is happy so we have to be happy for her."

Isobel should have been in her element to have all her children with her, however she was irritable, almost angry. She had managed to avoid Gideon when he came to the house to speak with Stephen. Stephen had been deliberate in avoiding Gideon knowing how uncomfortable he would be waiting for him. He did not return to his mother's home until later that night. Her anger stemmed from the fact that Stephen had not confided in her any part of the reason for his meeting with his father. She had no idea what plans he had for the future but she was afraid Gideon would influence Stephen to join him. She was jealous and felt betrayed. Isobel was too angry to be nice or show interest in Mary Granville. When the prospective in-laws David and his parents Gordon and Mary Granville came to the house to pay a courtesy call Isobel scowled and added little to the conversation. Arabella wished her mother was more like Mary Granville.

◆

Gideon was extremely angry when he reached Isobel's home for the second time, and demanded to see Stephen. As he entered the wealthy home where he and Isobel had started their married life he could see nothing of the beauty in the morning room. More and more American families were calling this room the parlor. All around him were mementoes of a past life; pictures of the young boys as babies, books long waiting to be read or reread. Ornaments of their pleasure and business trips. Elegant furniture placed around the room that was not as comfortable as it looked. Several expensive pieces of crystal, vases, and small sculptures decorated small tables. He had always been uncomfortable in this room while it had been a favorite place for Isobel. Overcome with rage Gideon saw none of the beauty.

Stephen knew exactly why his father demanded to see him. He had hoped this latest incident would stay quiet until after the wedding, he did not want to spoil Arabella's wedding. It would be up to his father how much was revealed. Jason Gould had warned Stephen this could blow up, however they agreed to go forth with the venture, regardless of the outcome. Although it might put a damper on the wedding Stephen almost looked forward to the confrontation.

Gideon was waiting in the morning room when Stephen entered. Gideon could not contain his wrath. "You little bastard do you know what you have done?"

Removing the cheroot clenched between his teeth and with all his attention on the cigar he then turned to Gideon. Smiling Stephen answered "I know exactly what I have done! I now own fifty-one percent interest in Walcott Mining Enterprise and as such I influenced the company to move its accounts to a more...uh shall we say acceptable managing firm. Old Mr. Walcott has an aversion to mixed ethnic relationships. Your affair with Alana Montoya-Luna will be the ruination of you!" spat Steven menacingly.

Speechless Gideon could only stare at his son. This had been no accident, it was a deliberate attempt to undermine and ruin Gideon! "But I have worked for years to bring that company to fruition." Smiling Stephen said, "And to think it took me such a short time to break it! And by the way you might want to look into your investment in the Mountain Coastal Railroad. My friend, mother and I now own the majority of that stock." Turning his back on his father he said matter of fact, it is time for me to dress for my sister's wedding. You may see yourself out." With these words Stephen left his father staring at the wall, a blank frozen look on his face. Gideon saw his life dissolving in front of his eyes.

It was difficult for Stephen not to turn hand springs! He had done it! He had broken Gideon and at this point in time he could not tell anyone. Not even his mother. He still had one more company to acquire then he would surprise his mother. But first thing after the wedding he would approach Gavin and Mark to set the next phase of his plan in motion.

The day of the wedding dawned bright with the perpetual California sun. When Gavin and Mark arrived at the church they found a large crowd gathered out front. The two entered a side door to the church and quite by accident Arabella was exiting another door. Happily she stopped and greeted her uncle and brother as she might not get the opportunity to talk to them later. She dismissed her bride's maids from their work of preparing her gown to have privacy with Mark and Gavin. After his greeting Mark asked Arabella if everything was alright. "Oh how I wish Mother and Father were not fighting and this day would be perfect," she said, after asking the men to sit. "I suppose if they can retain some semblance of civility I shall be satisfied." Gavin was struck by how much the young girl had changed into such a beautiful young woman. She was five foot seven a good six inches taller than Isobel. Reddish gold curls hung long and shining, almost to her waist. Curls framed around her delicate features of lovely cheekbones and full lips. Beautifully spaced green eyes looked from perfect formed eyebrows. Today on her wedding day she was radiant, a most beautiful creature. A prayer for her happiness emanated from her uncle's heart.

Gavin could not help comparing Moria with some of the women he saw. Her grace and beauty would have put most of them to shame. She would have loved this occasion and he could not enjoy the event for missing her.

———◆———

Lorelie sought out her uncle and brother, "Have you seen father? Earlier today he came to the house to talk to Stephen but he left before I could talk to him. He is not here, in fact Mother just informed me that Stephen will walk Arabella down to the Alter. I just know something terrible has happened, "said the distraught girl. Shaking his head Mark said, "We have not seen Gideon since we arrived in California."

It had been several months since Gavin had seen this niece and she too had grown into a beautiful young woman. Today anxiety marred her lovely face. Tears were near the surface of her beautiful brown eyes.

Turning around Lorelie ran to her mother, "They have not seen father. Oh, mother everything is wrong. We must find father and he must walk Arabella to the Alter."

Hatefully Isobel answered, "Perhaps he must see to his other family, after all this would not be the first time he chose them over his legitimate family. Don't worry everything will be alright, without him."

———◆———

A distraught Gideon left Isobel's house and began to walk towards the ocean. All thought of the wedding was gone from his mind, he was thousands of dollars in debt for Arabella's wedding and his life was becoming a shambles. He came to the road leading to the ships at the same time the wedding began to take place. Suddenly realizing where he was and the time he made the decision not to return to the wedding. It would be better to be absent than to enter late and disrupt the ceremony.

A very happy jubilant Stephen walked his sister to the Alter and into a new life. The wedding proceeded and the couple were off on a world trip and everyone returned to their life. Still no one knew where Gideon had gotten to. Early the next morning Gavin and Mark began the day by drinking coffee in Isobel's kitchen, they had checked out of their hotel rooms and brought their luggage to the house so they could visit with Lorelie. They both were curious to learn what Stephen wanted to talk to them about. Mark and Gavin were excited to be on their way home, they were always reluctant to leave the ranch. They were waiting until time for a carriage to take them to the railroad station. They were both so anxious to be on their way home that they were ready to leave an hour early. When they got to the station in Red Lodge they would almost be home.

They heard voices in the next room and took their coffee into the dining room. They both kept a close eye on the clock on the mantle as they were sitting in the dining room of Isobel's home drinking coffee with a couple of Isobel's house guests while waiting for breakfast as Stephen entered. Mark believed there was a swagger he had never noticed before, he also noticed that Stephen had signs of alcohol use, too much alcohol use. He reeked of whiskey already this morning. Jovially Stephen asked." I wonder if I could talk to the two of you privately in the morning room."

Gavin and Mark rose from the table and followed Stephen across the hall into the morning room and closed the door.

Almost gleefully turning to face his uncle and brother, Stephen said, "Did you see Gideon, (he no longer referred to him as father) at the wedding?"

Both men acknowledged they had not talked to Gideon the day before. Gavin said, "I saw him come into the house and come in here with you but I did not see him leave."

"That is because he slinked out the back door" said Stephen with a smug grin.

"And why would he do that?" asked Mark.

"Because I have beaten him in business," answered Stephen barely able to contain his glee.

"What do you mean?" Demanded Gavin with a sinking feeling that he was certain meant trouble, just when he had hoped the wedding had brought the family closer; at least talking to one another.

"I own a majority percent interest in the Walcott Mining Enterprise and mother, a friend and I own the majority of the stock in the Mountain Coastal Railroad. I would imagine today he is in his office calling his minions to see what else he has lost," stated Stephen gleefully.

"Is this what you wanted to talk to us about?" asked Gavin angrily not at all liking the gloating Stephen. He might dislike his father but Gavin could see that Stephen was enjoying getting the best of his father too much.

"No, what I wanted to tell you is that my share of the ranch is for sale. I no longer want to be part of the ranch and I want to invest more in mining. I believe the days of ranching are past, that there is no future in ranching."

"What price do you have in mind?" asked Gavin suspiciously.

Reaching for a small tablet Stephen wrote a number on the page and handed it to Gavin who in turn handed it to Mark.

Mark said, "I can't meet half this price no matter how much I want to!"

Gavin turned to Mark saying "you now have ten percent stock in the Broken Anchor, your sisters each have five percent and Philip has ten percent while Gideon and I each own thirty percent and Stephen has ten percent. You and I have never taken a wage like the other stock holders have. Let's get an accountant to take a look at what you are worth, what the actual ranch is worth then all of us will know where we stand. Is that alright with you Stephen?"

Stephen had hoped to be able to settle the matter quickly but rather than rock the boat and lose a chance to make some money he answered, "It sounds fair to me." "Mark do you mean to tell me you haven't taken a wage for all the years you have worked on the Broken Anchor?"

"No, just necessities like clothes and a new saddle once. And I signed a note for some more land but that is almost payed off."

"Boy you couldn't get me to wrestle those cattle for nothing," stated Stephen his speech more than a little slurred.

Dismissing his brother Stephen turned to Gavin and said, "Let me know when you get an accounting for the ranch and we can go from there. I have to go now, but I'll wait to hear from you."

After Stephen left Mark sat wondering to himself if he had enough equity in the ranch to buy Stephen's share. He could not believe that there was not a future in ranching even if there was a sheep war looming on the horizon.

Finally Gavin said, "Mark I believe you have more than enough equity to buy twenty percent more of the ranch. When we get the results from an accountant and we know what the percent is worth you might want to contact your sisters to see if they want to sell their combined ten percent. You would then own thirty percent while Gideon and I own thirty percent. I can make you a loan so you can buy out your brother and sisters. While we are at it I am going to approach Philip to see if he wants to sell. He has no apparent interest in the ranch. If you could buy out your brothers and sisters you would have the majority interest in the ranch, no one could take it from you. Isobel has given up any interest she has in the ranch and it would have to come to her through Gideon."

It was a few weeks before the accountant finished with the books at the Broken Anchor, when Gavin approached Philip about selling his share of the ranch. Always in need of money Philip saw the chance to demand double the worth of his share. Without hesitation Gavin said no thanks and left Philip wishing he had not been so greedy. Once again Philip had overplayed his hand but he would sell. He would wait a few weeks then he would talk to Gavin and take the amount offered. His intentions were to take the money, go to Denver or San Francisco and never come back to the Broken Anchor.

Before the summer began Philip sold Mark his ten percent share of the ranch at the first offered price Gavin had quoted. Gavin felt certain that the future of the Broken Anchor was in safe hands. Nothing else changed. Philip continued his life style of running with two would be outlaws, Spike Johnson and Joey Baker who spent their days gambling at one of the nearby forts or towns.

After two long hard weeks on the range working cattle the riders returned back to the ranch headquarters. When Gavin and Mark reached the Broken Anchor Mark told Gavin he was moving out of his room in the big house and into the bunk house. The flair up Stephen and his father had would be more fodder for his mother's ire. He would need to be ready to take his turn to stand night guard on the ranch. He also found it a challenge to hear his younger brother stagger up the stairs to bed only an hour or so before dawn.

When he spoke to his mother of Philips actions she reminded him that it was none of his business what Philip did as part owner of the ranch. She had forgotten or chose to ignore the fact Philip had no claim on the ranch. He had never been required to work like one of the cow hands. He did not want to be around when Philip's fall came and fall he would, it was a matter of time.

27

MARK RECIEVES A SUMMONS

Summer was coming to the high country. The snow on the mountains had melted off several hundred feet. The geese had been going north for several weeks and Mark had watched a pair of hawks building a nest high in the broken off top of the tallest pine tree near the kitchen door. One of the rider's wives had taken over the care of the chickens and setting of the broody hens after Moria died and today she had all the older children cleaning the chicken house, probably with the bribe of donuts. This was a busy and best time of year for Mark.

A few more days and the men would have gathered all the cattle into the mountain valleys to brand and fatten before a roundup began. This was the time to recheck gear and equipment and enjoy the lull before hard work began. Mark had ridden into town for a few supplies and to pick up the mail. Some of the ranch wives had family elsewhere and letters were always welcome. He always let the women know when he was going to town, and was willing to pick up small items for the families. Sewing thread seemed to be the never ending item the ranch needed. The women put thread samples in an envelope that Mark dropped off at the general store for the owner's wife to match. He then collected the mail and sat on a bench outside the general store waiting for his supply list to be filled.

For a time the lives of the family appeared to settle down and all become normal again at the ranch. Then he opened the letter sent to him. When he first read the summons from Gideon he wanted to tear it to shreds and mail the trash back to Gideon. He read the letter three times hoping he had misunderstood the message but not so it was the same the third reading as the first. His Father was adamant that he come to California and if he did not Gideon would not support the expenses for the ranch. He again cursed the setup of the ranches finances. How could his uncle Gavin have trusted Gideon to do what was right? It should have been in writing. He loaded the ranch supplies and began the return trip to the ranch. He was anxious to talk to Gavin.

He missed dinner since he had read the summons over and over waiting for the men to return when he got back to the ranch from town. He went to the kitchen where Anna had cleaned up after dinner. She asked if she could fix something for him. Absentmindedly he answered no then said perhaps a glass of milk. When she offered him a piece of apple pie he answered yes and thanked her. She offered to make coffee to go with it, he answered no to the coffee. He wanted milk, perhaps it would settle the bile that rose in his throat. Going to the cellar he took a jug of the morning milking and shook it vigorously, returning to the kitchen filled a glass. Anna told him to leave the milk in the kitchen as she would use it to start supper.

The contents of the letter ran through his mind as he ate. He would talk to Gavin as soon as he could. He made the decision not to go as he sat staring at the half empty glass of milk. So absorbed in though was he that he did not see the fly as it walked around the rim of the glass then stood on its front legs cleaning itself. Getting up from the table he stepped out on the patio and poured the milk into the pan for the cat. Returning to the kitchen he placed the pie plate and glass in the sink, and with a definite purpose picked up his hat and went to find his uncle.

He took the letter to Gavin as soon as Gavin unsaddled his horse and put the saddle on the top rail of the corral fence, Mark could hardly wait for his input. Mark hoped Gavin would tell him to ignore the letter but in his mind he knew that was not to be, they needed the money Gideon withheld from the ranch. After reading the letter Gavin said "Mark the ranch needs the money for new blood in our cattle herd, we do not know what Gideon has in mind but let's find out before we dismiss the summons." Leaving the ranch now was the very last thing Mark wanted to do. This was his favorite time of year. Oh how he hated the turmoil of his family. He believed this was not what his grandfather had intended at all. He believed his grandfather had meant the move to bring the families together. Just the opposite had happened to his family.

With Gavin's advice still in his mind Mark caught the stage from Red Lodge south to California a few days later. He was angry to be summoned away from the ranch like a school boy. He only hoped that Gideon would turn over the needed money to run the ranch back with him. He was amazed at the change in the landscape as he traveled southeast to the Montoya-Luna hacienda. He had to be honest with himself, his anger was not only his father summoning him it was the fact that he would be going to the hacienda not his father's home. He decided he would listen to his father then return to the Broken Anchor. Gavin had been right he would take the high road and not be like the person Stephen had become. Stephen lived on hate for his father.

--- ◆ ---

Mark was still irritated as he got off the stage in the hills far east of the City of Angels. Awaiting was a beautiful coach pulled by four coal black horses their coats brushed to a high glistening sheen. The coach stood at the gate to the entrance of the Casa Del Montoya-Luna hacienda which was located three miles from the gate. A young boy whom Mark guessed to be twelve years old jumped from the back of the coach and hurried to pick up Marks valise.

"Welcome Senior" he said.

"Thanks" answered Mark. He wanted to get this visit over with so he could return to the ranch.

Gideon had made it clear he would not pay or sign for the release of funds for his share of the cost to restock and run the ranch until he had talked with Mark. Each year he withheld his share of the cost to run the Broken Anchor until the very end although throughout the year a share of the profits were given to each member of the family. Mark could never understand why the cost of running the ranch had not been deducted from the profits to begin with but that was how Gideon and Gavin had started and so it continued.

Gavin had paid more than his share of the cost for the new herd of white faced cattle. The note was due on the newly purchased ten thousand acres of land that Gavin and Mark had bought and would soon become a part of the Broken Anchor. It was well known that Gideon would like to sell the ranch. It would have been much to his liking if he could divest his holdings along with his first family.

Mark resented Gideon for taking him away from the ranch. He was the only one of Gideon and Isobel's sons that had a true love for ranching. Stephen had gone east to study law and was not only a lawyer but a successful businessman and Philip still had not made up his mind what he wanted to do with the rest of his life. So far he had chosen poorly both friends and conduct. As the coach raced along the road south Mark saw a few beautiful golden colored horses grazing in the hills of emerald green grass. Reaching up and tapping the driver's seat of the coach he asked the driver to stop. He was surprised how well the man spoke English when he jumped from the coach and asked if everything was alright.

Mark could not take his eyes from the golden horses grazing a few yards from the road.

"I have been admiring your beautiful golden horses he told the driver. I have never seen such magnificent animals. What is this breed?"

"These are the well-known Palomino that Don Carlos Manuel Montoya-Luna raises. He has bred the stallions and mares of the ranch for their disposition and color. His horses have been shipped to Spain, France, Denmark and many other countries. The Montoya-Luna horses are known for great stamina as well as beauty."

As the men stood watching the herd a dust cloud rose over a low hill to the east. As the riders drew near the driver smiled a wide greeting to the riders.

Mark stood in absolute fascination at the sight of the six riders. Each wore wide brimmed sombreros, elegantly embroidered jackets of green, red and blue, tight black trousers with a slit on the outside of the pant leg and an insert of cloth the same color of his jacket. Their horses were all as beautifully attired as the riders. The color of the saddle leather complimented the color of the golden horses. The white silvery manes of each horse reached to the middle of the horse's chest while their white tails reached nearly to the ground. Over each horse's hips was a cape that came almost even with the stirrup and it was inlaid with silver. Each bridle and saddle was adorned with so much silver Mark wondered not only at the extreme cost but the extra weight each horse carried. The tapaderos over each stirrup were polished and fastened with silver buckles.

They were true Californios, Mark had heard that term for the Spaniards of California. The young riders stopped in a row in front of Mark, each tipping his sombrero to the young stranger. "We are pleased to have you visit our hacienda and we welcome you said the man who appeared to be the older of the riders although he was younger by a couple of years than Mark. I am Alejandro Juan Montoya-Luna and this is my brother Mateo Juarez, who appeared to be about the same age as Philip now in their teens. The other four riders were young also. These four are our cousins when they behave he said, waving a hand at the four young boys who sat grinning at Alejandro. My father has sent us to welcome you."

"Thank you, you live in a beautiful part of California, but I am amazed at the horses. I have never seen such animals they are truly magnificent. The driver tells me they are called Palomino, I have never seen such horses" repeated Mark.

"My great, great grandfather started this herd with a select stallion and certain mares that had the golden coats. He spent his life improving the breed and as you can see he mastered his efforts. They are the choice of Kings and Royalty all over the world. Not everyone can own one of our horses, they are very expensive to own and we are careful who we sell our horses to" answered Alejandro." Mark still did not know he was talking to his half-brother. At no time present or future was it ever explained how the two men were so close in age. The affair between Gideon and Alana had begun long ago.

All the while the men talked each rider's horse stood as a statue hardly moving, only their eyes and ears alert. The driver said "let us continue to the hacienda your father is anxious to see you. A mysterious look in his eyes.

They approached the hacienda from the west, the headquarters lay sprawled in a small valley below. The layout was such that it would be advantageous to defend. A wide river ran open on three sides and the ranch buildings lay behind a bulwark of a six foot high three foot thick adobe wall. The ranch was exceptionally clean with small boys picking up dried sticks and even leaves from trees. As the group dismounted in the door way of the large patio that surrounded the house Gideon came forward and griped the hand of his eldest son. Mark noticed the grey at the temples and beard of his father.

"It's so good to see you I am so glad you came."

"Did I have a choice? I believe it was more of a command!" answered Mark trying hard to maintain control of his anger. Why are you here, why are you not at your own home in San Francisco?"

"I didn't mean for it to be a command. As far as my house where you boys were born I no longer own it. I am afraid I lost it in the... ah... take over. Referring to Stephen and Isobel's ruining his business, but I believe we have a program that I think you would do well to be involved in!"

"Who is we?"

Don Carlos Manuel Montoya-Luna, myself and your brothers here at the hacienda!"

"Angrily Mark answered "I didn't know I had brothers in California!"

"Mark you have known about Mateo for some time, Alana and I have two sons, Alejandro and Mateo. They are your half-brothers. Come into the patio we need to talk."

Holding his temper, Mark followed his father into the cool shaded wide patio.

Gideon motioned for a young boy to take Marks valise, with instructions to take it to the guest room in the north wing. The room where Mark would stay for the time he was at the hacienda overlooked the grazing ground where mares and young foals were kept. This was not an accidental instance. Gideon had planned well, he intended Mark to fall in love while he was in California.

In the cool shade of the patio a girl brought a pitcher of cold fruit drink. Mark waited for his father to broach the subject he seemed nervous to start.

"As you know Isobel has made it difficult for me to continue making the kind of money I had made for years..."

"I believe you know why!"

"Yes, and I never meant to hurt her, but I fell in love with Alana a long time ago and each time I asked your mother, for a divorce she became vicious and abusive. We just cannot live together. Ours was a marriage of convenience. "

Mark had no answer for his father. He knew his mother was difficult, so why had they married and had five children? Why not each go their own way and be happy instead of living together in constant anger and fighting?

"Mark Don Carlos Luna has made me see I was wrong trying to force you and Stephen to come into business with me. I realize now you should be allowed to make certain decisions and choices without my force or interference. I am sorry for so many things that I have done wrong. I have been unfair to your mother and our children and I have been unfair to Alana and our sons. There are things I cannot change but there are some that I can. I can support all of my children in their choices of their lives."

"Mark I wanted you to come here to see what Senior Montoya-Luna has done with the Palomino horses. I now own thirty five of these fine horses and I believe they would do well in Nevada. At this time I did not release funds from the ranch account to the Broken Anchor until you could actually see the horses. I can help you start a herd with a few mares. You could increase your herd perhaps double in a year with the help of Senior Montoya. If the ranch would invest in a stallion I believe the ranch could prosper with these horses. If the ranch will prosper so will your sisters and brothers, don't make up your mind yet, ride and get to know the horses first. We will talk of this later." Gideon did not know that Stephen and Philip had sold their share of the ranch to Mark. Gavin held the lien for a portion of the land added to the ranch. Mark decided to say nothing at this time of the change at the ranch.

What he did ask was, "why would Senior Montoya want to help the Broken Anchor?"

"He is trying to save his horse herd and he believes this could not only save the horses he owns but will improve the herd with the proper management. If he does nothing he could lose his herd to the Mexican government they are becoming more aggressive towards the hacienda. He has shipped some of the prized animals back to Spain, he is afraid that the ships will be stopped and the horses confiscated."

The rest of the afternoon was spent talking of inconsequential subjects of the family however father and son stayed away from the subject of Isobel. The time passed quickly and soon the bell rang telling them the evening meal was ready. Entering the large open room richly decorated Mark saw many large comfortable chairs and couches. Several men who were seated rose when Gideon and Mark entered. Senior Carlos Manuel Montoya-Luna the scion of the highly regarded Spanish family introduced himself and his son Raul, Raul's sons Marco, Luis, Pablo and Manuel. Senior Montoya-Luna was of stately slight build giving the impression of being much taller than he actually was. He carried himself ramrod straight. It was apparent Senior Montoya-Luna was proud of his son and his grandsons-all of them. He then introduced the sons of

Gideon and Alana Alejandro and Mateo. Gideon had not said anything, watching Marks reaction. It was the third time for Mark to see his half-brother Mateo.

After the introductions four beautiful women came into the room and Senior Montoya-Luna made the introductions, his daughter Alana Maria Montoya-Luna, his granddaughter, Mercedes Ines Montoya-Luna, the daughter of his dead son Raphael. Alana's Sister Lucia Sofia, and another young girl Consuela Lopez-Acosta who was the friend of Lucia. Mark felt out of place in his dress suit which seemed plain next to the beautiful costumes of the Spanish men. One thing was for certain the Californios knew how to dress.

Senior Montoya-Luna passed out glasses of wine to each of the men including the younger boys. In a soft melodious voice he explained to Mark the wine was made on the ranch grown from their own grapes. Mark could not remember seeing so many stunningly gorgeous women in particular the young Mercedes. Her long black hair was done up in a most pleasing style fastened with a blue shell comb that matched her gown. It seemed each time Mark looked in her direction her lovely eyes were on him. He felt warm and he didn't think it was the excellent wine served at Senior Montoya-Luna's table.

When the main course was finished and the table waited on desert Mercedes asked Mark if he had seen the golden horses. He told her he had seen some of the horses on the way to the hacienda but not up close. He was surprised when she suggested they ride out among the horses tomorrow so Mark could see all of them. Mark was pleased at how easy it was to talk to this dark eyed beauty who was extremely knowledgeable of the horses. He found himself telling her of the wild horses at the ranch and the highland cattle they imported and raised. They talked longer than Mark had ever talked in total to all the girls he knew.

Early the next morning near sun rise Mark walked out onto the prairie as close as the horse herd would allow. They were truly magnificent animals. Their coats glistened in the early morning sun. He still had to wonder what his father wanted and why he had been summoned to the hacienda in California. He could have simply refused to release his share of the operating money he and Gavin had agreed on years ago to renew the cattle herd or he could have sent the money and been done with it. His mother had been sufficiently upset at his going to see his father however Gavin had told him he should go in respect to his father's request at least once. After this trip Mark would have to decide if he wanted contact with his father.

Mark had been surprised at the cordial reception he had received at the Montoya-Luna hacienda. Even his half-brothers had treated him well however his father had not gotten around to discussing his reason for having him come to the southeast of California. He was sure it wasn't for him to see the scenery of California. He was impatient, he wanted answers and he wanted them now. Gavin had taught him patience and so for the time being he would quietly wait.

Returning to the patio Mark sat down in the shade near the gate. So many questions passed through his mind. While he loved Nevada he could easily love this sun bright country. But he would never leave the ranch, he was homesick now just thinking of the Broken Anchor. So far the visit had been cordial and quiet but he had to wonder what was going on at his home ranch. Also he would have to face down his father if he disagreed to whatever proposition Gideon had in mind when he got around to revealing it.

◆

Always on his mind was the growing unrest between the cattlemen and the sheep men. He agreed with Gavin and Tater there was plenty of room for everyone. The Broken Anchor riders had been told to avoid the conflict to which two riders quit the ranch to join the hot headed cattle ranchers. Gavin intended to avoid trouble as long as possible. Everyone loses in a war.

Rumors of the unrest had surfaced before he left. Some of the small ranchers were adamant that the large cattle ranchers should stop the sheep ranchers from settling east of the Big Thunder Mountain region. The range covered some several thousand acres, one would think there was enough land for everyone. To which Gavin agreed with Tater that there was plenty more land for families. Mark wasn't certain how he felt about the sheep men for one thing he did not care for a couple of the more vocal cattle ranchers which in turn put him on the sheep men's side. There were thousands of acres that no one was using so why not allow new comers to settle. They all had been new to this country at one time. And his own grandfather came from sheep herding background in Scotland.

"Are you worried or upset Senor Mark?' asked a soft voice from the shadows at the back of the patio.

Startled Mark turned to see Mercedes and her duenna sitting silently in the shade.

"Uh no Ma'am but I am wondering what is going on back home."

"Are you what you call the foreman of your ranch?"

"Oh no Ma'am my uncle is my boss."

"Please call me Mercedes."

"Yes Ma'am, uh Mercedes."

A young boy the one Mark had seen yesterday removing debris from the ranch yard come onto the patio and spoke in Spanish to Mercedes.

"Senior Mark would you like to ride out to the horses before breakfast? It will be at least two hours before the meal is served."

"Yes Ma'am…Mercedes I surly would. I can't seem to get enough seeing those golden animals."

"Our horses are ready answered, Mercedes."

There were two horses saddled and a man and woman were mounted waiting. Mark was more than pleased with the horse that had been chosen for him. The horse not only had beauty and grace it was also highly disciplined. The gait was more than satisfactory and when halted the horses stood completely still. The two hours passed all too quickly. When they returned to the hacienda Mark was famished. The breakfast meal was not as formal as the evening meal had been. Alana, Gideon, Mark, Mercedes, Senior Montoya-Luna and Lucia Sofia were the only ones at the table. Mark was wondering where everyone else were when Senior Montoya-Luna told them the other men were rounding up the horses.

When breakfast had been completed Gideon, Mark and Senior Montoya-Luna walked down to a large corral when the first Palomino horses arrived. These were mares with small foals and were driven into a pen for safety. Next came the geldings that were used on the ranch. They were beautiful but it had been decided they were not breeding stock. The last to arrive was the flashy fiery stallions. One in particular was especially eye catching. A tall well over sixteen hands stallion darker than the other horses stood out as a very special animal. Obvious pride shown in Senior Montoya-Luna's eyes as he explained this horse was of the original line his grandfather had started with. Some of the stallions were ridden but this horse was special and it was apparent to Mark just what his job was, to produce quality foals. The horse circled the corral in a high stepping prance that made Marks heart beat faster, the horse was magnificent.

"Senior Montoya-Luna they are the most beautiful horses I have ever seen!" said Mark with enthusiasm from the heart of a true rancher.

"That is why your father and I wanted you to come here to see the horses for yourself. We would like to offer you a partnership in raising more of the horses. We are running out of grazing land and your government will not allow me to buy more land. Since the local authorities are aware your father is a partner and a friend of mine he has been stopped from buying land also. It is a political game that is meant for me to lose. I have lost one son so I am careful to keep our young men under control as well as I can. This corrupt government will take all my horses if they can get away with it. The time will come when I will be forced to give up everything to them, but I must save the horses" said the old man tears choking off his voice.

Gideon had joined Senior Montoya-Luna when he began to talk to Mark. "Mark there are rumors that the government is planning to confiscate these horses. We need to get as many as possible away from the hacienda as soon as possible."

Senior Montoya-Luna said, "Your father and I are prepared to send the herd home with you and share on a fifty-fifty basis. My men including my son and grandsons would drive the herd towards Nevada. Would your Uncle Gavin bring men to drive and protect the herd through the mountains? If the herd was started before the local politicos could get to them we could get them out of the country."

"Uncle Gavin has gone along with everything I have wanted to do at the Broken Anchor. I should wire him..."

"Don't do that said Gideon sternly, there are spies everywhere!"

Sadly Senior Montoya-Luna said, "I would rather turn the herd loose in the mountains and the desert than let this corrupt government get them!"

Mark stood watching the horses in the corral, he had never taken on a project of such great proportions but the more he saw and heard the more he realized it was something he really had to do. He would wait until he was out of the local jurisdiction then wire Gavin that he was bringing the horses home.

Turning to Senior Montoya-Luna he asked, "How soon could we leave here and what do you and father believe is the best route to take the horses?"

Quickly the men returned to the house and retired to Senior Montoya-Luna's office with Raul, Alejandro, Mateo, Marco, Luis, Pablo and Manuel to discuss the plans to move the horses. They decided they needed to be well away from the hacienda before anyone really knew what was happening. They would leave all the older geldings on the ranch along with the old mares that more than likely could not make the hard fast trip. Senior Montoya-Luna had made secret arrangements to send the stallions he could not send north and some of the very young stock to relatives in Spain, a total of ten stallions and twenty-five mares. It was the only way Senor Montoya-Luna could manage to save the work of three generations. By the time they returned to the hacienda the ship would have sailed for Spain.

In the dark of early morning when Mark left his room he found Mercedes waiting in the hallway. "Mark would you please take my mare Bella with you?"

"But Mercedes you love that horse, what if something should happen to her on the trail?"

"I have thought of that but I would prefer that to having the local rabble get hold of her! Please Mark I beg of you take her away!"

Marks heart melted at the sight of the distraught girl in front of him. "Mercedes when the political unrest settles I will bring Bella back to you. In fact I will come back and I want to ask you a question that we will have to talk over with your grandfather." Mercedes smiled thankful her mare was going to safety with someone she trusted.

Mark was sorry to be leaving the hacienda and Mercedes. He had never been in love before but if having your heart do a flip flop and your breathing stop every time that special someone came into view then he was in love.

———————◆———————

It was still dark when the stallions were moved out of the ranch on their way north. Vaqueros from the ranch would lead the horses five to a man for the first part of the move. Within a short period of time young mares with foals followed an older mare with a bell tied around her neck leaving the ranch. Raul Montoya-Luna and the six cousins were in charge of the stallions and finding the best trail, grazing and water, while Gideon, Mark and trusted ranch hands would drive the older mares including Mercedes horse Bella. Mark did not question the reasoning for the division of the herd or how they were moved. The vaqueros knew the horses much better than he did. Their planned route was known only to Senior Montoya-Luna, Raul, Gideon, Alejandro and Mark, there could be no slip-up. Mark himself decided he would take the position of riding drag to make certain the stragglers kept up.

———◆———

Less than a week later a fat sergeant named Gomez riding a rather small horse at least too small for a man of Gomez size, and his troop of federales rode onto the ranch and past the hitching rails, stopping just short of the tiled patio, showing their disrespect. "Go get Senior Montoya-Luna, Gomez shouted to the small boy sweeping the patio. Tell him General Calderon's men are here!"

Alana and Mercedes followed the boy out to where Gomez had dismounted without invitation. "My father and my brother are not here," Alana told the ugly, dirty Gomez!

Anger flushed Gomez cheeks, he did not relish riding any further and he was certain by the stance the two women took he would not be invited to rest overnight. "Where are the horses, he asked accusingly seeing the empty corrals and where is your brother?"

"My father and my brother have moved almost all the horses to the pastures at the foot of the mountains for the summer."

"All of them?" Shouted Gomez in a high pitched squeaky voice.

"Well of course not all of them as you can see there is part of the herd," said Alana pointing to the horses some distance from the hacienda, hoping Gomez did not realize the herd was made up of old mares and geldings.

"General Calderon sent us to tell your father he must bring in half of his mares and stallions and turn them over for military use. He will be most displeased if he has to go to the mountains for them. When will the old man be back?" asked Gomez brimming with disrespect.

"I do not know" said Alana truthfully since the women had no idea where the men were at the moment or when the men would return.

"You lie, I should shake the truth from you!"

"I don't think General Calderon would like it if he had to deal with a fat disrespectful sergeant! It is to his best interest to remain in the good graces of the King of Spain who as you may or may not know is my father's relative, answered Alana angrily and that said she and Mercedes retired back inside the house.

Gomez was disappointed and extremely angry it was near hatred for the women to be disrespectful in front of his men when he had not been invited to spend the night. He would have enjoyed being in the company of the lovely women of the hacienda and would have enjoyed the good Medera that Senior Montoya-Luna served. He was not looking forward to the long ride back to the army post and to have to tell General Calderon he was returning without any of the horses. He had hoped Montoya-Luna would send riders with the horses to return with Gomez. It would have been a feather in his cap to deliver the horses personally. To return empty handed would do nothing for his already strained relationship with General Calderon.

Seventy or more miles to the northeast of the hacienda Senior Montoya-Luna, his men, Gideon and Mark drove the horses north towards the Broken Anchor. Avoiding the towns the men kept the horses from the public eye. Mark or one of the men went into the town for supplies. When they reached the larger town of Kingston Valley Mark sent a wire to Gavin and hoped Gavin would come running. Senior Montoya-Luna had expressed the desire to return home as soon as possible. He did not like leaving the women of his family for long, there was always danger of roving bands of outlaws, not to mention the Mexican Federales. Once the herd was inside the state lines of Nevada Mark began to breathe easier.

———◆———

A young rider from Red Lodge rode hard and fast onto the Broken Anchor asking for Gavin. Opening the telegram it read, "Come running. On the trail to Rock Point to avoid towns. Large horse herd need help. Mark" Within the hour Gavin and a dozen riders left the ranch on the trail to meet the herd. Many questions raced through Gavin's mind including why were the horses being brought through the mountains? Large horse herd, where did they come from? Why the mystery? Who was helping Mark with the horses now? Why avoid towns?

When Gavin and his men were a few miles north of Rock Point Gavin sent a rider ahead to spot the herd. Gavin and the men had rode hard to meet Mark and their own horses needed a rest until they knew where to meet the herd. Seventeen miles south of Rock Point the two parties met. Montoya-Luna's men with the stallions had skirted the desert. The herd was tired but in good shape. Gavin and Gideon had not seen one another since well before Arabella's wedding and had not talked about important matters since long before that. They had much to say to one another. Each man thought the other looked older. The two brothers walked off to one side of the camp to talk and to make up for lost time apart. Gavin found that Gideon was no longer arrogant but had mellowed and appeared to be sincere in helping the Broken Anchor establish a new herd of Palomino horses. He asked Gavin about his other four children since he had no direct communication with Stephen and had not seen any of them.

Gideon thought Gavin had lost weight and was older and sadder looking. He knew what the loss of Moria meant to Gavin. As the men sat at their camp fire that night Gavin was impressed with Senior Montoya-Luna's decision to save his horses, and he was most proud of Mark for making the choice to help when it would have been so easy to avoid trouble and return home. He could have gotten even with Gideon at the same time, for revenge is a dish best served cold. Had the Montoya-Luna men been caught by General Calderon's men they more than likely would have been killed at the very least imprisoned. It was difficult to predict what a corrupt government would do. The herd especially the mares with foals reached them the next day. The decision was made to allow the horses to rest and graze for a couple of days. They were well inside the Nevada border and there had been no sign of anyone following the herd. The Broken Anchor crew would take the horses from Montoya-Luna's men and the pace would slow down.

Montoya-Luna's men had a fire of their own they shared with the Broken Anchor ranch hands. They had delivered the herd to the Broken Anchor men and tomorrow they would be returning home. Senior Montoya-Luna allowed the men to drink their native alcoholic beverage called pulque, a milky sour yeast concoction that when offered to Mark and Gavin they found much to dislike. They were neither one drinkers so as soon as the man who offered them the drink left they set their cups down. All of this was observed by the sharp eyes of Senior Montoya-Luna, "It takes time to develop a taste for pulque, I, myself am not fond of it."

The men from the Montoya-Luna hacienda along with Mark and Gavin sat talking, telling one another of their life and customs. Finally Mark got the nerve to ask Senior Montoya-Luna about the golden horses and how he had come by the beginnings of his herd.

The old man's eyes sparkled as he began to tell the story of the golden horses. "Our herd is direct descendants of horses owned by Queen Isobel of Spain. She wanted these golden horses to live on forever, they are an old breed that was used during the Crusades. Most ranchers use selective breeding just as we do. Their color ranges from a dark gold to light almost yellow, but the manes and tails will always be nearly white. The first horses were brought to Mexico by the conquistadores. We have not found anything our horses cannot do. Since they are so versatile they are coveted by rulers and leaders all over the world. My family brought our first horses from Spain with us when we obtained our land grant. My grandfather was a small child and well he remembers the golden horses when they were turned out on the green pastures after the ship ride. Spain wanted people to settle in the new world."

"In raids across the border the Indians obtained some of the horses and they mixed with the wild horses. My grandfather returned to Spain and brought back more horses. He returned with five blooded mares and a stallion from the linage of Queen Isobel's own stable. That was all the horses we were allowed to buy. Of course he didn't buy them from her but the linage has been kept as pure as can be managed. Any stallion that is deemed unworthy is gelded and sold. They kept only the best for breeding. I have followed suite, it is unthinkable these horses would be badly treated or the pure bred lines die out." Mark listened mesmerized by the story.

Early the following morning Senior Montoya-Luna walked out to the stallions and called to the dark golden one. The horse immediately left the herd and came to him. This stallion had the atavistic instincts of his ancestral linage. He was forever on guard when in a different situation. Licking sugar from Senior Montoya-Luna's hand the big horse nuzzled the man. With tears in his eyes Senior Montoya-Luna returned to his riding horse, he waved goodbye as he, Gideon and the other men from the hacienda began the return trip home not knowing what was in store for them.

———◆———

The Broken Anchor riders almost fought over who would lead the stallions, the men were amazed at how well behaved the horses were. On the other hand the mares were protective of their foals. Gavin thought they would do well on their ranch. Senior Montoya-Luna had made Gavin and Mark an offer they could not resist taking, it was an opportunity to start a Palomino herd of their own. Oh how Moria would have loved these fiery golden horses thought Gavin as he rode alongside the herd. His thoughts deep in sorrow for his dead wife and what might have been. At times he ached to hear her laughter again.

The next few days were spent at a leisurely pace for men and horses. The last night on the trail had caught the riders and their horse herd just outside of Red Lodge, one more day and they would be home. Gavin sent Mark and two to the men into town for supplies and mail. The men had lived on rather sparse rations since starting the herd north, Mark sent a coded telegram to his father telling him they were almost to the ranch speaking of the horse Bella as a person that she was well and happy. He knew Mercedes would be worried for the safety of the horse. After sending the telegram the men bought a large ham, sugar, coffee and several dozen eggs before returning to the herd. They had another day before reaching home, but tonight the men would eat supper of something more than beans and biscuits.

Mark had difficulty not thinking of the coming meeting with his mother. She would not be happy with his news of the ranches partnership with his father and the golden horses or his impending marriage.

———◆———

Isobel was standing at her window when the golden horses came into the ranch yard and into the corrals. They were truly beautiful animals and she wondered how Mark had come into possession of such animals.

When the horses were settled into corrals and fenced pastures Mark went to see his mother.

He was not looking forward to telling her that the Broken Anchor was now partners with Senior Montoya-Luna the father of the woman Gideon was living with instead of his legal family. In the big kitchen of the Heritage Mark drank coffee and ate pie Anna had set in front of him. Her husband had been one of the men to go meet the herd and she was glad he had returned safe and sound. Isobel sat silent agitated, angrily disapproving until Mark was finished. "You know this is a ploy by Gideon (she did not say father) to win you to his side don't you? And you are being foolish and playing right into his hands" Said a very angry Isobel.

"Mother I don't see sides, this fight between you and dad is his and your affair. You are both my parents and I will not join in or take sides" said an exhausted Mark! He decided he might as well get everything out in the open, get Isobel's rant and rage done in one fell swoop knowing she would be extremely angry. "Another thing Alana has a niece Mercedes, she asked me to bring her mare Bella north for safety. When this political uprising is over in California I will take Bella back to Mercedes and I will marry her if she will have me, if her grandfather and she agree."

"You cannot mean to marry an Indian/Mexican! Shouted Isobel. I won't have it!"

Shocked Mark shouted back, "she is Spanish not Indian or Mexican, and yes I am going to marry her if she will have me. Mother the Montoya-Luna family can trace their ancestors back to the old King of Spain, many years back. Mother you can't continue with this hate and bitterness. Arabella has asked you to come visit her but you can't put your hate aside long enough to think of anything else. Please Mother be happy for me! Stephen is making a life as a lawyer go to him and help him if you can, do anything instead of brooding in the tower of this house."

Isobel could not believe what she heard from her son who had never in his life raised his voice to her before. Well if he did not want her around she would go visit Arabella and Stephen! Once she was gone and he had time to think it over he would come to his senses and forget this Mexican girl. What was so appealing about these women that father and son were besotted by them? Well she really didn't want to know since she had no intention of ever having any interaction with this girl Mark said he would marry. Within the week Isobel began plans to go to San Francisco to visit her daughter and son in law David and her son Stephen. She would open her town house and begin with parties and social gatherings.

It was a somber Mark that asked to talk to Gavin. He was sorry he and his mother had quarreled however he was still determined to ask Mercedes to marry him as soon as it was safe to return her horse to her and the horses that belonged to Senior Montoya-Luna. Gavin refrained from talking about the affairs of his brother and sister in law, he did however tell Mark he had to do what he thought was best for him, that no one could live his life for him; that he could not live his life the way someone else wanted him to. He had to take happiness where he found it, life was short, shorter for some and he had to make the most of it while he could.

———◆———

28

THE SHEEP ARRIVE

The summer months found the horses doing well. The men had begun to train the yearlings and were amazed at the intelligence of the horses. The horses Senior Montoya-Luna had indicated should be gelded if they did not reach their potential were added to the ranch remuda all but one. His coat was the color of honey but he did not measure up to the Montoya-Luna breeding standard. Mark and Gavin came to the same conclusion, Tater Fletcher! The horse was not as big as some of the stallions but he was deep chested and could run with amazing speed. He was fiery however well-mannered under saddle. They took the horse to Tater as an offering for all the help he had been to them over the years and with his help at the ranch getting the horses to safety on the Broken Anchor. The two men were rewarded with the look of appreciation in Tater's eyes when he saw the honey colored horse. Tater hid the tears in his eyes as he examined the horse. It had not been gelded and this horse when crossed with his paint and Appaloosa mares would produce good ranch horses, and they would not be in competition with the Montoya-Luna horses.

To save Tater embarrassment Mark and Gavin pretended a need to check the cinches on their saddles on their horses and prepare to return to the Broken Anchor. They had ridden for nearly half an hour when Gavin burst out laughing. "That's the first time I ever saw Tater speechless."

Every once in a while thought Mark it was possible to do something for someone that made up for the anger and hate that seemed to be so ready and available in the world even in his home. As Mark and Gavin rode back home they languished in the lime light of the man they had made so happy with the honey colored horse.

Mark could not get Mercedes off his mind and with the help of Gavin had laid out the plans for a Spanish type house south and east of the Heritage. Should Mercedes not agree to marry him he would live in his own home. Later that day Mark and Gavin and two of his men were at the coral watching one of the hands top off a young colt. The young rider from the north came riding hard into the ranch. Jumping from the sweating horse the rider Wes, a narrow faced wiry man that was given to become excited, hurried up to Gavin and Mark.

Turning to Gavin he said, "Boss I followed that wild horse herd like you wanted and they went into the Gotome canyon. As I was leaving the canyon I saw a herd of sheep moving into this end of the canyon. I watched that sheep herd and billy-be-damned I aint never seen nothing like it in my life. That Mex whistled and the dogs drove them sheep right up into the narrow mouth of the canyon..."

"He aint Mex he's Basque," said Ben another slow talking southern Alabama Broken Anchor cowboy dismissing the sweating rider.

"As I was saying, said Wes giving Ben an angry look, when he whistled again the dogs laid down till he told them to start."

"How many riders they got" asked Mark?

"There wasn't any other rider's the Mex or whatever he is was on a horse leading a pack horse and only him and two dogs herded the sheep. I aint good knowing about sheep but I'll bet there was at least eight hundred head." Gavin thought for a while and finally said "Well, the canyon is almost the only easy way to the open range on the other side. If the herd doesn't stay in the canyon there is no harm, we won't use the canyon until late fall." And the subject was dropped.

———◆———

29

PHILIP

Well as usual Mark did it again, the golden knight was the hero again! I had gotten the same summons to go to California with Mark. I had no intention of being at the beck and call of Gideon. I ignored the letter the day it came and went off riding to town with my friends. Besides I would have had to explain to my father why I was expelled from the new college at Elko in the new state of Nevada.

When I looked in the mirror I began to believe I did not belong to this family. I was different than my siblings. Mark was tall and lean, Stephen was bulky not tall and was short tempered, at least with me. I seemed to tend to run to fat. I have to admit I hated all kinds of exercise and I seldom walked if I could ride. I did not consider myself obese but I was much heavier than I should be. I would have liked to be a professional gambler and when I became successful I would work on becoming slim and handsome. I was easily angered but I had learned to not allow myself to give into anger. I had come out the loser in fights so I became cunning and deceitful. Well maybe I did belong in this family after all.

Not only did Mark return with a herd of expensive horses, Gideon had sent all of the ranch expense money back with Mark. Philip thought to himself if I had gone all it would have been good for was a long ride and probably a chewing out for not having gotten a start on my life's profession and for flunking out of the college at Elko. I simply was not ready to settle down or face my father.

Sometimes I would spend all week at Fort Halleck or Fort Ruby or any one of the nearby towns with my friends. It sure beat chasing smelly cows. When I returned to the ranch broke, I was deeply in debt to a gambler that was an expert at three card Monte I would stay out of Mark and Gavin's sight. I was very good at getting money from my mother. I had spent the money I got for my share of the ranch and why would Mark want to go into debt to Uncle Gavin for more of the mountainous canyon country was a mystery to me. I knew Mark had said I should work for my money, and my answer was why? Who cared how many cows the ranch had? Cattle took too much work and I hated the smell and the men got up so early and worked late sometimes past dark.

As I sat on the veranda on my mother's side of the house I watched a couple of cowboys working with one of the young golden horses. Our side was sparsely furnished with a couple of chairs. Aunt Moria had decorated their side with a round table, four willow woven chairs and potted plants that were moved into the hall in the winter that made the entry pleasant. My mother admired what aunt Moria had done but made no attempt to improve our side. Mark had left instructions that the mare Bella was not to be ridden. Mark wasn't the boss yet and if I took a notion to ride the mare I would! The next time Mark was out on the range that is exactly what I would do. I was thinking about going to go visit Stephen. I always enjoyed the company Stephen associated with, and there were always enchanting women at the parties. I needed to get away from my gambling problem also. What I needed was a new fresh start to forget my yesterday's problems and start over.

The sun had almost reached the position where it would start moving to the west when the two young riders rode into the ranch yard. Deep in thought and wool-gathering for my new plans I did not see the two riders until they drew rein at the hitch rail in front of the house. The two young men Spike Johnston from the Bar J and Joey Baker from the Half Moon ranch stepped off their horses and bounded up onto the veranda. "We are going to Red Lodge for a drink tonight want to come along?"

"Hey, yeah sure."

Running to the barn Philip picked up his saddle and looking at the golden mare Bella, considered riding her, then on second thought he decided he would do that when he was certain Mark was gone from the ranch for a long period of time. He had no desire to tangle with his older brother. He didn't want to think about what would happen if

Mark returned and the mare was gone. What he wanted at present was whiskey and women.

Saddling one of the ranch geldings he spurred out of the ranch yard with Spike and Joey hard on his heels. The three malingers rode hard giving their horses only short rests until they reined up at the saloon in Red Lodge. At midnight the three men decided to stay overnight with some of the girls from the saloon. With hangovers the three would-be toughs returned to the bar in the saloon the next morning. Their breakfast consisted of more whiskey. The more they drank the braver they became. Spike Johnston began telling how his father and older brothers weren't going to stand by and watch the sheep men take over good grazing land. The more they drank the louder they got. Philip with slurred speech said "what we could do is run them woolies over a cliff and get rid of the cowboy…"

Spike and Joey found that statement funny and laughed uproariously. "Sheep herders' aint cowboys said Joey, don't you know nothing? They's called "damn sheep-men! You just ask my daddy" The three planned and drank far into the night again. The plan was hatched that they would attack the first flock they came upon. The next morning the three loafers began riding towards the Big Thunder Mountains where they knew a flock was camped. Philip had overheard the cowboy telling Gavin and Mark the sheep had taken the short cut through Gotome Canyon to the mountains. It was late afternoon when they reached the McGill flock.

───────◆───────

THE BASQUES

The Basque country was not an area that interested the Normans or Arab Moors and so was more or less left alone. The Basque people could claim a homeland but did not have a nation of their own. They were claimed by Spain or France whichever country was in control at the time. The Basque homeland, a hundred miles across was made up of forests and rocky peaks, where the people raised livestock on farms to eke out a living in the Pyrenees Mountains. Their country is known as Euskal Herria and the people have lived there for more than thirty plus millennia herding sheep and livestock and farming, since the Stone Age as witnessed by cave paintings in the Pyrenees Mountains. The Basque people have a unique language they have maintained for hundreds of years. The Basque language is called Euskara, it is unrelated to any European language. Basque is the only remaining language spoken in Europe since the Roman Conquest.

Basque culture came to the attention of the United States president John Adams and was a form of model to the American Constitution. The Basques under Spanish occupation in 1512 became autonomous. They were recognized as Europe's first whalers and as such were expert sailors and navigators. It was Basque sailors under Spanish rule that guided Columbus's three ships to the new world.

The Basque influence in Nevada came about largely from the gold rush era. Young Basque men headed to the Americas especially South

America then on to North America seeking opportunity to earn enough money to return to their home country to buy land and settle. Those who settled in the Americas were the second, third or more sons of large families. The first son inherited from the father therefore any other sons had to make their own way in life. In the Basque society the younger family members were encouraged to migrate to other parts of the world. They in turn when settled would send for other Basque members. It was soon discovered that more money could be made raising and selling meat to the miners than panning for gold. By the middle of the 1800's there were many Basque itinerant sheep herders. Many herders accepted sheep instead of wages. Once they had a herd they began to graze and roam the public land in the Great Basin, land claimed by the U.S. Government, these were called tramp sheep outfits.

Once the sheep owner was established he sent back to the part of the Basque country he came from for relatives or friends to come to the American west. Like those who came before them they knew very little of the country they were going to. There were names of towns mentioned or spoken of or talked about but without knowledge of English and little or no education about all they brought with them was the knowledge of livestock.

The term sheep herder has become synonymous with someone who came from the Basque region. It was assumed he was a sheep herder and was expected to know sheep while in truth they were from rural areas and knew livestock. However the Basque had other desirable qualifications such as the desire to succeed by extreme hardship and hard work. Many young men learned from an established sheepherder the art of raising sheep. Some of the Basque immigrants became just as well adapted at raising cattle and horses. They were true stockmen.

While some cattle ranchers resented sheep Gavin MacDougall believed that sheep and cattle do not compete for the same food. He knew cattle to be grazers, and sheep were browsers. Each preferred a different type of forage. His ranch the Broken Anchor would do nothing to discourage the new comers.

Once the sheep herder arrived in America the ranch owner outfitted his new employee with hopefully a well trained herding dog, many of the dogs knew more about herding than the men. They also were given a pack burro or mule, a pack saddle with canvas pack bags, bedroll, a canvas tarp, cooking utensils, rifle, a sheep hook and other needs for his nomadic life. If he was lucky he might have a riding horse however most of the herders preferred to walk. The herders had to get used to the great distances the sheep traveled, the silence, the physical elements of working with animals and always being alone. Some found it difficult to withstand the loneliness and succumbed to a condition known as txamisuek-jota or "struck by sagebrush" in which they would not want to meet or talk to strangers and became reclusive. Hard work was not something new to most of them, however herding sheep was to some.

They had to learn how much to allow the dog to work the sheep or the sheep became "dogged sheep" and became nervous with the overuse of the dog. The sheep would then lose weight and the ewes would have smaller lambs. In the spring the pregnant ewes along with the rest of the herd was driven to lambing grounds. The ewes were sheared after their lambs were born. The lambing grounds must be located where there is grass and water and protection from cold prevailing mountain winds. Males were castrated and all had their tails docked for cleanliness. The mothers and lambs are marked in paint with the owner's brand.

The first part of the trail into the mountains must go slow enough for the lambs to keep up. By the time the lambs were old enough to keep up with their mothers the herd might travel ten to twelve miles per day browsing and moving as they go. The herd was kept overnight on their bedding grounds on an open hillside. The herder keeps track of his herd with a black sheep per a certain number of white sheep. He counts the black sheep and if the number of black sheep are present then the herd most likely was complete. If a black sheep was missing the herder took a dog to hunt the lost black sheep and his followers. There was always the threat of coyotes, wolves, mountain lions or bears that would steal lambs.

During hot weather the sheep left their night bedding grounds at sunup. The herder would start to check the herd long before they started their move. Older ewes wore bells around their necks that helped keep track of the herd. In the mountains the sheep feed downhill to water, rested during the heat of the day to midafternoon then fed back up hill till dark to their bedding ground. To pass the time when the herd was browsing and there was no danger from predators a herder might pass the time doing arbor glyphs or tree carving. It was never determined if the carvings on the Aspen trees was from boredom or loneliness, to record events or as a marking for their return trip back to the ranch. Whatever the reason a black scar would build up on the white bark of the Aspen tree when carved and the marks would widen as the tree grows.

Some of the herders also built rock markers or even monuments called arrimutilak or stoneboys and their exact purpose is not truly known, they are found throughout the western United States. This practice seems to be unique to the American herders since it was not practiced in the Basque region. It would appear it was passed from one herder to another. For whatever the reason the carvings and markers were left to posterity.

———◆———

The Basque women who settled in the American west became reputable workers and business women. Some were wives, mothers and sisters of the sheep herders. Once the Basque men arrived in the U.S. they soon sent for wives, mothers, sisters and sweethearts. While the men were herders the women worked in the Basque hotels, some actually owned the hotel where they served Basque food and drink.

The Basque inheritance followed the patriarchal line in the social order and the Basque women faired better than other women in other cultures who came west. Women were often the person in the family to handle the finances and often were considered to be partners and a substantial influence in major decisions both in the home and farm or business. The men were often gone from the home for long periods of time with the sheep and it took a strong willed woman to keep the business and the home going.

The Basques were known for being honest and reliable, stoicism in their everyday business, loyalty and integrity. Through the strong matriarchal domination the best qualities produced the strong sense of family. The women were successful at running hotels and boarding houses and their success was a boon to the community where they lived. Their hotels and boarding houses were used by neighboring ranches where children were boarded during the winter of the school year. Ill or injured people convalesced or pregnant women spent their final days of their pregnancy to be near a doctor if they could afford it. The hotel provided a homey atmosphere with home cooked family type meals, and guests played a card game called "mus" and a form of handball called pelota.

———◆———

THE RAIDERS

Old Bob McGill started his first sheep ranch in Wyoming then relocated into the Utah Territory bringing two Basque brothers Bernardo and Pedro Ibarra as herders. Since Bob could not walk or ride long distances any longer the brothers took turns gathering supplies and herding the sheep. The older brother was herding the sheep when the three young toughs rode into his camp. He was extra cautious of the sheep since word had spread of the objections of the cattle men to having the sheep arrive and a part of the flock belonged to him. He had come to America from his Basque homeland located between the borders of Spain and France ten years ago. He had taken all his wages in sheep and had become partners with Bob McGill when McGill decided to relocate from Wyoming where winters were extremely harsh. It was a good partnership and Bernardo had encouraged his brother Pedro and sister Grace to come to America since they no longer had relatives in the old country. Their sister Grace had started an upscale hotel and restaurant in Red Lodge that catered to the people traveling on the stage line. Her husband had been killed in a mining accident. They had one child who was crippled, mother and daughter made a good living running the hotel and serving meals. Pedro was just beginning to build his flock. He had left two days before with a third of the McGill-Ibarra flock. The brothers would meet later in the summer, join the two flocks and bring them to the home pastures for the winter.

When Old Bob became immobile Bernardo and his wife Anna moved him into their home to care for him. Not only had the move from Wyoming been difficult for the old man, he was getting progressively more incapacitated. Old McGill could still weld power in the state coming from a wealthy family. He had made a will that would give the Ibarra brothers the flock of sheep and the ranch. The remaining McGill family in Scotland would know nothing of the will that Bob McGill left, himself considered a black sheep of the McGill family, until the old man died.

In Northern Nevada and other north western parts of the Western United States, Basque immigrants were closely tied to the sheep business. Those that were experienced with livestock found their life was better outside the gold mines. They could make more money per day by raising sheep and providing the gold camps with meat. They could still have the hides and wool from the herds. The miners found the Basque immigrants to be dependable.

◆

The morning the three young outlaws rode into the McGill-Ibarra brother's camp Bernardo was not surprised they were there. Rumors had been rampant that the cattlemen were displeased with more sheep coming into the valley. Joey spoke up first, "What you doing on cattle range sheep man? He asked drawing out the word sheep man with disgust. Don't you know this is cattle country and there aint no place for sheep. Now why don't you get on your horse and leave? We will take care of your dogs and these woolies!" With that the three men drew guns and began killing the sheep. The dogs barked and ran at the raiders trying to drive them off and were promptly killed for their effort.

Bernado watched in horror as the sheep dropped dead by the dozens. He got to his horse and left before they decided to kill him. He memorized brands and description of the men and horses. Since he spoke very poor English he would have to draw the brands of the horses and the descriptions of the men. The men reloaded their guns and continued shooting, wounding and killing the sheep. They looked for the herder and decided he had hid in a cave somewhere too scared to come out. Tiring of the blood bath the three killers rode around the dead animals and headed for Fort Halleck to the north.

They finally stopped in a grove of Aspen trees to rest their horses. They saw strange writings on a large tree. "Now look at that said Spike sarcastically these fools don't know trees is for firewood not for writing on." And with that he took out his hunting knife and began to remove the writing on the tree. "Damn sheep men! He repeated over and over." The men stayed at Fort Halleck for three days before Philip ran out of money and returned to the ranch. Again he avoided Mark and Gavin. He ate his meals with his mother showering her with attention and compliments and then returned to his room. He wondered what he would do for money while she was in San Francisco. Isobel planned to leave in a week or so.

As the three outlaws, Philip, Joey and Spike killed the sheep the herder watched long enough to identify them. He returned to the McGill headquarters to report to his boss then rode to town to report to the nearest sheriff which was Red Lodge. Sheriff Dave Beldon and his deputy rode into the hills to the place where the killing ground was located. Dead sheep lay everywhere. Very young lambs stood amidst the dead animals bawling for their mothers who could no longer answer. Buzzards sat perched on the dead animals. The lawmen smelled the copper smell of the blood of the mass of the dead and decaying animals before they topped the hill and pulled their neckerchiefs up over their noses before getting any closer to the scene below. A pair of wolves were laying down eating as coyotes slinked at the farthest edge of the dead animals.

Overwhelmed by the destruction Sheriff Beldon drew his gun and fired at the black cloud of buzzards. How could anyone be so stupid as to kill innocent animals for the sheer pleasure of killing? It would be a pleasure to haul them into court. From the information from the sheep herder he was certain he already knew who the guilty parties were. The fly in the ointment was Judge Wittenberg. He was a close friend of both Tom Baker and Bill Johnston and they were well known for wanting the sheep gone, Beldon read Joey and Spikes handy work written all over this deed. He figured Philip MacDougal was the other killer but his uncle and brother were not against the sheep men and would not stand for this nonsense.

A week after the killing spree Sheriff Dave Beldon and his deputy rode onto the Broken Anchor ranch yard and asked for Gavin or Mark. Philip had no way of hearing what was said but he could tell Gavin was angry and Mark joined them. The four men turned towards the house. Too late Philip realized he was trapped on the veranda.

Almost reaching the house Gavin spoke sharply to Philip, "Sheriff Beldon wants to talk to you."

"We have a complaint that you, Spike Johnston and Joey Baker did some sheep killing over on the McGill ranch, what have you got to say?" asked the sheriff.

"You got no proof I done anything," answered Philip belligerently wiping his dripping nose on his shirt sleeve.

"Oh I am afraid we do, that sheep herder may not speak good English but he can draw a picture and has drawings of the brands on the horses and enough of a description to know it was you and those two thugs you run with."

"They was only sheep," answered a callous sullen Philip.

"They are McGill's ranch property and you are under arrest!" Said the sheriff pulling hand cuffs from his belt.

Philip answered in a timorous voice no longer the cocky smart aleck, "Uncle Gavin you can't let him do this, as he again wiped his dripping nose on his shirt sleeve."

"He not only can but will," Mark said harshly, angry that another black mark was being lodged against the Broken Anchor yet again by Philip.

Philip turned dark malevolent eyes on the men. At this moment in time he truly hated his uncle and his brother.

Isobel came outside as sheriff Beldon with Philip in tow stepped off the porch. "Sheriff I have been listening from inside the house. I agree to pay for a third of the damages now if you won't take him to jail.

"Can't do that ma'am it's up to the judge."

"Then I would ask you to allow me to be responsible for Philip. Philip will turn himself into your office in forty-eight hours. He must have a lawyer, you must agree to that." Gavin and Mark stared at Isobel in disbelief, she might as well been with the killers, she was aiding Philip again in his outlaw ways.

The sheriff looked to Gavin for confirmation. Reluctantly with an imperceptible nod Gavin gave consent to Isobel's request. The family was being torn apart and while he wondered the outcome of this latest prank of Philips he had to take the chance. If Philip did not turn himself in he would drag him to Red Lodge and the sheriff's office. Gavin had a low opinion of his spoiled nephew. Sheriff Beldon said to Gavin, "more men have died from associating with the wrong crowd than being shot."

Philip went to his room after the sheriff left, refusing to talk to his mother all through her pleading. Saying he had a headache he began to plan his escape, but before he left he would seek revenge on Mark. There had only been contempt from Mark since he had flunked out of the University of Nevada. He blamed his teachers, his parents, his brothers everyone but himself for failing at school. Late into the night he planned his revenge and escape.

Before dawn the following morning Philip entered the barn and looked into the stall where Mercedes horse Bella stood knee deep in bedding in a clean stall. Going to his own horse he found the horse with very little bedding in a dirty wet stall, begging for food and water.

Anger flooded over Philip. Why had Mark taken such good care of a stranger's horse and had done nothing for his brother? It wouldn't have hurt him to have taken care of Philips horse. For that he knew how he could hurt Mark. He went into the tack room and returned with two pieces of wire. Entering Bella's stall he knelt down and wrapped and tightened a piece of the wire around each of the horse's front feet just above the hoof and smoothed the hair over the wire. The mare stood perfectly still. One thing could be said of the Mexicans they knew how to train horses he thought. He piled bedding around the front legs of the horse and quickly left the stall.

Saddling his horse without feeding or watering it Philip left the ranch at a dead run heading for the stage at Red Lodge. The stage was late by almost an hour when he got to town. Being careful to stay hid he waited at the back of the livery stable. He needed a drink badly but could not leave the safety of the barn, he was afraid the sheriff would see him. He would not have come to Red Lodge if there had been another stage line going through the area.

It was almost sunrise when Gavin and Mark heard the commotion in the horse barn. Both men and a cowboy from the bunkhouse ran to the barn. It was obvious the mare Bella was in distress. Looking into the stall they could not see anything different although the horse was extremely agitated. When she lifted her foot up in pain they saw the much swollen leg. Mark reached the mare first and saw the wire cutting into the horse's leg. Gavin saw the wire about the same time and hurried to the tack room for a pair of wire pliers. Together they managed with great effort to get the wire off the horse's legs. Mark rubbed and massaged the legs until finally the mare could stand quiet. Now the question who and why would anyone do this to an animal? They believed there was not a rider on the ranch that would treat an animal this way.

The cowboy that went to the barn with Mark and Gavin returned to Bella's stall, "Philips horse is gone."

Mark and Gavin looked at one another and said "Philip" in unison!

When he was certain Bella was alright Mark fed and watered his own horse. He went to the bunk house and returned wearing his gun. All Gavin said through anger was "don't do anything foolish." Nodding to Gavin Mark swiftly stepped aboard his horse and left the Broken Anchor. Life would not be the same between the brothers where there had always been mistrust and contempt was now hate. Philip had not only put the Broken Anchor in a bad situation but had done harm to an innocent animal. He hoped he could catch up to Philip before he got on the stage to San Francisco. If not he would run the stage down. He would bring Philip to justice. He might not be able to make him pay for the torture of the horse but he would stand trial for sheep killing.

Mark reached Red Lodge only minutes before the noon stage was due to arrive. Going to the stable he searched for Philips horse. The horse had not been taken care of, it was still saddled and there was no hay in the manger. Pitching hay to Philip's horse Mark began searching the stable for his cowardly brother. He found Philip hiding in the livery loft. The livery owner had found Philip's horse and had gone looking for the owner and to report to the sheriff. People did not just leave their animals and disappear. Jerking the crying, whining Philip to his feet Mark hit him several times before his anger subsided. The crying, whimpering Philip nauseated Mark. Mark gripped Philip by the collar and hauled his brother to his feet by the nape of the neck like a puppy and marched him out of the livery stable and began forcing him towards the sheriff's office. He turned him over to Sheriff Beldon went to the telegraph office and left town. The stage pulled in, loaded and left as Philip watched from behind the bars of the jail.

It seemed there was never to be peace on the Broken Anchor. On the ride home he made the decision to go forth with his life and marry

Mercedes. He would have preferred to bring her into a calm safe quiet life, however he knew that would never happen as long as Isobel lived on the Broken Anchor. If she could not accept Mercedes then he intended to isolate himself from his mother. Gavin had told him several times how short life could be and that he needed to do what was best for him. He would leave immediately to go to California.

Mark returned to the ranch anxious to see if the horse Bella had permanent leg damage. He was met by his mother. "What have you done to Philip?" asked the angry Isobel.

"I turned him over to the sheriff," stated Mark going through the barn and out into the back corral, where he found Gavin walking Bella up and down the length of the corral.

"I don't think the horse is permanently hurt, said Gavin but it's a good thing she was discovered when she was. What about Philip?"

"I delivered him to the sheriff. He was running away as usual! He will stand trial with those other two when the circuit judge gets to Red Lodge."

Turning to his uncle he said to Gavin "I am going to return to the Montoya-Luna ranch and ask Mercedes to marry me. Instead of taking her horse to her I will bring her to her horse. I was going to wait until spring but my house is finished and I want to marry Mercedes if she will have me. I have hesitated hoping mother would relent but that is not going to happen. I sent a wire from Red Lodge to Senior Montoya-Luna telling him of my intentions. He wired back for me to come to the hacienda. I am leaving on the next stage."

Isobel was livid! How could Mark do that to his brother? Her anger had reached a very deadly level as she returned to her rooms. Isobel had followed Mark to the barn and overheard him talking to Gavin. She began to plot how to stop Mark's marriage, she would remove him from his position on the ranch. She would fire him, leave him as outcast as Philip. Suddenly she remembered she no longer had any say at the Broken Anchor in fact Mark was equal in owner ship as Gavin and Gideon. There was the possibility that if she angered Mark she could be removed from the ranch. Still she tried to think of a way to punish Mark. She would stay at the ranch to see what kind of wife he had. There were still ways to take revenge. She stopped one of the cowboys and asked him to return to the house with her. Going to the ranch safe she removed a stack of money, peeling off several bills she told the cowboy to go to Red

Lodge and pay Philips fine. She told the cowboy to keep twenty dollars and give the rest of the money to Phillip but not to ever tell Gavin or Mark she had paid him or paid Philip's fine from ranch funds. How dare Gavin or Mark discipline Philip?

Isobel had divested her holding in the ranch and until now had been glad. At this very moment she wished she still had at least some ownership, she would enjoy jerking it from Mark. She still thought of Philip as her little boy who could do no wrong. It was just a boyish prank with the sheep and Mark had no right to get involved!

Philip sat on the jail bunk cussing his brother for turning him over to the Sheriff. What would it have mattered if Mark had given him some money and turned him loose? He could be many miles west on his way to Stephen. Someday he would make Mark and Gavin pay for what they did to him. Just wait someday he would get even.

The rider from the Broken Anchor stepped into the sheriff's office late that afternoon holding the door open as he was followed by Sheriff Beldon carrying a supper tray for his prisoners.

"What can I do for you?" he asked the rider.

"I was sent to pay Philip's bail."

"It's gonna take $100.00 to get him out. You got that much on you?" asked the sheriff hoping he did not.

"Yes," answered the rider as he peeled off the bills, handing the money to the sheriff. "My boss will need a receipt for this."

"Never thought Gavin would want a receipt."

"Gavin is not paying this bail, Mrs. MacDougall is bailing her son out."

"That figures" said Beldon. To himself he thought she will do him no favor with all the mollycoddling she does. He has to learn to take responsibly for his actions.

The sheriff unlocked the cell and swinging the door open said, "You are free to go Philip. I would advise you to stay away from Spike and Joey. If you were so inclined you could learn a trade or get into one of your fathers business and make a good life for yourself. You may get out of this scrape in good shape but you may not be so lucky next time."

"Yeah, yeah just give me my belongings and my gun so I can get out of here."

"I take it you don't want your supper before you go?"

"No I don't want that slop" said an angry Philip slapping the tray off the desk and onto the floor.

"That will be another three dollars" said the sheriff to the Broken Anchor rider." The two men in the other cell groaned seeing their supper spilled all over the floor.

The rider handed the money to the sheriff and walked out of the office to his horse. Philip was on his own.

Philip left the sheriff's office and headed to the nearest saloon. As he walked in he saw his friends Spike and Joey sitting at a table half way to the bar sharing a bottle of whiskey. "Bring me a glass," he yelled at the bartender. "Where have you guy's been while I was in jail thanks to my brother?" asked Philip bitterly.

"We been waiting for you to get out. We knew your mother wouldn't leave you in there for very long. We paid our fines when we heard that sheep man had identified us. If you had come in the sheriff wouldn't have had to go after you, that's what made him mad. You gotta learn not to kick a law dog, that's where you got into trouble." Said Joey.

"Oh shut up! Did that Broken Anchor rider come in here? I know mother sent me money, I have to find him." Going to the door Philip stopped a youngster and flipping him a coin told him to go to the livery stable and tell the Broken Anchor rider to come here and hurry. "I ought to fire that rider for not waiting for me instead of me having to go to him!" Like Isobel Philip had forgotten he no longer had any say so at the Broken Anchor. He and his mother were free loaders at the ranch.

The youngster soon returned telling Philip the rider had returned home. Philip was furious. He did not have enough money to get him to California. He would wait a day or so then go to the ranch at night and get money from his mother.

◆

The man that walked into the saloon stopped just inside the door waiting for his eyes to adjust to the dark interior. No one paid any attention to him until he walked to the bar ordered a drink and turned to face the room, his left hand holding his drink, his right elbow resting on the bar, his hand near his six gun. His eyes dark as obsidian were flat, expressionless; the eyes of a killer. He was of medium height, well dressed in new black corduroy pants, blue wool shirt and black neckerchief. His guns were carried low, tied down and he stood mesmerizing the room. The flat serpentine eyes fell on the three young men at the table to his right. It irritated him they appeared to not have noticed when he entered the saloon. That was one thing he could not overlook, being ignored. Taking his drink he walked over to the table where Spike Johnson, Joey Baker and Philip sat. The outlaw Piney Malone had a U.S. Marshall trailing him. If he could hook up with a partner or two it might slow the Marshall down long enough for him to put some distance ahead of his pursuer.

"Who's the leader of this gang" Malone asked jokingly.

"I am bragged Spike, why who wants to know? Who are you?" The three young toughs were drunk enough they did not realize they had not received an answer to their question.

Without being asked Malone sat down at the table. The men spent several hours talking and drinking until finally Piney steered the conversation back to joining up. "I got no special reason but I was looking to join up with an up and coming bunch that is out to make some good money."

"We are going to make some quick money. I had this plan for us but I aint had a chance to talk it over with my men," said Spike looking through drunken hazy eyes at the new comer.

"What did you have in mind?" Piney wondered how these three found their way to town.

"The bank," said Spike slurring his speech.

"How much is in it?" asked Joey.

"Don't know but should be enough to give us a new start. The real money is in banks in bigger towns."

Malone had gold dust in his saddlebags he had stolen from a miner, but no one would know for some time, at least until the body was found. He would throw in with these three jokers just to see what they could do and to help cover his tracks. "What is your plan?"

"We take the bank when it opens tomorrow morning and then head west. Philip will hold the horses he is no good with a gun and us three takes the bank, real easy, but no killing."

Oh yeah thought the egomaniac Piney, just leave all the witnesses to identify them. Not if he could help it.

The four men returned to the livery stable unsaddled their horses then bedded down in the loft. Early the next morning the men woke and after making certain there was no one in the livery stable they went over the plans for the robbery. There were parts of the plan Philip did not remember at all. The men rode their horses through town to the café. There were several horses tied at that hitch rail so they rode across the street to the bank and tied their horses to the hitch rail at the bank then returned to the café for breakfast. They watched the bank until they saw the manager open the doors, raise the pull down shades and turn the sign to read Open. Unhurriedly they walked across the street as though they were going to get their horses.

Philip untied the horses mounted his horse and held the others ready to run. He thought it took a long time to collect the money when he heard several shots in the bank. Suddenly the three men burst from the bank, running for their horses. Joey was holding his shoulder as he mounted. Piney turned his horse back along the side of the bank, across a couple of streets and down an alley. The other three fled down the main street of Red Lodge heading west.

Piney was waiting in a small grove of trees a mile from town when Philip, Joey and Spike rode up. "What was that all about shouted Spike, I said no shooting."

"Listen you little punk from now on I am giving the orders, you got that? If we left witnesses we would have every law dog in the territory on us. I've bought us some time. We are going to head west, stay away from towns and especially the Forts. Once we are in California we are heading northwest away from big towns. Philip kept his own council he would leave these men as soon as he could and go to San Francisco to seek refuse with Stephen.

When they reached the lower Humboldt River Joey told them he was going home he needed a doctor he had already decided he wasn't cut out for outlaw life. The other three rode hard west, staying south of Fort Grant.

◆

Two days later as the outlaws rode west a buckboard entered the town of Red Lodge. Bob McGill had received word that the bank had been robbed by the three sheep killers and another man. That meant that Joey Baker and Spike Johnson would not be brought to justice for the killing of his sheep. He still had an alternative. He was on his way to the bank to buy up the Johnson Bar J lien on the ranch and he intended to foreclose, he would drive the Johnson clan out.

There was no lien on Bakers Half Moon ranch but he owed a large sum of money for the cattle he had just purchased. McGill bought up that loan also. No cattle no ranch.

Before the sun set Sheriff Beldon sent two deputies with written papers notifying the Johnsons to vacate the property of the Bar J within two weeks. Two other deputies had ridden to the Half Moon with notice to bring the ranches cattle to the rail head north of Red Lodge. Both ranches were about to no longer exist. The owners and grown sons would have to hire out as ranch hands or move on.

The sons of both ranches had ruined their families. McGill was relying on Gavin and Mark to handle Philip should he return to the Broken Anchor, but in time his behavior would bring him down, one way or another.

❖

Beldon and his posse returned to Red Lodge. They had followed the outlaws as far as they could before losing the trail. Beldon had been very reluctant to turn back however as one of his deputies pointed out if the outlaws were caught the arrest outside their jurisdiction would be thrown out of court and he had a good idea Isobel MacDougall would hire the best lawyer available for Philip.

Three days after the bank robbery U.S. Marshall Colin Nelson rode into Red Lodge and up to Sheriff Dave Beldon's office. "Sheriff I am looking for a killer by the name of Piney Malone, I have papers on him, he is wanted for murder, bank robbery, rape and kidnapping a young girl" said Colin Nelson handing the wanted poster to sheriff Beldon. Nelson was so tired he found it difficult to think. He had set out to hunt Piney Malone as soon as he turned in the two wanted men he had hunted down and turned them over to the Denver office.

"This man was here a few days ago, he joined up with three young local thugs, and they robbed the bank and killed the manager. We know they are headed west but we lost the trail on the Lower Humboldt River," said Sheriff Beldon grudgingly. He always hated to stop chasing an outlaw.

"Those boys don't know who they have joined. Malone has a habit of ending partnerships with a six gun. He is a real egomaniac!" Well thought Beldon now we know who the fourth man was, a known killer. "Those boys are in real danger. There will be bounty hunters after Malone and those boys will be included," said Nelson.

Wearily Marshall Nelson took his horse to the livery stable where he had the horse stabled and grained. He and the horse had gone as far as they could this day. He bought supplies, ate a late noon day meal and decided to get a hotel room and sleep for a few hours. The girl behind the hotel counter wasn't more than a child. She spoke broken English but appeared to be in charge. Through a side window he could see a woman hanging wash on a line. The young girl came from behind the counter with a room key in her hand.

She limped badly from a twisted wretchedly crooked foot and leg. Now Colin realized why she held down the hotel counter and the older woman did wash. Although he knew very little of the Basque people that had settled here he believed these were Basque women running the hotel. The room the girl took him to on the second floor was located at the end of the hall. She opened the door for him to enter, handed him the key and stepped back. Colin stepped into the room it was clean and simple with a clean quilt covering a sagging bed set on wooden posts, two tall posts at the head two short ones at the foot. There was a small round table with a coal oil lantern, a chair that was worn but once had been plush upholstered. On the other side of the room was another small table with a basin and pitcher of water, a clean white towel and under it a chamber pot, above the table was a small mirror. He acquainted himself with his room's location to the street below, locked the door then hung his gun belt on the head post and fell across the bed.

He slept for several hours straight hardly moving. It was late for the supper hour when he woke up starved. He entered the lobby of the hotel and rang the bell. The woman came to the counter and Colin asked if it was possible to get something to eat. She noticed the Marshall's badge and told him in broken English she would prepare something. He followed her to the spotless kitchen where she set out cheese, sliced bread, a cold meat loaf and began frying eggs.

Colin ate the meat, cheese and bread while the eggs were frying. After six eggs he told her he believed his hunger had been squelched. He rose from the table leaving a very hefty tip and walked out onto the hotel porch. The lights were out in the other businesses along the street. The town was quiet except for a barking dog somewhere a couple of streets over and the ever present noise from the saloons. He began walking to the livery to check on his horse.

Reaching the stable he found the owner sitting in the door whittling on a stick watching the last color of light of sun set on the mountains to the west. Colin engaged the owner in conversation about the bank robbery. From what the man told him he knew for certain that Piney Malone had joined the three young cowboys. Since the stable owner was new to the town he did not know their names but he gave Colin a very good description of the horses the men were riding. After tending to his horse the Marshall returned to his hotel room, washed off and read for a while from a book he always carried, a law book.

Colin Nelson woke before daybreak, dressed and silently left his room. Through the half dark dawn he walked to the livery to take care of his horse and to saddle it ready to begin trailing the outlaws. He returned to the hotel, in the hotel lobby the young girl was sweeping the floor. She asked if he would want to eat, remembering last night's fair and the fried eggs he followed her to the kitchen. He was back in the saddle before it began to come light in the east and by the time the sun hit its peak in the zenith he was many miles down the trail headed west and the quarry he was trailing. He was pretty certain the outlaws were headed for Donners Pass, it would be the most isolated shortest area to cross into California.

◆

The Malone gang, Spike was no longer the leader, camped in an isolated canyon. Spike was sulking over the fact that Malone had taken over the leadership of the gang. Muttering to himself he shot a hateful glance at Philip. Philip had said nothing when Malone announced he was the new boss. Malone tired of Spike's constant mumbling raced across the camp and lifted Spike by his collar shoving a gun into his face. His cold dark obsidian eyes held death only an instant away.

"Now you listen to me I'll not listen to any more of your whining, you will do as I say when I say it or we can end it right now, you got that? I've left better dead men than you behind me one or even two more won't make a difference, his hard dark eyes staring Spike down and glancing at Philip for his reaction.

Spike nodded his head in acknowledgement as Malone shoved him back down into a sitting position. Philip nodded with his head down, realized he had gotten into something deep and sinister. He had never intended to get involved in a bank killing and now here he was with Malone a killer that promised to kill them unless they did as he said. Spike nor Philip could begin to match guns with Malone.

Malone taking over the leadership did not believe they were being followed. He had watched when the Red Lodge posse turned back. They made camp where the horses could graze and they had water. They had a bad streak of desert to cross to get to the San Joaquin Mountains. Once in those mountains they would be safe until the past crimes died down. He was certain the Marshall was looking for a lone man not three, it was too soon for him to be looking for bank robbers. He might even by pass Red Lodge.

They camped three miles from Cherry Creek a small town that didn't have a sheriff. Malone became overconfident and felt safe enough that he did not set a night guard. The moon in the first quarter had just enough light to show three bedrolls.

Marshall Nelson stepped slowly and quietly among the sleeping men gathering their pistols and long guns. Going to Malone he kicked the man's foot, shouting "OK up and at'em boys we got a long ride back to Carson City and your new home. Malone you won't have to worry about it since they will hang you soon after you go before the judge. By the way the body of the miner you killed was found. That will be added to your other crimes."

Malone could not believe his dumb luck, first he got mixed up with three stupid cowboys and now he let the Marshall sneak up on him. He must be getting too old for this life. They weren't at Carson City yet and there might still be a chance to escape. That plan fell apart when they found themselves tied to their horses and the horses tied head to tail with neck ropes and no bridles.

———◆———

The Judge in Carson City looked down at Spike and Philip and saw two young men who had fallen under the influence of an older outlaw. The banks money was mostly recovered. When presented with wanted papers the Judge sentenced Malone to hang at sunrise the next morning. The Judge released both young men with a stern warning to mend their ways and should they find themselves in his court room again they would regret it vigorously. Spike and Philip left the courtroom as quickly as possible. Spike headed east back to the ranch. Philip turned southwest to San Francisco.

———◆———

32

THE SPANISH WEDDING

Mark was informed by his father in a telegram that the rein of Colonel Calderon had ended when the Colonel had been hung for theft and treason. It seemed he believed what he confiscated should be his. The Mexican Government not wanting to enter into a fight with Spain and their people agreed to a settlement on land grants in the U.S. and assured Senior Montoya-Luna that his horses would not be taken. Also one of the men from the Montoya-Luna hacienda had seen the fat ex-Sargent Gomez sweeping out a saloon in a little dusty town in Mexico.

Gideon also told Mark it was safe to return the horses the Broken Anchor held for safe keeping. Mark and the Broken Anchor riders left early the next morning to reverse the route they had taken more than a year previously, it seemed like years. They would be met by riders from the Montoya-Luna hacienda, Mark would release his men to return to the Broken Anchor. Mark would have liked his uncle to be at his wedding however the sheep and cattle war was heating up and Gavin believed he needed to be at the ranch. He had gotten the aid of Anna and the ranch wives and they were planning a real barbeque for the newlyweds return.

The men from the hacienda met Mark and the Broken Anchor riders a hundred or so miles north of the hacienda. When they arrived at the gates of the hacienda east of Los Angles they were greeted by his half-brothers Alejandro and Mateo and two of the cousins Pablo and Manuel who were waiting anxiously for the golden horse herd. They had waited to hear of the return of the golden horses for several days. But Mark had not pushed the horses hard, wanting them to be in the best shape possible. Mark thought the younger boys looked pretty smug. For a few seconds he thought it was some joke, on him but he gave them the benefit of the doubt.

"So you are going to marry our cousin? Asked a jovial Alejandro. We will be happy for this as she has moped around ever since you left," he said with a sly grin.

"Maybe she misses her horse Bella" answered Mark, trying to hide his pleasure.

"I think it is not the horse she misses" said Mateo smiling.

When they arrived at the corrals of the hacienda Mark was taken immediately to Senior Montoya-Luna's office where he found a much older appearing man. "Mark are you certain you wish to marry my granddaughter? Marriages of our culture are usually arranged however Mercedes has turned down all offers for her hand in marriage and insists she will remain unmarried until she hears from you."

"Senior Montoya-Luna it has been difficult for me to think of anything else. I have had a Spanish house built on the ranch with only Mercedes in mind. If she refuses me I will live alone, I cannot think of another woman in my house. I would like very much to clean up before I see Mercedes or we make any announcement."

"Of course come to my office when you are ready." Glancing out the window Mark saw Mercedes petting one of the golden horses and almost wished he had brought Bella to her. It would be a sweet reunion when they got home. "Then there only remains to make the announcement to the rest of the family. Mark I am very pleased that the Broken Anchor are partners with the horses. The ones you have returned to us are in very good shape, it is hard to remember they have made that long trip twice in going on two years and look so good."

It was a very nervous Mark that washed up and changed clothes in preparation of seeing Mercedes. It was into a solemn room that Senior Montoya-Luna and Mark entered, the senior nodded to a servant and glasses of wine were passed out. "It is my pleasure to announce that Mark has asked for Mercedes hand in marriage. Alana please ask Mercedes to join us."

Mark's heart did several flips when the girl entered the room followed closely by her duenna. Her grandfather asked her "Mercedes

Mark has asked for your hand in marriage. While this is a rather unusual procedure these are unusual times. In the old country it would be a year before the marriage ceremony took place. He has stated he has a home ready for you. What is your answer?"

"Grandfather I believe I have loved Mark since I first met him. It would be my greatest honor to accept his offer of marriage," answered Mercedes.

"Mark, General Calderon and several young men have bid for the hand of my granddaughter. When she refused one of them became abusive when we moved the horses out of his reach he became impossible and has made threats to me and my house. I want you to know this and be aware. The young man's family is powerful, however it would be most unwise for him to follow you to Nevada but I believe you should know of him.

"I will take extra care to watch for him and protect Mercedes" said Mark.

"We will go into my study with Raul, your father and my two daughters Alana and Lucia. We will attempt to explain how the Spanish wedding is done. Your wedding to Mercedes will be somewhat different than usual. Mercedes has expressed her desire to have a simplified ceremony because she does not wish to make you uncomfortable. Everyone on our hacienda and the neighboring haciendas will attend, it is not unusual to have as many as two hundred guests, however there will not be that many here, explained Senior Montoya-Luna. Mark breathed a sigh of relief in his mind two hundred people was a lot of people!

"As per our custom the wedding will begin late in the day, at 5 pm and continues most of the night into early morning whichever way you wish to look at it. There will be the traditional Flamenco music and dance. The music is played on a Spanish guitar that has six strings and was invented in Andalusia about a century ago. Flamenco music comes from the Gitano's or gypsies. We are telling you this because some day your children will wish to know," said Senior Montoya-Luna.

"Our weddings do not consist of bridesmaids or groomsmen said Alana in a soft melodious voice. The bride as she has expressed it will wear the traditional Mantilla that can trail several feet behind her traje de novia, her wedding gown. The bride and groom exchange coins as a symbol of the wealth and finances they are to share equally. Their wedding rings called alianza are worn on the ring finger of the right hand." no one else is in attendance. They have no Best Man or Maid of Honor. The groom's mother accompanies him down the aisle." Well thought Mark that has been taken care of thinking of Isobel. Had she been there Isobel would have refused to participate in the ceremony.

"After the wedding, at the reception there are traditionally six places, the bride, groom, and their four parents." Continued Senior Montoya-Luna.

"The bride and groom circulate among the tables with baskets of small gifts for their guests," said Lucia softly. At your table should you wish it will be you, Mercedes, your father, our grandfather, Alana and myself?"

"Before you return to Nevada you will present your Actade Matrimonio or marriage certificate for a civil wedding so you can receive your Family Book where the date of your wedding is recorded as will be the births of your children," said Senior Montoya-Luna.

"We will leave you to discuss all this with your father" said Raul as the group rose to leave the room. Mark realizing he would not have the support of his quarrelling parents intended to have no one but Mercedes and himself at the table. "If it is permitted I wish only Mercedes and myself at the table. I believe it will save possible trouble in the future." He said, thinking of his mother and her anger.

Mark wished Gavin was here, it was he who Mark wanted to talk to although they had discussed the marriage, and Gavin told Mark to follow his heart, saying happiness was precious sometimes fleeting always fragile.

When the room had emptied Gideon began to speak, "Mark we have never been close but I want you to know how much I am aware that you and Gavin have made a success of the Broken Anchor. I never cared if the ranch succeeded. I wanted you boys to come into business with me and I know now I was wrong. Alana has taught me to value family, I am just so sorry it took me so long to learn. I want you to know whether or not you and Mercedes marry I will support you in whatever you do" with these words Gideon arose and left Mark alone in the room.

A servant came in bringing a pitcher of cold fruit juice placing it on the table in front of Mark. Turning to the girl he said, "Senorita would you please ask Senorita Mercedes to join me."

Within minutes Mercedes entered the room. Gathering his nerve Mark knew he had to make Mercedes aware of what ranch life was like.

He had to tell her all the good and bad of what she was letting herself in for. As much as he hated doing it he had to tell her of Isobel and the fact she was against the marriage. They talked well into the night keeping nothing from one another. When they finished talking Mercedes duenna awoke and Mercedes helped the elderly woman to her feet and they left the room. They found Senior Montoya-Luna and Gideon with the other men waiting to hear what the young couple decided.

"Senior Montoya-Luna, father, Mercedes and I are going to wed in one week. We want a very small, quiet wedding. Then we plan to spend a little time in either Los Angeles or San Francisco or Sacramento. Perhaps visit all three before going to the ranch. I want Mercedes to choose the furniture for our home. We will have it shipped directly to the ranch. This will be the last time we will have time to ourselves until next year after the round up. As soon as it is day light I am going to go into town and send a telegram to Gavin letting him know I will not be home for a while. I will also telegraph mother of my decision." At this news Gideon had a sad worried look come onto his face. The cousins looked very pleased.

"We will dispense with the custom of cutting the grooms tie into many pieces to auction off" said Raul.

Mateo spoke up saying "but we will still get to throw rice and flowers at you."

———————◆———————

149

33

MARK'S RETURN

A week after their arrival at the ranch the newlyweds were greeted by most of the neighboring families, business people and the families of the Broken Anchor to a gigantic barbeque. The delicious smell of roasting meat and good cooking greeted the couple from the bridge over the lake. Isobel had not attended the barbeque. It was the same old thing with nothing settled, nothing gained.

When Mark and Mercedes returned home to the ranch from California he went to see his mother to talk to her of his marriage. He had invited her to come to his home to meet his wife or as he told her they would come to her. Isobel soon made it clear she was not interested in either choice instead she began a ranting tirade on Gideon and how he was intentionally luring Mark away.

Once she reached a full head of steam in her anger she accused Mark of being disloyal to her, of being selfish in going to see Gideon although she knew funds had been withheld and it was in the interest of the ranch to speak with Gideon. She accused Mark of accepting the bribe of the golden horses, of being stupid for marrying the girl she refused to accept as being Spanish, that the marriage was not valid, legal or worth her time to acknowledge.

Mark left his mother's home vowing to never return. He went to see Gavin who could always put things into perspective. This time however he could not understand why Isobel was so adamant in refusing to be civil to her eldest son. He finally said to Mark, "You have to live your life as full as possible, build your family and allow your mother to go down this path of destruction she has set herself on. You do not have to engage yourself in her hate. Avoid her fits of temper while at the same time being civil to her, as difficult at times as that seems."

Mark returned to his home, Mercedes did not have to ask if he had been successful in his talk with his mother, the sad look on his face said it all.

---◆---

After Mark built his home south of the Heritage and Moria was killed Isobel decided to switch upstairs rooms with Gavin. When they came to the Heritage, Hamish and Maeve had moved into the finished part of the house, three rooms with the children and Fiona. As the house was worked on the north side became completed. When first arriving at the house Gideon and Isobel had taken over that part of the house at the insistence of Moria and Gavin. Isobel believed Gavin and Moria's side was larger but in fact was the exact same size. Gavin allowed the move across the hall, storing his belongings in a storage room. He did not return to the part of the house he had shared with Moria. He moved into the bunk house with the riders. There were too many memories in their bedroom of Moria. However he was not totally dumb as to her reasons for the move, she wanted to be able to watch what went on at Mark's house. More so now that Mark was married. Her hate grew to impossible peaks.

Isobel walked restlessly from window to window on the top floor of the Heritage. Little by little she took over the whole top floor of the house. Daily she watched as two or three of the ranch women went to Mark and Mercedes home with fresh milk, eggs and choice vegetables and apples from the root cellar. One of the ranch girls had quit working in the big house and was now helping Mercedes. Isobel seldom saw Gavin now, he spent long hours on the range for which she was glad. She still blamed him for Philip being driven away. She avoided Mark at all cost since he had returned from California territory with his Mexican or Indian or whatever she was wife. Why Mark had to build such an ugly house so close to her home angered her, a quarter mile away was too close since he married. Isobel had seen the girl through a spyglass walking in what passed for a garden or walking to the lake, her lake. She had seen workmen digging, leveling and hauling dirt from the river area for days. Now it appeared they were planting small trees or bushes. The girl had brought two women with her from California. There always seemed to be one or two of the ranch wives visiting at Mark's home.

An angry Isobel continued her walk from window to window. She saw Mark and Gavin at the corral as one of the wranglers worked a golden horse, the same horse, Mark had tried to give her. However it reminded her of Gideon and she had returned the horse to the herd. Again passing the window facing Marks home she saw Mercedes in the garden directing the workmen. The duenna sitting nearby under a small tree. The slut was wearing her Indian mantilla, who was she trying to impress out here where there was no one of influence. Hatred flared in her eyes. That woman reminded her that Gideon was still alive and she was dying of loneliness. She had gone to San Francisco after Gideon left the ranch to see her lawyer to be absolutely certain everything was still on course. He had attempted to persuade her into returning her accounts for him to manage. She had refused to even discuss the possibility with him. Her intent then as now was to ruin Gideon MacDougall regardless of how or who else it hurt.

She felt utterly betrayed by so many, by Mark when he brought the Palomino horses back to the ranch and now this marriage, these were just more physical ties to Gideon. She thought to herself she would not take Gideon back if he begged on bended knee. Hatred was now her ever constant companion. Since Moria had been killed she never rode again to the lake or on the trails they once rode. She seldom heard from her children. Arabella was busy with her reign in society, Lorelei had become a religious fanatic and she did not know where Philip was.

Stephen had no time for his mother. He was going to make a bid for a high political office in California. There was no time to lose he had to work long and hard. He believed he could count on Gideon to try to stop him. In fact the opposition had knowing of the family feud put out the word that Gideon was backing the opposition. Perhaps once Stephen announced his candidacy Gideon might change his mind but he doubted it. Stephen believed he would only have to work harder to win the election and again beat his father. Too much of his future depended on how the election came out. At times Stephen resented both his parents. Had they not been so determined to hate one another they could have put their time and effort into his campaign. Instead they appeared determined to destroy one another. Why had he been born into their world? He also had a useless brother, Philip that was always hanging around. Even Arabella's husband was working for the opposition. Her in-laws were determined to see their man win the election. Well, let them all turn against him he would show the world that Stephen MacDougall was a force to contend with.

Arabella hated politics and was ashamed of her parents. Her father was off somewhere with his illegitimate Mexican family; her in-laws insisted they were Spanish of high quality. Regardless they had replaced her family and she disliked her father for it. Each time her mother came to visit she spent all her energy railing and ranting against Gideon and looking for a way to seek revenge. Arabella often wondered if things might not have been different had her Aunt Moria not been killed. It seemed many things changed after Moria died.

Arabella wanted children but as time passed that appeared to become less and less of a possibility. Her marriage was not what she had envisioned. Her husband seemed to prefer the company of the men at his club to spending time with her, and they seemed to quarrel more frequently. If only she had children to fill her lonely days.

Isobel had tried to talk to Stephen and Arabella of her betrayal. She tried to make them understand how she felt about the golden horses that were running on the ranch that they were just a way for Gideon to make a more and tighter hold on her, to take Mark from her. Philip had agreed to her complaints and situation then asked for more money. His only thought was more liquor, women and parties. She was truly alone.

◆

34

PRESTON RAID

The various and odd collection of men settled into a cold camp back in the mountains where they could take turns memorizing the lay of the land, some of the raiders were strangers to Nevada. The men were gathered southeast of the town of Gunsight in a hidden canyon. As darkness gathered more riders rode in bringing with them more and more whiskey. Taking a head count the leaders motioned for Bill Johnson of the Bar J to step over to a more secluded area where they were standing, a short distance from the rest of the men.

"Have you heard of any other cattlemen joining us? We can't wait much longer. We need to get to the Preston sheep outfit soon after 2 am, they will be off guard by then."

"The last I saw of Caleb Marsh he was too drunk to ride so there's no use waiting on him." They had planned all week for this raid. They had to stop the westward movement or the sheep would take over the whole state of Nevada.

Looking over the thirty of more men Johnson answered "I think this is most of the men, I am more than ready to go! It's time we put a stop to this sheep business. Johnson and Baker were in this raid for revenge. Bill Johnson now worked for another rancher as did Tom Baker. Johnson no longer had a ranch while Baker had a ranch but no cattle. They blamed the sheep men for their problems not their own hatred and lack of parenting. Even their wives had abandoned them. Baker's wife had returned to her family back east. Mrs. Johnson had moved to the town of Red Lodge and now worked in one of the Basque hotels.

Silently the men mounted their horses and followed the outlaw leaders, the ranchers did not know the leaders who had gathered the riders. They only heard the men were from Wyoming where another cattle and sheep war had been recently fought, again. The leaders were seasoned fighters. The riders followed the Copper River east to a point in the Big Thunder Mountains to a trail that turned north they followed the Pine River until they were almost in sight of the Preston outfit. They removed the torches tied to their saddles and gathered for last minute instructions.

The outlaws plan was to hit the sheep ranch hard, kill anything that moved and burn the rest. Leave no witnesses. After lighting their torches the raiders rode out of the deep arroyo within sight of the barns.

The kitchen door opened and bumped shut, sounding loud in the early morning silence. Mrs. Preston had forgotten to have one of the boys bring in a bucket of drinking water after supper. As she walked to the well to draw the water she saw the horse men with torches. She sounded the alarm as she ran screaming to the house for her husband and sons. The bullet hit her in the middle of the back as she reached the kitchen door. She fell half inside the kitchen blocking the door way.

Preston and his two sons raced to the windows and began firing on the raiders. They could already see three of their men sprawled to the side of the bunk house. One by one the out buildings were burning, the blaze reached high into the sky lighting the nearby trees.

The house was set ablaze and as the three Preston men attempted to flee the inferno they were met with a barrage of gun shots not unlike a firing squad. The Preston family was wiped out in a matter of a few short minutes killed in cold blood. As many sheep as could be forced into a large barn was locked in and the barn set on fire, killing all inside.

Within thirty minutes from the time Mrs. Preston saw the raiders and raised the alarm the raiders had finished their grisly work and had turned back to the mountains.

The following morning two neighbors down the mountain who had seen the fire came to the Preston Camp. There was nothing to be done but to bury the dead. Every building had been burned to the ground and every living livestock and person on the ranch was dead.

As the men finished with the burying detail they each decided it was time to sell their sheep and move on. They would report the raid to the new sheriff of Gunsight, gather their sheep and move north to a less populated area. And pray for the best, their camps were not as large or well protected as the Preston camp was and it had been destroyed.

Even before the Preston raid could be reported another raid was being planned at the saloon in Red Lodge.

◆

35

PHILIP

I spent my days before the problem with the law at the saloons of the nearby towns, usually in the company of my two buddies Spike Johnson and Joey Baker. Since the killing at the sheep herder's camp my arrest and the bank robbery I had been on the run and instead of returning to the ranch I headed to California to stay with Stephen. I truly despised my brother but Steven was my passport at the time for a leisurely life until my latest trouble blew over.

When I arrived in California I found Stephen was not home and I was denied entrance by Stephen's house staff. I was told Stephen had been called to New York at the summons of Jay Gould. With Stephen's home closed I found I did not have funds to live at a hotel. I went to my sister Arabella's home intending to stay until Stephen returned.

Arabella welcomed me into her home however her husband was not so welcoming. He told their friends I was deceitful and cunning a truly unlikeable person. I was oblivious to my brother in-law's feelings and proceeded to make myself at home.

A week or so later I found the liquor cabinet unlocked and well stocked and proceeded to attempt to drink it empty. When Arabella's husband returned home I received a cold reception. I moved out going to a lesser known hotel and signing in under Stephen's name. The hotel knew the name but not the man so I was given complete acceptance. I then began opening accounts in clothing stores where I had several suits made. I managed to get a line of credit at some gambling houses. Life for Philip MacDougall was good while it lasted.

When Stephen returned he found a tall stack of bills that he knew nothing about. It did not take him long to have me found and brought to him. It was a very angry Steven that I faced, I didn't know why, he had the money and could afford to help his brother. As always Steven found Philip a sniveling, whining coward when confronted. Without a second thought Stephen closed all accounts and had Philip removed from the hotel at the end of two months, telling his brother to get a job any job but he was no longer liable for any of his debts.

Instead Philip went to a disreputable gambling house, obtained a line of credit again in Stephen's name and attempted to recoup his losses. The men at the table had no gentleman's agreement concerning the game and on Philip's third attempt at cheating the last card he turned over was an ace of Spades long known as the death card. That card had already been played. He scrambled to his feet struggling for the gun he carried but seldom practiced with. He was dead when he hit the floor. He died as he had lived begging for someone to help him.

The newspapers reported the name of Stephen MacDougall being killed and soon Stephen knew what Philip had done. He had his brother's body retrieved and returned to the ranch for burial. Then he had to set about to re-establish and repair his name and reputation. Philip's latest episode would most likely cost him his possible political position.

It was an angry Isobel that confronted Stephen after the funeral at the ranch. She attacked Stephen with the question asking "if you are as successful as you to want us to believe; why did you allow your brother to sink so low into the gambling world?" She was taking no blame whatsoever for her culpability in Philip's failure or for her enabling his vices. Isobel attempted to scold Stephen. Stephen had no time for his mother's accusations and left immediately to return to California. He determined that if he never saw the ranch again he would be happy.

Arabella and Lorelei only stayed overnight before they too left their mother's home. Arabella did not tell her mother of her experience with a drunken Philip, there was just no use trying to reason with her.

Gideon had not been notified by Stephen of Philips death and the burial had been performed the day the body arrived at the ranch. Gavin believed Isobel and Stephen had done this to prevent Gideon's return to the ranch for the funeral. It would seem there was no limit to which

Isobel and Stephen would go to hurt Gideon, revenge was the name of their game.

———◆———

Sitting under their favorite tree Gavin and Mark discussed the happenings of the past few months. They were sorry for Philips demise but felt he had plunged headlong into the life he choose. They were not surprised at the outcome. Their lives were quickly changing. There appeared to be a range war shaping up that was taking all their time and energy. The cattle men who were not against the sheep men were finding themselves under attack. Gavin and Mark had tried to stay neutral however they had been dragged into the war when they found some of their cattle and horses randomly killed across the ranch. The sheriff still had not caught the culprits. The men of the Broken Anchor became gunfighters when night raiders attempted to attack the Broken Anchor. The valley was at war. Gavin hired more men whose sole purpose was to guard the Palomino horses and the expensive herd bulls. All the workers rode as two man teams on the ranch, a rider had his horse shot from under him. No one ever saw the shooter.

———◆———

36

ISOBEL'S RE-CREATION

Before her marriage Isobel had been one of the great beauties of San Francisco. While she was rumored to be wanton and flighty she had held herself pure. She was known to tease to the point of madness and most of the rumors were false allegations made by jealous rivals. She had left more than one of her rivals beaus dangling while she skipped off with another. Remembering her life before marriage made her sad. If only she had not fallen under the spell of Gideon MacDougall she would now be living in a social whirl wind in San Francisco. She had always been aware that she had married beneath her status. She believed love made fools of some women and she was one.

Perhaps it was not too late. She went to a full length mirror at the end of the great hall upstairs and took stock of herself. Her figure was still good, perhaps fuller now but she had worked to regain her youthful figure after the birth of her children, all five of them. She decided with some pampering her hair and skin could be improved. Since she had given up riding her skin was milk white. Suddenly a thought came to her, she would go to Paris and be recreated; then return to San Francisco and turn society on its ear.

A storm was building over the mountains the rain pounding at the house and the windows. Isobel hardly noticed the rain sliding down the glass and forming rivulets. The storm had begun to compete with the excitement that was building in Isobel. The rain was almost comforting as though it was a human wrapping her in its security.

Going to the door of her rooms she called to Anna to come help her pack. She took only dresses that would do until she could shop. She would leave immediately, go to San Francisco book passage on the next European bound ship and begin to make a new life for herself. She felt alive for the first time in years as she chose her wardrobe to get her to Paris and the fashionable salons. She was taking only two portmanteau, she would buy trunks for her new wardrobe. She was going to leave her old life behind and create a new more exciting one.

◆

Isobel remained in Paris for six months. This was six months in which the house keepers, Anna and Juanita could laugh and talk without waking or disturbing Isobel. Their young children could play in the yard near the house without being told to stay quiet. The women made donuts or bear claws for the men and children, something Isobel had ordered stopped. They were free to visit Mercedes and walk with her to the lake.

One day as Mark and Gavin sat on the back steps eating bear claws Mark mentioned to Gavin that one of their men, Ben, had seen Tater Fletcher. He was riding with the lady that ran the boarding house on the stage line that ran through Fort Cameron to Red Lodge. Her brother was one of the Basque herders who ran sheep north of the Copper River to the north east. The rider said she was a very beautiful lady, he had met her while his wife stayed at her boarding house to be near a doctor when their first child was born. Ben said she was a "larrupin" good cook." "She is no wandering petticoat, although not highly educated she is an honorable woman."

Finally Gavin said, "Do you think it is serious?"

Mark answered, "If what Ben said is true it is. He said the lady was riding the honey colored horse we gave him, Tater was riding the Appaloosa stallion he had captured a few years before. To give up riding the Palomino told the men more than words could say. Gavin smiled and said, "Yep ole Tater is smitten alright that horse is a sure sign. I am truly glad for him, he deserves the best. Good looks and good cooking too he is one lucky man."

◆

As the passenger ship eased into the docks at San Francisco Isobel began to set her plan into motion. First she would check into the Pacific Palace Hotel with her many trunks and boxes. She wanted to continue to be pampered and from there she would sweep San Francisco off its feet. If the rumor mill was still as active as it had always been she was certain her old enemies would know soon enough she was back and she intended to make society sit up and take notice. She had not felt so alive for so long every nerve in her body tingled.

The following evening Isobel swept into the Opera House where she had suffered humiliation a few years before. Isobel entered the room with panache few women could equal. She took her place in one of the seats closest to the stage. She did not go to the family box. She wanted to be where she would be seen not necessarily where she could see the play. With her opera glass she discreetly scanned the audience. She spied the Count Manchelli at least he passed himself off as a Russian count and clinging to his arm was his wife Pricilla; the woman who had spread vicious rumors and lies when Isobel was a girl. Now that would be a coup! She imagined how angry Pricilla would be to find Isobel and the Count in a rather compromising situation? Mentally she made a note to find out where they spent some of their leisure time. Scanning the audience at intermission she saw two more nemesis for possible revenge. Her life could have been so sweet these days but Isobel lived on hate for everyone she perceived who had wronged her in the past, even the distant past. Revenge was her constant companion.

A few days later Isobel found herself seated next to the Count by no coincidence, at a lavish dinner party. He was a very handsome man and easy to talk to. She hung onto every word he said and pretended to enjoy his jokes immensely all the while discreetly watching Pricilla do a slow burn. She had entered the drawing room after dinner to find the Count and Pricilla in a near argument. She had quietly slipped off to the opposite side of the room and came back near them from a distance. While she pretended to be interested in the conversation of the group she had joined she was listening to their quarrel. Turning she met the eyes of the Count and flashed him a dazzling smile. Later as the evening progressed Isobel made certain the count was watching as she slipped out into the garden pathway that was lighted with colorful Chinese lanterns. The cool breeze from the ocean was invigorating and she had never felt so alive.

She slowly wandered about the garden, found a bench and sat near a rose bush of blushing pink color. In a very short time the Count followed her. She teased a while then allowed herself to be taken into his arms and kissed knowing full well the result. As if on cue Pricilla appeared on the garden path.

"You wretched fool, how could you let yourself fall into her web of deceit?" spit the angry wife.

Shocked and stuttering the Count stepped away from Isobel as she turned with a lascivious smile at Pricilla knowing full well her actions was the impetus of a quarrel between husband and wife.

Leaving the Count to explain his dilemma to his angry wife, Isobel returned to the dinner party. She was viewing the extensive art collection her hosts had accumulated when someone appeared at her side. Turning she looked into the deep blue eyes of the most handsome man she had seen for a long time. She found his presence electrifying. Speechless she finally said "hello" as the man asked if he could get her something to drink. She could only nod her head. When he returned with a cup of punch he said "you are Isobel MacDougall are you not?"

"Yes how did you know?"

"I recognized your picture with your sons from Gideon's office. We had a business venture a few years ago." Isobel finally answered with something she could not remember saying, she felt giddy as a school girl.

"Let us go out on the veranda for some fresh air."

"I don't know you, even your name," said Isobel being coy.

"I am Leonard Devaroux, we uh... I arrived here a couple of years ago. Why haven't we met before now?"

"I live on a ranch in Nevada, I came to San Francisco to visit my son and daughter."

"No husband in the picture?"

"No husband in the picture," lied Isobel.

For the next five weeks Isobel and Leonard spent all day and most of the nights together. They took in the opera, theater and all the most prestigious social events most at Isobel's expense. Isobel felt like a debutant again. Then one morning she woke up nauseated, she sent word to Leonard she was indisposed. As the day wore on the feeling passed and she blamed her illness on sea food she had eaten the night before. When the same symptoms occurred the next two days Isobel began to panic. It just could not be happening, fate would not be so cruel! How could this happen and now? She was just past forty years old, and she believed she was past child bearing age. Getting control of herself she began to plan. Gideon wanted a divorce she would agree immediately in fact she would send word for him to meet her, the sooner the better. She did not believe it was necessary for her to see a doctor to confirm the pregnancy, she had given birth to five children and knew the signs well. The fewer who knew of her predicament the better.

As the day wore on Isobel became more convinced she could pull off a marriage to Leonard Devaroux without anyone realizing why. He had sent word he would pick her up at seven-thirty for dinner. She would order dinner served in her suite and they would spend the evening planning their future. They could start their married life in her San Francisco house until they arranged to buy the home that would be known for magnificent parties.

She realized she knew very little about or what Leonard did for a living. Was it mining or railroads or ranching perhaps all three and more? She spent the rest of the day planning a beautiful romantic evening. She lighted the candle sconce along the wall providing a light that enhanced her beauty. She began to believe that Leonard could not resist her proposal.

At seven-thirty the knock on the door announced the arrival of her lover. A glance in the full length hall mirror confirmed she was beautiful. Opening the door the light in Leonard's eyes told her she had planned well and her choice of gown had been an excellent one.

"Come in, I hope you don't mind, I took the liberty of ordering dinner. I thought we could spend the evening here."

After the dinner had been cleared away and Champaign poured, Isobel sat down next to Leonard on the divan. "Darling there is something I wish to talk to you about." And so Isobel explained to her lover how their lives were forever about to change.

Devaroux sat stunned. A baby! Finding his voice he said "this is impossible! You cannot be pregnant and I cannot marry you, I...I have a wife and family in New Orleans. No this cannot be happening now. I have just closed the biggest deal I have ever made with the railroad. I was going to tell you tonight our little play time is over, I am being sent back east now that the deal has closed. I am sorry Isobel I am sorry...!" And with that announcement Leonard Devaroux fled from

Isobel's room and life leaving behind a crushed broken woman. Isobel felt dizzy, humiliated, lost and angry. She spent the rest of the night going from tears to rage to utter fear. The next morning very early she left San Francisco to return to the ranch.

———◆———

37

DECEPTION

Two weeks later found Isobel back at the ranch shuttered on the upper floor, more bitter and resentful and revenge minded than ever before. She was more alone pacing from window to window in her endless rounds of her self-imposed tower prison.

After another of the latest fights with Gideon and her disappointment and angry outburst with Mark Isobel isolated herself in the sanctuary of the connected rooms she called her home at the Heritage. It seemed her life was one disappointment after another. She was truly alone her children no longer lived in the over-sized mansion. Mark and Mercedes lived in their house down the valley. Isobel made it clear she would not allow Mercedes to live or visit in "her" home. Gideon had left San Francisco again without a divorce to live permanently in California at the hacienda with his mistress Alana Maria, after his discovery at the Pacific Palace by Isobel. Everything was the same as before, almost.

Now Isobel was even more alone but carrying the unwanted love child. Oh life was cruel! Why her? She was so alone and unhappy. Arabella and Steven were living in San Francisco she seldom heard from them. She missed Philip but seldom ever visited his grave. Loralie was at the mission in Santa Fe New Mexico. She would never dream of being friends with the wives of the ranch workers like Moria did. She was truly alone.

There was no one to talk to, even to see other than the cook/

housekeeper. She stood at the upstairs window of the house watching night close in. The mountain lion called from high upon the side of the mountain. Coyotes moved across the valley. The pine trees became black spears in the moon light. Somewhere outside she could hear the night insects chirp. The wind whispered in the cottonwood trees planted by the mother in law she had never met. The large leaves of the trees of the cottonwood flicked into one another as the wind in the canyon rose and fell. She went to her rocking chair to start another long, lonesome night of worry and crying.

Owls called from near the river, a mournful call, sad, almost as sad as she felt, cold, sad and alone. The Apache and many Native people believed that the call of the owl in the evening was a bad omen, the call in the daytime was a malicious warning. Be aware in the hearing of the owl in the evening the call of evil approaching unexpectedly. She became angry to think she was living among ignorant superstitious people. She awoke in the rocking chair she had slept in for the past two nights, the chair she had slept in for years when her children were ill and she waited for the long night hours to pass, waited until the day light hours would reveal if the sick child was getting better or dead.

The next morning rising stiffly from the chair she walked to the window and looked down on the activity of the ranch. The washer woman hung clothes on a wire line stretched between two cottonwood trees. Three ranch hands rode from the ranch out towards the river and the north range. Two men walked toward the corral where the young horses ran about kicking at one another. Anna, the house maid that Isobel was so careful to avoid walked down the driveway to the hitch rail calling to one of her children, and Anna had several children.

All this activity and not one soul looked up at the windows where Isobel had isolated herself from the world, not one person on the ranch appeared to know she lived there or even cared. The sun shone on the small grouping of workers homes north of the Big House.

———◆———

Isobel heard the carriage as it crossed the bridge at the river. She did not recognize the carriage or anyone riding in it, there were at least three women in the large carriage holding parasols. The carriage stopped at the home of Mark and Mercedes. Unconcerned Isobel picked up her sewing and sat in the rocking chair in front of the window, she enjoyed the warm breeze as it moved the curtains. Finally she put her sewing aside and leaned back closing her eyes in sleep.

She was awakened sometime later and from the position of the sun she knew she had slept for quite some time. The sound of carriage wheels in the driveway had awakened her. She saw the carriage had stopped in front of the mansion and from her advantage point high above she saw Gideon descend from the carriage. One of the women closed her parasol and Isobel recognized Gideon's mistress. Alana Maria Montoya-Luna! The woman left the carriage and walked to the corral where the latest golden colts were gathered. She had overheard talk that some of the young horses would be shipped by rail to the Montoya-Luna hacienda within a few days. Gavin and Mark were excited they could now ship livestock by railroad and no longer had to make the long overland drives. Isobel had no interest in the workings of the ranch. She would not give a care if they all left.

Her knuckles turned white as she gripped the back of the rocking chair, she was overcome by a breath taking blackness and when she looked again the carriage had turned around and was again returning to Mark's home down the valley. Gideon had come into the house. She had left San Francisco without seeing him after she had summoned him regarding her giving him a divorce. Shaking and livid with anger Isobel remained in her rooms now considering all that had happened she would never give him a divorce, not over her dead body. A soft tap on the door announced the presence of Anna. Opening the door Anna did not meet Isobel's cold stare when she was told that Gideon wished to speak with her.

"You can tell him I have nothing to say to him." Silently Anna turned to leave as Isobel slammed the door closed. She began to pace the floor. How dare he bring his whore near her? She would find a way to bar him from coming onto the ranch ever again. Oh how she wished she were a man she would hunt him down and kill him for the way he had treated her and she considered it his fault she was in the predicament she was in now.

She heard Gideon on the stairs outside her door. As he entered without knocking Isobel flew into a rage, screaming at him "Why did you bring your whore here? Get her off my property!"

Gideon remained calm saying "she came to see her niece who is having a baby, which by the way is your grandchild! Isobel I have divorce papers that would put an end to our quarrelling like this. Would you please just sign them so we can each go on with our lives?"

Isobel shouted profanity at Gideon when he mentioned divorce. "So you can marry your whore you mean, and make your bastard sons legal you mean?" No I will never sign such papers! I will kill you first!" Isobel again flew into a rage as she ran at Gideon screaming obscenities clawing, kicking and biting at the man she so despised. "How could you bring that whore, that slut, that...that tramp to my house?" She screamed clawing at Gideon's face.

Before he could ward off the attack Isobel had raked at his face with her finger nails, all the while spewing vile and vicious threats at Alana. Finally Gideon got hold of Isobel's wrists forcing her onto the couch by the window that overlooked Mark and Mercedes home. She glanced out the window and saw Alana and Mercedes walking along a path towards the river. Rage renewed itself, "you filthy dog you brought that slut here to humiliate me screeched Isobel." Her face twisted into an ugly mask of hate.

Continuing to hold onto Isobel's wrists Gideon tried to reason with the woman he had grown to hate. She was the proverbial albatross around his neck, he could not remember the last time they had been in the same room together and not quarreled. How he wished he had never met her! As so often in the past he wondered how much of the gossip about her was true.

"Alana came here to see her niece and that has nothing to do with you! The baby Mercedes is having is your grandchild can't you understand that? If you ever had enough sense to be concerned about your family now is the time. But you would rather shut yourself up in this hell hole of a tower and feel sorry for yourself. I came here to tell you I have filed for a divorce and whether you sign the papers or not it is going to happen..." With the words divorce ringing in her head Isobel flew into a renewed rage and threw herself clawing and gnashing her teeth at Gideon.

Gideon shoved her away from him as she hit and clawed at him. With a final shove she fell on the bed. He was shaking with anger as he left her there in a crumpled heap sobbing. Humiliated that he had lost his temper, he left the room and slowly descended the staircase. He returned to Marks home where he waited for Alana to return. It was afternoon when Gideon, Alana and Mercedes duenna left to begin the long trip to return to their home. Mercedes elderly duenna was returning to California. A much younger girl would replace her, as she would care for Mercedes and the new baby. If the baby was a girl she would become her duenna and remain with her as long as she was able. Also a young woman had come to help Mercedes in the house. The people in the carriage would again stay overnight at Red Lodge. Gideon wanted to get to San Francisco as soon as possible and file the divorce papers. Isobel was poison. His life would never be the same. This had been a waste of time to think he could talk to her but he had to try to free himself from her hatred. He had no doubt the woman was dangerously demented.

❖

It was dark when Anna brought the food tray to Isobel's room, knocking gently on the door. There was no answer. It was past midnight when the storm broke over the mountains. Thunder rumbled and built into a crescendo that shook the house. Lightening flashed and struck the cedar trees on the mountain behind the house. Isobel could not remember such a storm in all the years she had lived at the Heritage. The raging of the storm was equal to that of the woman lying on the bed. Gideon would pay for this, oh how he would pay for this yet another humiliation. He would find he could not throw her away like a piece of bread crust. She would never allow him to marry Alana or be happy. Finally with the passing of the storm she fell asleep.

Several hours later Isobel woke from a sound exhausted sleep. She struck a match and lighted the candle inside the globe lamp on her bedside table. The little porcelain clock with pink roses read three-thirty a.m. She rose from her bed still fully clothed to light another candle, taking it to her dressing table. Her hair had come undone and hung in loose hanks on her shoulders. There was a bruise on the side of her face that she had no idea how she acquired. She had never in all her life looked so disheveled, frumpy, ill kept, she thought to herself. "I look like I have been raped!" she said aloud. The thought like the root of an evil vine took hold and grew exceeding fast in her mind.

Raped! She could make everyone believe she had been raped by Gideon! His sons would never again speak to him. Mark would send his

Indian wife and the yellow horses back to California and she need never be reminded of them again. She had no intention of ever seeing the baby Mercedes was carrying, she did not care if she had delivered. She would have been happy to hear mother and child died in childbirth!

She sat down in her rocking chair to think. She knew exactly what she was going to do. If she was careful she could make everyone believe she had been raped by Gideon and the baby she was carrying could be passed off as his. No one would ever find out she had entered into a love affair with Leonard Deveraux! When the time came she would figure out what to do with the child. It was certain no one would expect her to allow it to live at the ranch. It could be sent to a mission somewhere.

She left her chair and returned to her dressing table. Taking hold of her dress at the neck with both hands she tugged until the dress tore down to the waist. She quietly walked around the room turning over chairs and small tables, removing pictures and mirrors from the walls and placing them on the floor. She laid pillows from the sofa and chairs on the floor. The room was in complete disarray, it truly looked as if a fight had taken place. Steeling herself to the pain she clawed herself across her chest. Going to the window where she kept a round two inch in diameter stick that was long enough to prop the window open she picked it up. She struck herself first on one arm and shoulder then the other. For good measure she struck herself on her legs and thighs. Unable to bear the pain any longer she laid the window prop on the overturned rocking chair, blew out the candles and laid back down on her bed without undressing. This was how she wanted to be found.

She had no idea what time it was when she heard footsteps on the stairway. Bright sunlight had spread across the room, the day was clear with the passing of the storm. She hoped the bruises she had inflicted on herself had time to take effect.

———— ◆ ————

Stephen had entered the political field with less money than his opponent. Although he had won the election by some miracle he found it difficult to keep up appearances. He had come to the ranch in hopes of selling some of his mining stock to his mother. If she would buy his stock the majority of the stock would remain in their control. They would not have to deal with an outsider. Going back to the ranch was not something he wanted to do it was something that had to be done. It was the only way he could hold his position in California as his rivals closed in like a pack of wolves.

His intention was to see his mother, make a deal and catch the train within twenty-four hours of arriving at the ranch.

He called to his mother as he ran up the stairs to her haven of hate apartment, where she now spent all of her days alone.

She heard the voice of Stephen calling her name. She rose from the bed and pulled a robe about her. She was careful to have her arms uncovered showing her bruises. Opening the door she saw her second son staring at her.

"My God mother what has happened to you? Anna said you had not touched your tray from last night and she was concerned that you were ill she did not say anything about this. Who did this to you? How could something like this happen on this ranch with so many people here? Talk to me, tell me what happened!"

"Gideon!" she sobbed.

Isobel continued with her plan to get back at Gideon. Slowly and dramatically crying she told of his coming to her rooms of the beating and the rape. She left out any and all of her part in the encounter. She did not tell Stephen she was hitting, kicking, clawing, biting and yelling or that Gideon had only tried to hold her away from him, to fend her off. The account she gave was that Gideon burst into her rooms and began attacking her for no reason. Her lies of rape came easily as she became the innocent victim of a brutal man seeking revenge.

Livid with anger and believing his mother's lies Stephen allowed all the hatred from the past to came to the surface and he vowed he would kill his father for what he had done. Slowly he led his mother back to her bed. He closed the drapes and left the room. He found Anna and questioned her about what had happened. Yes his father had been here yesterday afternoon late. No she had not heard anything out of the ordinary, but she remembered she had gone to gather eggs so she couldn't have heard anything. After talking to Anna he then went to find Mark. Mark was in the corral with a new horse from the wild horse herd. The ranch was breaking some of the wild horses for the Army. Stephen ran up calling his name. "Its mother you must come quickly.

Turning the horse over to one of the ranch hands the two men raced back to the house.

They entered their mother's darkened bedroom. Mark opened the drapes and looked into the battered face of his mother who appeared to be semi conscience. Her self-inflected bruises had darkened and spread still more.

"My God what happened here?" Looking around he saw the room was in shambles, pictures off the walls and on the floor however nothing was broken. Isobel managed to look a pitiful sight as slowly and dramatically she raised herself from her bed and repeated her story of Gideon's attack.

Sobbing she said, "I was...I've been raped!"

Stephen and Mark could not believe what their mother again had just told them.

Mark was incredulous, unable to comprehend her story.

"Gideon yesterday!" Isobel afraid she would let something of the truth slip and seeing the effect of her condition with her sons asked them to leave, saying "I want to take a bath."

Silently her sons left her rooms.

Sitting down at her dressing table she began to remove the rest of the pins from her hair and brushed it back into place. She smiled at her reflection and almost hummed a favorite tune as she congratulated herself on the ingenious plan she had set into motion. She could cover her pregnancy and get revenge on Gideon in one fell swoop. Her sons believed her and she was certain everyone else would also. She just had to be careful how she repeated the story. If she pretended she was unable to talk about it perhaps there would not be too many questions.

38

MANY TRUTHS REVEALED

It was two days later when Gavin and several of the Broken Anchor riders returned to the ranch from the north range. Mark was waiting to talk to Gavin. Mark had not gone out on the range with Gavin. Mercedes was very close to her time and Mark was loath to leave her. Everything on the ranch, and in the valley seemed wrong only his life with Mercedes kept him going. His mother's rape was utmost on his mind. Also the valley had night riders raiding both sheep and cattle ranches. Someone was bound and determined to start a war between the cattle ranchers and the sheep herders. They went to sit under the same tree where they had talked so many times over the years. Mark repeated his mother's story to Gavin who sat blank faced, speechless, and unbelieving. Finally he said, "Mark it is hard for me to believe Gideon did such a thing, he has never been a violent person. Granted he loves a good board room fight but has never been violent!" said Gavin unbelieving.

"I would not believe it myself if I had not seen Mother the next day. She was truly beat up."

When Gavin asked to see Isobel he was told she was too tired to talk to him. He was the one she would have to be careful talking to when repeating her story. Gavin was a very savvy man.

He had been out on the range for several days and though he should have been dead tired after hearing of the rape he could not go to sleep and was wide awake, alert to the settling noises of the bunk house, sleeping men and the noises of horses in a nearby corral. This was often the end of his days lately. He had distant distinct memories of his father and mother, and Moria and the sea.

Finally sleep took over and he slept later than usual. He dressed quickly and headed to the cookhouse to eat breakfast with his riders. The cookhouse was empty. He cooked himself breakfast of bacon and eggs, he would leave to go out with the men after he did one more chore. Finishing breakfast he went to the house to see Isobel. She was still too tired and now she professed she was too ill to see him. He did not want to push the issue or make any demands on Mark who was staying close to Mercedes. Finally he saddled up and joined the men on the range. He had a strange feeling about this happening.

The next day Gavin went again to see Isobel. This time she could not put him off. He asked her to repeat her story or what she could remember to him. She assured him she remembered everything! Through sobs and tears she told him Gideon had used his fists to beat her. Gavin was puzzled that the bruises were smaller than what should have been fist marks. He had seen and patched up men who had been in fist fights aboard ship they looked nothing like the marks on Isobel. Gavin began to see holes in her story but he thought that was due to trauma that she was getting confused. Pictures still stood against the walls looking more like they had been placed instead of falling. The room was still in shambles as if she liked having the chaos around her. He sent a telegram to Gideon to meet him in San Francisco. He had to talk to Gideon. He had to hear his version of the altercation before making any decisions. If Gideon was guilty then he had to pay for his actions. If he was innocent then what was the reason behind the charade?

Gavin told Mark he was going to go see Gideon, he had to hear him out before they did anything drastic. A few days later the two men met in San Francisco. Gideon was thunder struck at the news he was accused of raping Isobel! Gavin didn't know if it was because Gideon was his brother but he believed him. There was something amiss with Isobel's story but there was no way to prove different just yet. Gideon told Gavin to return to the ranch and they would just wait to see how this played out. Gideon hoped that Isobel would slip up and they would know what she was up to. Gavin would remain silent for the sake of Mark and his siblings. Isobel became aware that Gavin remained silent and watchful. He made her dreadfully nervous so much so she was afraid he had guessed something. She had to be careful if this scheme was going to work.

───────◆───────

Night riders continued to raid the valley. The cattlemen had formed a Cattleman's Association and some of the hot-heads prodded by Johnston and Baker were demanding revenge. They blamed the sheep men for the loss of their ranches, they never mentioned the fact that their sons had committed a crime so heinous old Bob McGill sought compensation. At the last meeting two more ranchers had joined in with them. There was talk of starting their own vigilante association, talk that was fueled by anger. They were determined to drive the sheep men out. Three sheep ranches had lost herds of sheep scattered to the four winds deep in the mountains and more herders had been killed by the night riders just last night.

The Broken Anchor had been sending their riders in pairs from the beginning of the dispute. It was an almost nightly occurrence that the cattle men were shot at although no one had been injured or killed. At least two riders had their horses shot out from under them. The Broken Anchor riders posted on the north side of the property reported they saw a large group of riders carrying torches riding East on the other side of the Copper River.

Gavin had gone to meet with the Governor of the state when the killing began. The Governor sent U.S. Marshals to the territory and sent troops from Forts Ruby, Grant and Halleck to assist. The elusive night riders continued to burn and kill the sheep and the herders. They seemed to always know where the law would be. Gavin and Mark had started relay riders that would eventually end up reporting to them or the Marshalls of any activity.

The U.S. Marshalls set the trap for the night rider vigilantes and the riders rode into it. The law men chose a ranch that was farther from the forts than some of the burned out ranches. With Gavin and Marks permission the trap was set in Gotome Canyon. The night riders had taken the longer route to the sheep ranch and their return trip through the canyon was a short cut return. The sheep owners had a traitor in their midst. Someone was keeping the cattlemen posted of the goings on at the sheep ranch, the number of men there, and where the herd was grazing.

To be able to convict as many as possible it was determined that everyone would abandon the Zabala ranch to safety. The night of the raid produced only a quarter moon but enough light for the raiders to do their dirty work. They set fire to the ranch but were stymied by the abandonment, not a sheep or person was on the ranch to confront them.

When the raiders reached the narrow part of the canyon they were confronted by the U. S. Marshalls who demanded they surrender. Instead they chose to fight not knowing there were soldiers in the surrounding rocky hillsides. Eleven of the raiders were killed, nine were taken into custody. The two men leading the raiders were Spike Johnston and Joey Baker. Their fathers were the most outspoken of the ranchers against the sheep men. It was only by chance that Caleb Marsh was not with the raiders the night they were arrested. He was too drunk to sit a horse and had been left behind.

Two weeks later Caleb was shot by the wife of a rancher when she heard the chickens being stirred up and believed a coyote or fox was causing the disturbance. Caleb was killed while stealing chickens.

After the Preston camp was raided and the family killed, the sheep driven into the mountains, the Marshalls were called in. A very uneasy truce began to settle over the valley as the trial for those arrested for the burning of the latest ranch began. The highest ranking judge available sat on the bench at the raider's trial. Both Spike and Joey were sentenced to terms in prison. The hoods found in the raiders saddlebags was a main contributing factor to the conviction of all the raiders. Gavin feared it would not last.

◆

When Stephen returned to San Francisco he went straight away to Arabella's home. Telling of how their mother had been beaten and raped by their father. Devastated Arabella could not in any sense of the word comprehend that her father could have done such a thing so despicable. Not the father that let her and Lorelei take galloping horseback rides on his shoulders sometimes, not the father who read to them when he was home sometimes. Not the father who picked them up when they fell or cried. Not the father she thought she knew; until Isobel convinced the girls their father was a truly bad person and she drove him from the ranch.

She left within days to return to the ranch to comfort her mother. Surprised she found her mother in an almost good mood. She had expected to find her bitter and hateful towards Gideon as she had been when she had last seen her mother in San Francisco months before. She was also surprised to discover as the baby grew her mother flaunted her pregnancy and repeated the story of the beating and the rape often always with tears. As her pregnancy grew she dressed in such a way as to show off the baby as she began to take long walks around the ranch. She garnered as much sympathy as possible. She found her mother's story almost rehearsed. Arabella could almost believe her mother enjoyed the attention she was receiving.

◆

Arabella spent the summer attending her mother. She returned to her own home less often as Isobel grew larger. It had been six months since the alleged rape and her mother was getting very large. She still took walks around the ranch and repeated her story often. When she spoke of Gideon it was with hate and malice, her audience believed this was natural.

One afternoon while Isobel slept Arabella walked over to Mark and Mercedes home to see their baby again. She would be returning to San Francisco soon and would miss the child. She had visited Mark's home several times since coming to the ranch always while her mother slept and never telling Isobel of the visits.

Arabella found Mercedes an intelligent girl who was easy to talk to and whose company she truly enjoyed. The baby Fiona Marie was a happy beautiful child. Most of all her brother Mark was beside himself with happiness with his little family. He and Mercedes talked often of having more children.

On this day Arabella had stayed longer than she intended to, wanting to be back at her mother's house when she awoke. As she entered the kitchen she was met by an angry Isobel who had seen her coming from Mark's home.

"Have you been to the house of that slut that's married to your brother?" yelled Isobel. At this angry outburst Anna laid her dish towel on the table and made a dash for the back door going outside.

"How could you disrespect me and go see that woman and her brat? Have you no shame as to enter that Mexicans house? If you are going to go against my wishes you can just go home, I don't need any more disrespect!" With this violent outburst Isobel went upstairs to her rooms and slammed the door.

Arabella left the kitchen crying to find her Uncle Gavin to ask him to take her to Red Lodge the following day to catch the train home. She saw Anna sitting under the tree at the edge of the patio peeling potatoes. "Anna does mother get angry like that often?" she asked.

"Oh yes and it seems like her temper is even shorter now that she is carrying a child. It's not good for the baby for her to become so angry. If it weren't that my family needs the extra money I earn working here I would not return to this house at all."

"Anna I am going to return to my home in San Francisco but I will return when mother's time to be delivered of her baby is near. I am sorry she is so difficult, but perhaps she will mellow when the baby arrives. I wish she could see how happy Mark is with his family then she might understand why he loves Mercedes and Fiona Marie so much."

Thinking of Isobel Anna nodded agreement to Arabella but in her heart she knew this was not true. She considered Isobel wicked and could not wait until the time when she could quit this job forever and not have to deal with the woman.

When Arabella returned to her mother's room she found her mother had gone to bed and was sound asleep. Tip toeing to Isobel's rocking chair in the sitting room adjacent to the bed room, she sat down to wait for her mother to waken. She had slept and rocked for some time when she heard a slight noise outside her mother's door. When she opened the door she found Anna leaving a basket of Isobel's linen being set to one side of the door and returning downstairs. Arabella took the basket into the room and began to fold her mother's undergarments.

After folding the clothes Arabella took a stack of petticoats and camisoles to the chest of drawers that was located in an alcove of her mother's rooms. The clothes in the drawers were tossed about. She began to straighten the clothing into neat stacks. As she moved the tumbled camisoles in the third drawer down, she found a beautiful Egyptian mother-of-pearl box. She and her mother had seen these boxes in the jewelry store on a shopping trip but her mother had not bought the expensive box.

She held the beautiful beech wood box up to the sunlight where sunbeams danced on the intricate arabesque inlay work with hundreds of hand cut pieces of mother of pearl a design from the seventh century. If she remembered correctly what the jeweler had explained to them was they made beautiful jewelry boxes. The box was approximately seven inches by six inches, four inches high. The inside of the box was lined with velvet. Arabella was fascinated with the beautiful piece of art work. She noticed when she opened the box that one corner of the lining was turned up. She lifted the corner and the stiff lining came out revealing a small book in the bottom that fell out. The book opened to a page that was very much dog eared. Unable to prevent herself she read the pages.

As she read her face turned red with embarrassment. This could not be her mother, and who was the man she was with? According to the dated pages she had been with the man weeks before she had returned home. The last entry had been made the day Isobel had expected Leonard for dinner and she would tell him of their baby and her plans to ask Gideon for a divorce. She had written in notes for opening her house in San Francisco. Stunned Arabella stood transfixed absorbing what she had just read. Suddenly like a flash of lighting it hit her that her father was not guilty of raping her mother, the baby was not Gideon's child!

Without a second thought she shoved the diary into her pocket and left the room. She found Gavin and Mark repairing one of the barns. Gavin looked up as Arabella rushed up to him, handing him her mother's diary. Anger had replace embarrassment as she paced back and forth in the corral waiting for her uncle and brother to read the diary. No matter how much her mother hated her father, rape was a serious charge and something despicable for a woman to accuse a man of doing.

Gavin spoke first, "I could not believe that Gideon was guilty of what Isobel accused him of. She lied to cover her indiscretions. I am going to go to town and send a telegram to Gideon and to Stephen. I am going to hold on to this diary, Gideon has a right to know the truth," said Gavin taking his saddle off the corral fence.

"Uncle Gavin may I go to town with you, I am returning to San Francisco today if possible" said Arabella crying as she began running to the house to gather her belongings.

Gavin returned his saddle to the corral fence and took the halters down for the carriage team so Arabella could go with him.

When Arabella returned to the house she told Anna that she was to stop taking trays to her mother, she could come to the table for meals or else. There would be no more pampering and walking on egg shells just to please Isobel. Going into her childhood room Arabella shoved her clothes into a large valise. She was leaving her room when her mother walked in unannounced. "What do you think you are doing? What is going on?"

Pushing past her mother into the hall she said, "I am going home and I may never come back except to see Mark and his family."

"What do you mean going home?"

"You know Mother! I am going to catch the train at Red Lodge and return to San Francisco. You are on your own Mother I know everything."

"You don't understand, I need you here to take care of me, wailed a tearful Isobel"

"No you can take care of yourself! You have been doing very well taking what you want for as long as I can remember," answered Arabella angrily as she descended the spiral staircase.

Dumbfounded Isobel could only stare after her daughter. What could have changed her from the obedient dutiful daughter into such an angry girl?

Suddenly she became fearful of her diary, had Arabella found her diary? Running to the alcove she found the stacked clothing, the open drawer and the empty Egyptian box. The diary was gone! Angrily she swiped the neatly stacked clothing off the top of the chest onto the floor. She had to think. What to do now? She sat down in her rocking chair and that was where she was sitting when Gavin and Arabella went down the road, across the bridge towards town. Mark rode past on his horse to his home without looking towards the huge brooding house called the Heritage.

◆

39

RAID ON THE ZABALA CAMP

The raiders had gathered at the saloon in Red Lodge a few days earlier. The raiders had become over confident as they planned the raid on the Zabala sheep camp. They believed the elderly man swamping out the saloon floor was a Basque who did not speak English, therefore they talked freely in front of him. When the men in the saloon in Red Lodge left the old man went to the sheriff's office, he was told that the sheriff was in the lower part of the county at the Broken Anchor. He was trying to get a posse together to hunt for the raiders that was destroying the sheep ranches, they had killed the Preston family and another U.S. Marshall was on his way but they needed men to join them to help.

The old man then went to the livery stable and asked the owner to send a rider to the Broken Anchor with a message to Gavin MacDougall. The message asked for Gavin to find him when he got into town. Only an hour later that morning Ben from the Broken Anchor rode into town for the mail and supplies. Happily the livery man passed the message on to Ben as he had not found a boy to deliver the message. Going to the saloon Ben found the old man Charlie who told him he had important news but they could not talk in the saloon. Ben asked the old man if he had eaten dinner yet and offered to set him up to table at the Big Dipper café.

Charlie could hardly believe his ears when offered a good meal. When the two men walked into the café it was almost empty, the noon crowd had finished and left. Old Charlie was overwhelmed by the choice of food so Ben asked for a regular meal for himself and asked the waitress to bring Charlie a portion of everything and a pot of coffee.

As soon as the girl returned to the kitchen Charlie told Ben of the planned raid on the Zabala sheep camp. Although he did not know all the names he gave a good description to the point that Ben recognized the ranchers. The leaders were still unknown to either man. The raiders had kept the actual date of the raid close to the vest but they knew when they would meet. The next full moon. Ben thanked old Charlie, paid the bill and asked the waitress to wrap Charlies left overs on his plate for him to take home. He would also eat a good meal for supper.

After picking up the mail and supplies Ben hurried back to the ranch as fast as the light wagon could travel. Reaching the ranch Ben found Gavin and Mark and relayed the information to them. The men were still at the corral when several riders rode onto the ranch. Sheriff Dave Belton stepped down from his horse at Gavin's request and asked for the men to join himself and Mark under the trees. He sent one of the ranch children to ask Anna to make coffee. Sheriff Beldon introduced the two strangers as U.S. Marshals. They told Gavin and Mark they were trailing two men wanted for murder and were fugitives from Wyoming. When Gavin told the men of the information Ben had brought back from town and the description Charlie had provided they were certain the men they hunted and the leaders of the raid were one and the same. The Sheriff would put a man out near the agreed meeting place to alert the sheriff of when the raiders gathered.

The deputy watched for three days from a tree covered cliff up on the Big Thunder Mountains as several riders gathered and built a camp. A cabal of dissidents set out to deal death to the sheep ranch. Their arrival was reported back to the sheriff. The marshals deputized several men and moved out towards the Zabala camp. There was a total of twenty lawmen in the posse. Sheriff Belton requested Gavin and Mark be deputized and join them. The lawmen were watching a short distance from the trail back in a copse of pine trees. When Gavin and Mark agreed to join the lawmen Gavin made a suggestion, since the raiders had to be caught in the act, have Zabala move his sheep and people to safety. They would not be able to save the buildings but they could prevent anyone getting killed. The Marshal sent deputies to stake out the Zabala camp.

The next night soon after midnight the raiders readied themselves to move out. When the torches were lit the raiders moved towards the house and buildings. They stayed within a deep arroyo that allowed the raiders to ride three abreast. They came out to level ground shooting and yelling. Torches were put to every building, the fences, corrals and gates were pulled down, piled up and set on fire.

The raiders seemed not to notice that there were no animals or people on the ranch, the ranch was silent not even the sound of animals. Some of the raiders were so drunk they almost set themselves on fire. Finally having every bit of fencing and all the buildings burning the raiders prepared to leave, they were still not aware there had been no resistance. Believing themselves undetected they prepared to return to Red Lodge by way of Gotome Canyon. The canyon would be a short cut and would be cutting off several miles of travel.

It was nearing dawn as the raiders came through Gotome Canyon. When the raiders reached the narrow part of the canyon they were confronted by the U.S. Marshall's. Weary and some hung over from their nights work and the whiskey causing sleepiness they were unprepared when the Marshals and the sheriff's men closed both ends of the canyon at a narrow curve. The Marshall's identified themselves and told the outlaws to throw down their guns in surrender. Instead they chose to fight not knowing how many Marshalls there were in the surrounding rocky hillsides. It became like shooting fish in a barrel. Several raiders were killed, and more taken into custody one of them being the war promoter from Wyoming. Spike Johnson and Joey Baker were among the leaders. What were they doing here? Gavin thought they should still be serving jail time. Their fathers had been the most outspoken of the ranchers against the sheep men. Hoods found in their saddlebags was a main contributing factor to the convictions of all the raiders. Again the local judge gave out light sentences which angered the Marshall's and the sheriff. Gavin made a mental note to try to get an honest judge elected to office.

One of the U.S. Marshalls told the outlaws the next time he would personally drag them to headquarters in Denver where they would appear before an impartial judge. As Gavin and Mark rode back to the ranch Mark commented that he hoped this was the end of the dispute but he doubted it. Gavin could only agree as they rode silently home.

◆

KILLING ON THE BROKEN ANCHOR

The men on the Broken Anchor returned to the work of the ranch, but they still worked in pairs as they searched the canyons for stray cattle in preparation for the roundup to ship cattle by rail to the Kansas stockyard. The Broken Anchor was preparing for a major shipment. It would be their first since Joseph McCoy had begun a shipyard in Kansas City and shipped beef to Chicago.

Two weeks later Ben one of the night guards rode hard into the ranch. He dismounted as Gavin and Mark came out of the cook house. "Boss some of our stock has been found in the little dead end canyon that we usually don't even look at. Since we are gathering cattle for shipment to Kansas City we are careful to check every canyon, since the ranchers don't seem to be able to provide all the beef the rail road wants. There are four or five of the golden horses, one prized bull and several young cows in there. They have all been killed and chopped up. I left a couple of our men with the killing so you could see exactly what we found!"

Mark and Gavin hurried to their saddled horses and riding hard returned to the killing site. The location was an out of the way place that had taken some doing to drive the horses and cattle into. The Broken Anchor cowboy was right to call it a killing ground.

One of the Indian drovers said there were plenty of tracks and they all led to the north towards the Copper River. They found where the killers had stopped and covered their horse's feet. Then they lost the trail.

Mark went to his horse and flung himself into the saddle telling Gavin to send back to the house for supplies and extra horses, saying "I am going to go get Tall Bear, if anyone can track these killers he can!" Gavin moved the men away from the dead animals to preserve what tracks he could.

The riders with extra horses and pack horse arrived shortly before Mark returned with Tall Bear and a younger version of the Indian who was introduced to the other men as Toby, Tall Bears son. The Broken Anchor riders had heard of the almost mystical powers of tracking the big Indian had but few had ever seen him work or even met him. Tall Bear dismounted and walked back and forth across the trail then he began to circle far out around the dead animals and drew the circle tighter as he got closer to the dead animals. He stooped several times, picking up tiny unfathomable something, as the men watching saw nothing. He turned back to where Gavin and Mark had stopped their horses. Tall Bear held out his hand to Gavin, there were very tiny bits of white in the Indians hand.

"What is that Tall Bear?" asked Mark.

"Sheep, the killers used sheep skins on the feet of their horses to cover their tracks." Whoever killed their livestock were in close proximity to the sheep men or they were trying to throw blame on them.

The men took the sandwiches Anna had prepared for them and waited for Tall Bear to give the signal that he was ready to ride. Tall Bear spent more time walking around the dead animals looking for tracks he mounted his horse and continued to follow the faint trail. He then returned to where Mark and Gavin waited. "Five or six riders. Holding out his hand he held the casings of a sharps rifle saying not many men carry a sharps anymore. Most have traded for the Winchester guns .44/40 or the '73. Come we follow tracks."

The Broken Anchor cowboys strung out several hundred yards behind Tall Bear and Toby who was also a good tracker. The trail led towards the Copper River. They reached the Copper River at dusk and found where the killers had built a fire for coffee then rode into the river.

The killers had traveled in the river for several miles. He believed the killers would remove the coverings from their horse's feet, follow the river for a few miles then exit to the other side one by one and melt into the surrounding area. Mark soon believed the men they were following were from the Norton Box N and from the old Johnston Bar J both on the north side of the Copper River. Then Toby found where they left the river and continued northwest in the direction of Fort Halleck. The Box N and the Bar J were due west.

It was near dark when Tall Bear called a halt and they made camp near the Applegate trail where in 1843 immigrants left Fort Hall in Idaho traveling south along the Humboldt River to the California gold fields. "We will be getting into rocks tomorrow and harder to follow," said the tracker setting his plate aside he rolled up in his blanket and could soon be heard a soft snoring.

The men were up and ready to ride as it became light enough to see the trail. Tall Bear again led off with Toby following the outlaws into the rocky trail. The killers had believed themselves safe and removed the coverings from their horse's feet. Now the trackers looked for rocks marked and nicked by horse shoes. They also looked for signs of moved large rocks or piled up brush where the killers had hid the sheep coverings from their horses feet.

They followed the trail for mile after mile when Tall Bear pulled up. Mark rode up to the Indian who was now off his horse searching for tracks. Over a very small fire for coffee Mark asked Tall bear what the chances were of catching up to the men. Tall Bear thought for a long time then said "we will only know who they are if they make a mistake. They could split up and ride miles up or down the river before leaving the water."

"We would still not know who they are" answered Mark.

"No but I will go till my friend Mark says stop."

Mark talked to Gavin and they made the decision. "We will search one more day and if we don't come up with something then we will return home. Agreed? The men all nodded in agreement.

Mark had trouble going to sleep. He believed war had been declared on the Broken Anchor. He had begun to think the Broken Anchor would not survive this latest tragedy. He would send a telegram to Senior Montoya-Luna as soon as he could to inform him of the disaster. The horses killed belonged to him. One of the cattle had been the prize bull the Broken Anchor had high stakes in. Someone knew of the value in dollar amount and the importance to the Broken Anchor herd of this animal. His off spring would have brought huge sums of money to the ranch in turn to pay off the debt for the last cattle the ranch had bought. It was a revenge killing, someone hated the Broken Anchor. Gavin added it may have been jealousy also.

Early the next morning Tall Bear and Toby left the camp in search of tracks. Just as the men of the Broken Anchor were mounting to follow the tracker returned with the bad news. "They have been crossed over by a cattle herd. I will ride ahead and catch up with the herd and ask if the drovers have seen several riders. The consensus of Tall Bear, Mark and Gavin was the herd was headed for Fort Halleck up north on the Fox River. Gavin didn't like to leave the ranch with so many of the men away. Tall Bear suggested that he and Toby ride to catch the herd while Gavin and Mark return to the ranch. Ben, one of the Broken Anchor riders went with the trackers in case there were hardnosed men who still refused to talk to an Indian. Tall Bear would report the killings to the Commander at Fort Halleck.

It was late noon when the trackers reached the trail herd. The first drover pointed out the trail boss who told Tall Bear that five riders stopped with them a day earlier. They wanted to buy or trade horses but the herd was headed for Denver the trail boss could not afford to trade for tired horses. He could provide a good description of the men and had overheard them talking about Fort Halleck.

Tall Bear, Toby and Ben rode straight for the Fort. As they dismounted at the Commanders Headquarters a tall older soldier came out the door and stopped to talk with them. He introduced himself as Clay Daniels.

"We are tracking five men who killed live stock down south on the ranch called the Broken Anchor on the Copper River."

"You mean Gavin MacDougall's ranch?" asked the soldier.

"Yes, you know Gavin and Mark?"

"When I knew Mark he was just a button, bright and always full of questions. Gavin hired me and two other soldiers named Pickett and Jackson I think their names were, to help escort them the first time they went out to the ranch but that was many years ago. Fort Halleck was my first scouting assignment for the army and now I am back. How are the MacDougall's?"

Ben and Tall Bear told Clay the overall facts of the family. Sadness came over the old soldiers face at the news of Moria's death saying, "She was a very nice lady."

"And speaking of that time when I knew them they were stopped by an outlaw family by the name of Strader. By chance one of the men I think you are looking for is Zeb Strader. He and four other men swapped horses here a day or so ago. Think they were headed for Denver at least that was the talk, but you can't never tell about men like that. I found they would rather lie than eat when they are hungry."

The trackers, Ben and Clay talked far into the evening. There was no way to know the outlaws tracks now that they had changed horses and had a head start on them. On different horses it would be very difficult to find the men and no way to prove they had done the killing. Early the next morning Tall Bear, Toby and Ben talked it over and decided it was a very long chance that they could catch the outlaws, the hunt was over.

Reluctantly the three men turned back south from the Fort to return home. Tall Bear stopped at the Broken Anchor and reported to Gavin and Mark what he knew and also gave Clay's regards to the family. Gavin was not at all surprised to hear that Clay believed Zeb Strader was one of the men they had been tracking. Clay told them Zeb had been in and out of jail on a regular basis for years. He had even spent time in the jail at the Fort for drunkenness and mistreating a woman at the Fort. Gavin had to wonder if he was with the gang that had burned the Preston ranch out and had managed to escape capture after the Zabala raid and the trap in Gotome Canyon. He did not know how close to the truth he was.

———◆———

41

STEPHEN

There had been no word from Stephen since he left the ranch weeks ago. He had returned to San Francisco in such a killing mood towards Gideon. One night when he had become drunk and in the company of another lawyer he confided in the man of his hatred for his father and why. After hearing Stephen out the man had a few words of advice, hire an investigator such as the Pinkerton Agency to trace the parents, both Gideon and Isobel. The idea appealed to Stephen it would prove Gideon's guilt once and for all.

The man hired to trace the whereabouts and what had transpired the few weeks before going to the ranch found very little to report except that Gideon had gone to the hotel where he was supposed to meet Isobel only to find she had returned to the Broken Anchor. Gideon had returned to California then in turn had returned to the ranch for two days with Alana. He had gone to see Isobel and had spent only a few minutes at his old home, according to one of the maids.

The man Stephen reluctantly hired to trace his mother since returning from Paris had a brief case full of documents. He had sworn affidavits from influential people who swore to Isobel's outrageous conduct with several men including the Count Manchelli. One couple had been privy to the garden scene when Pricilla had found her husband and Isobel together. He had put together a damning dossier on Isobel.

The last document was sworn testimony of the hotel staff of the many nights that Leonard Devaroux had spent with Isobel at his hotel or at her suite in the luxurious hotel overlooking the ocean. Since he had skipped out on his bill the hotel had no reason to protect the man.

Stephen was stunned! What if he had taken his mother's word alone and gone gunning for his father without hearing him out? He was certain he would have believed his mother. With this latest information he had to talk to Gavin and Mark. He was thoroughly confused.

He had arrived by the midnight train at Red Lodge. He hired a carriage, he never liked riding western horses, and arrived at the Broken Anchor as the new cook was building a fire to start breakfast for the riders in the cook house. The man was called the new cook but he had been doing the bunk house and roundup cooking for fifteen years ever since Cricket had to quit. Saying very little Stephen sat down at the long table, his mind going in a dozen directions. He could not stop thinking about how he felt about his father and what might have happened if he had not talked to another lawyer about his situation. He had brought the Pinkerton papers with him, he would turn everything over to Gavin.

To think all these years he had believed everything his mother had told him! He was sure some was true but not nearly enough to separate Gideon from his children. He realized his mother lived on hate. Perhaps his father had good reason to leave his family, as it became apparent to him there would have never been peace. It was a surprised Gavin and Mark that entered the cook house and found Stephen sitting at the table drinking coffee. The two ranchers got themselves coffee and after general greetings they were surprised when Stephen pushed a portfolio to his brother and uncle. Gavin read Isobel's information and then laid it aside and picked up the second portfolio from Mark. When they were finished all three men sat looking at one another. Isobel had perpetrated a most serious crime against Gideon. It was hard to wrap their minds around so much hate. Finally Stephen spoke. "I am going to face mother with this information and then I shall return to San Francisco. I have been offered a job in England and I have decided to take it. I will leave in about six weeks I may never come back to the United States. It's a wonder any of us brothers could amount to anything living with so much hate. I might have killed my father in defense of Mothers lies, he said standing up. Goodbye Mark, Uncle Gavin I'll be leaving soon. Uncle Gavin divide my share of anything I have left from the ranch if there is any with Mark and my sisters. I'll never be back."

Stephen reminded Gavin of an old stoop shouldered man as he went out the door. Mark had said nothing at all. Finally with tears in his eyes Mark said, "Uncle Gavin I just have to go home and hold my wife and baby" as he rushed out the door.

Stunned by this recent discovery Gavin absentmindedly kept stirring his black coffee with a spoon. He could not believe the hate that had driven Isobel. Would it have been different if Moria had lived? He didn't know. His riders ate and left and still Gavin sat with cold coffee and the damning papers in front of him.

———◆———

42

LORELIE

Father Ramirez sat with his head in his hands looking at the list of names in front of him. Most of the named did not even have an address, some referred to someone else at the mission. The ages ran all the way from thirteen to seventy two. He himself was past sixty. How would he ever find the families of the dead? Perhaps those who were injured would be able to tell him once they recovered from their injuries.

So engrossed with the difficult task in front of him he did not hear the four people who entered the sanctuary. He knew they had been in the mission most of the day scrubbing the walls and floors after the massacre. Two priests had been killed in this very room hiding some children. Several of the nuns and novices had been lined up along the wall of the mission and killed. It had been a retaliation attack by the Indians and outlaws known as Comancheros. They were ruthless men who robbed raped, killed and had no distinction between Indian, Mexican or white. They were blood thirsty unprincipled rebels.

Some of the Indian children were from their own tribe that came to the school to be taught by the nuns. The Mexican renegades that were hold overs from the last regime had killed dozens of the Indians at the Mission in an attempt to drive the Mission out. At that time one of the outlaws questioned lied and blamed the priest and nuns for the Indian deaths, causing much bad blood between the Mexicans and Indians.

Then this massacre occurred. Two priests, twelve nuns and he still did not know how many novices were dead, there were several on loan to help doctors in the area. He had been sent as soon as his Mission to the north received word they were needed to help the doctors with an epidemic in the Arizona territory. Suddenly one name stood out MacDougall, Lorelei MacDougall. He knew a MacDougall once, a ranching family that had settled in Nevada. Father Ramirez had grown up north of the Copper River before his family moved to Arizona. He couldn't remember much about them but maybe this was a start. He went to the back room of the building where the storage of records were kept and after searching for several minutes he found the information he was looking for and the name Lorelei MacDougall. He knew the rest would not be that easy to locate but this was a beginning of a very hard task, an ugly task. It was a fifty-fifty chance that one of her parents would be dead so he decided to address the death notice to Gideon MacDougall.

◆

It was barely sunrise and Isobel was standing at the window of her rooms when the rider rode hard up the ranch drive. Gavin and Mark were in the corral. The rider shouted he had a telegram for Mr. and Mrs. MacDougall. Mark took the letter read it and turned white as a ghost. His hand shaking he handed the letter to his uncle. Gavin stepped to one side stopping the running horse in training and looked at Mark. "Go ahead to the house uncle Gavin I'll put the horse up."

After he read the telegram Gavin took it upstairs and knocked on Isobel's door. She looked angry when he told her it was a letter for Mr. and Mrs. MacDougall. She took the letter and read the short missive of her daughter's demise. Gavin returned downstairs to the veranda.

Isobel read the Priest letter, Lorelei was dead! She had hoped that the girl would come home to help her. Why of all the things she could have done did she have to go off to the wilds of New Mexico or Arizona wherever to work at menial jobs for no pay, in a sand, outlaw infested Mission, teaching Indian kids of all people? The thought had grown in her mind that once the baby was born perhaps she could send "the kid" back to the Mission with Lorelei. Fate had dealt her another cruel blow and she would have to make the best of it. She took the letter and went down stairs to find Gavin. She found him waiting on the porch, waiting in case he heard the anguish cry of the mother for her child. It was a dry eyed Isobel who came out on the porch and seeing Gavin handed him the letter, then returned back to her rooms.

Stunned Gavin read the letter again finishing as Mark came up onto the porch from the barn. He gave the letter to Mark and sat back down in the rocking chair. His mind went back to the little child who saved him when Moria was killed. The child who came to him telling him "don't cry Uncle, it will be alright." The beautiful child who led him into the sunshine from the dark depths of despair when his life became the darkest he had ever known, when he lost his beautiful wife Moria.

Mark looked up from the letter with tears in his eyes. He could not believe his baby sister, sweet gentle Lorelei was dead. He heard of the Indian attacks on settlers in the south-west but did not think they attacked the missions since it was the missionaries who taught their children.

Handing the letter back to Gavin Mark said "I have to go tell Mercedes. I will be back in a little while and ride to Red Lodge to send word to Dad, Stephen and Arabella.

"I will ride with you," answered Gavin.

Mercedes told Mark as much as she knew and had heard of the Apaches if in fact they were the tribe believed to have attacked the Mission. There were several different tribes in the southwest, he supposed they would never know. Mercedes also mentioned Comancheros, ruthless men who sold liquor to the Indians and coaxed them to join in the raids. They in general preyed on everyone they came in contact with. They were well known for stealing and selling women and young girls.

It was a heart sick Mark that left his family to go to Red lodge to send telegrams. It was past noon when Mark and Gavin reached the telegraph station located at the train depot office in Red Lodge. They sent the telegrams to Gideon, although Gavin wondered if perhaps the news of the massacre at the mission had reached Gideon already. They sent telegrams to Stephen and Arabella.

A rider from town delivered the telegram to Gideon as he was about to leave the hacienda to go to San Francisco. Stunned he read the telegram several times. Perhaps there was a mistake. He and Senior Montoya-Luna had visited Lorelei as they were returning from Mexico and a meeting with the new president of Mexico. In fact they had spent the afternoon with Lorelei and stayed the night at the mission before continuing to the hacienda the next day. He simply could not believe the sweet gentle girl who seemed to always be surrounded by small children was dead.

———————◆———————

Stephen looked at his expensive pocked watch as he got off the train from the east, it was five past three in the afternoon, a little later than the schedule but plenty of time to surprise his sister Arabella and still have time to meet his latest paramour for supper.

Stephen and Arabella were having tea in her luxurious morning room when the butler entered with a telegram on a silver tray. Arabella opened the missive containing the terrible news of her sister's death. The words swam before her eyes as the room filled with darkness and she slipped from the chair. Calling out for help several maids and the butler entered the room as Stephen picked Arabella up and placed her on a sofa. The maid brought smelling salts while another young girl brought a cold wet cloth.

Stephen stooped and picked up the telegram from the floor. He was stunned at the message it contained. He had not been especially close with his sisters growing up but Lorelei was the sweet gentle forgiving sister who never told on him when he tormented her. No wonder Arabella fainted this was devastating. He could have understood dying in a train wreck or a stage coach wreck but he could not understand an Indian attack. Didn't they have protection at the mission? Weren't there soldiers stationed close by? How could this happen?

The butler had sent for the doctor as soon as Arabella had fainted. Since Stephen was a relative the Doctor reported the girl's condition to her brother. "Your sister is four months pregnant and has been under my care to keep from losing the baby. This shock is not good at all. Send for her husband and mother in law, Arabella has become very close to Mary and she needs a woman with her now. The butler sent word to David Granville and his mother Mrs. Mary Granville. As the doctor worked to care for Arabella Stephen forgot the time. He knew how much Arabella wanted children this would be a hard blow to her if she lost her baby. The doctor shooed everyone except two of the household girls from the room. He had ordered a bed brought into the room and placed Arabella in the bed. She could not be moved again her very life was in danger.

It was later that the butler escorted a worried, haggard faced Mrs. Granville into the room. Arabella held her arms out to the older woman. Stephen was glad Arabella had a loving woman in her life, so different from their mother.

It was well past the supper hour when a weary Stephen left the Granville house. Lorelei had been killed and Arabella had lost her baby. It was truly a house of mourning. He had to wire his father and brother. As he waited for a return telegram he remembered the happier times at the ranch when his aunt Moria was still alive and before his mother became so bitter. The Sunday dinners had been disliked at the time but now remembering them he thought of them as being good times, the sheriff and his wife, the preacher and his wife and various ranchers and their wives and families would be guests, that was a happier time and now Stephen wished for the return of that time.

Gavin and Mark wired the Mission to contact the local undertaker to prepare Lorelie for transport home. They would go most of the way by train then one of the ranch buckboards would meet them at the new train stop south of the Broken Anchor.

They reached the mission at noon and was met by Father Ramirez. The old priest had a small bundle of Lorelei's belongings for them. He directed them to the funeral house and blessing them sadly returned to the mission. Gavin realized the old man could hardly keep from breaking down.

They paid for the funeral expenses and two men loaded the handmade wooden coffin onto the train. Neither man spoke for a long time, each deep in his own thoughts. At some point Mark remembered the bundle the Priest had given them, and he open it. Inside was a small gold locket given to Lorelie one Christmas by Gavin and Moria. A ring given to her by Gavin and Moria with a small red stone, her birthstone. A small diary given to her by her father filled with the early days at the mission. Letters from her father, Steven, Mark and Arabella. A letter from Mark and Mercedes with a snippet of soft dark hair that Mark recognized as his daughters baby hair.

There was nothing from Isobel or Philip.

They were met by a Broken Anchor buckboard at the train stop, reaching the ranch they found that Stephen had the arrangements made for a funeral. She was buried next to Moria in the small plot on the hill from the house. A party of ranch people were gathered to meet them. Gideon was there with Arabella and the Granville's from San Francisco. In too many short years another funeral cortege wound its way up the hill to the McDougall burying ground. Standing with the other mourner's father and uncle feared for Arabella. The girl pale and weak stood shaking between her husband and mother in law. Her father in law stood behind his family as if to catch anyone if they should fall.

Arabella's mother in law held the girl close to her. David held onto his wife from the other side. Isobel stood off a ways from the group. When the service was complete they returned to the Heritage where Anna and the ranch women had a meal ready for the mourners. Isobel had already left and walked alone back to the house across the meadow. At the house Mrs. Granville put Arabella to bed. It was a subdued group in the quiet house. Isobel had returned to her rooms.

The next day Gavin took the party to meet the train at Red Lodge praying the next funeral would not be Arabella. The girl was frail, Gavin was glad that the train stop at Red Lodge made the trip to San Francisco much easier than the old way by stage.

◆

43

THE RAID ON THE ETXEBARRIA RANCH

High in the isolation of the Fox Mountains near the California boarder Ander Etxebarria and his family had settled in an area he believed the white man had never seen at least had never settled on. The large family consisted of Ander, his wife Edurne, their sons Benat and wife Amaia and their two small children, Yosu his younger son and his pregnant wife Osane who was barely four months with child, Edurne's younger brother Kemen Abaroa and his wife Balere who was Anders younger sister. They were aware of the raiders and had driven them off at least twice in the past. Indians from the northern tribes had also attempted to raid the ranch and had found it a virtual stronghold. They had built their home in such a manner that the families were safe from almost any attack. It had been patterned somewhat like the Broken Anchorage's Heritage that Ander and Keman had seen when they went there to buy dogs from one of the Broken Anchorage's men Nacho, who raised the herding dogs.

The Etxebarria/Abaroa house was built as one story. The center of the house was a large divided area, a straight through hall front to back, a sitting room at the front end and the kitchen, dining area and family sitting room took up the back and east half. On the west side of the hall were two work rooms a spinning room and a carding room combined containing two spinning wheels with looms. A storage area was located just inside the back door. A small company parlor was located just inside the front door. The huge ranch house was located away from a cluster of out buildings and the families all lived under the same roof. This made the house easier to defend. The women of the family had hopes of more families coming to the area. They hoped for women neighbors.

While two women did the spinning two women did the carding and cleaning of the wool. All the women worked with the looms, designing their own patterns. Circling the entire house were sets of narrow two rooms built onto the four corners of the home. Each of these rooms consisted of a small sitting room and a bedroom, each room contained shuttered windows. The corner rooms provided each family privacy and security while allowing the occupants to fire in at least two directions from each bedroom. The home was built with the river on two sides and a wide open meadow and barns on the other two sides. The home was built in such a manner that anyone attacking was out in the open when approaching the house. The families had to be self-sufficient as they were miles from the nearest fort to the north and even farther from the town of Gunsight. They had to be able to live and protect themselves, they were on their own and they could expect little or no help.

◆

A month after the trial of the captured night raiders of the Zabala ranch the Etxebarria/Abaroa Ranch was attacked. Some of the sheep ranchers had banded together and hired men to ride with the herds, men who could handle guns and rode the surrounding hills keeping watch on the herds and herders. As the violence came closer to the Etxebarria/Abaroa ranch riders were hired to protect the family. The extra men were to keep watch over the ranch house and the families and the surrounding hills. The Basque ranchers took nothing for granted, they had not survived for centuries by running scared or being careless when trouble came be it from Spain or France or roving outlaws.

The women learned to handle guns, some as well as the men. The children were taught to seek shelter if shooting started. The families had built root cellars located close to the house that was functional and a safe haven in case of an attack. The Etxebarria-Abaroa ranch was located farthest from Fort Halleck or the town of Gunsight. They could not count on the law due to the great distance, they had to provide their own protection. They were on their own.

Ander Etxebarria had worked hard all his life, being born the third son of a third son had meant he would have to seek work away from the family farm. The farm land in the Basque nation was always left to the eldest son.

Kemen Abaroa the brother in law of Ander had fared no better, he was the fifth son of a third son. Soon after marrying Anders sister Balere the two men left their home land and traveled to South America where they worked on the ranches. They both saved their money with the intention of buying their own sheep ranch, they had worked two years when they heard of gold being found in the rivers of California. Reaching California they began searching for the elusive gold, they found little gold but realized there was money to be made feeding the miners. They found also there was free land, the men bought the sheep and started their own ranch in the wilderness. The families had prospered.

Ander and Kemen had come to the Nevada territory from California where they had searched for gold, however two years of wading in the cold mountain streams had not produced the gold they needed to bring their families to the new country. The two men used the gold they had to buy sheep and they began as herders for a large Eastern Company. They took their wages in sheep and soon had a flock of their own which they drove to the unsettled mountainous area where they staked out and built their ranch. They found an abundant supply of lumber and hired men to cut and help build the fortress of a home. Many of these men were disillusioned gold seekers. They also cut and sent lumber down to the more populated towns.

The mountainous region the men had chosen reminded them of their Basque homeland. Their families joined them, the women were used to the isolation of the mountains and soon were beginning to make clothing from the wool. The ranch was located eighty miles from Fort Halleck and nearly seventy miles in the other direction from the town of Gunsight. The women worked in the hotel that was now on the stage route until their home was finished and as the men built a sheep herd for the family.

During shearing time the large shearing shed was occupied by all members of the family all working together. In many ways the families and their workers made up a small community. Edurne and Ander Etxebarria had given their larger rooms to Benat and Amaia and their two children. Yosu and his wife Osane were expecting their first child. Edurne's brother and his wife made the fourth family.

When the workers returned to the ranch from delivering their last load of lumber they told of the raids on the sheep ranches. Ander called his family together in the large dining room and they began to make plans in case of an attack. He had advised his workers to have an escape plan from the raiders also. Many of the homes had cellars built under the floors of the houses.

With the bedrooms built at the corners of the house the men could defend their home with the help of their wives.

As expected the night came when the night raiders rode onto the Etxebarria-Abaroa ranch. The raiders hit the ranch full bore with the intention of pillage and tearing the ranch from the face of the earth and leaving no one alive. It was a continuing malicious effort to drive the sheep men from the entire state. The family was seated for the evening meal when suddenly there was pounding on the large double entry doors. Benat answered the door and one of the guard riders warned him of the oncoming raiders. Within a matter of minutes the pregnant Osane had taken Benat and Amaia's two children and started for one of the two root cellars. The rest of the family members armed themselves and were waiting for the raiders. Yosu helped his pregnant wife Osane into the root cellar before leaving he pressed a small gun into his wife's hands. Their eyes met not knowing if either one would be alive when the raid was over. Squeezing her arm he left and closed the doors being careful to leave no marks that the cellar was there. Inside Osane lite a candle that stood on a small table. Gathering the two small children to her she sat on a bench to wait out the raid.

Suddenly the cave vibrated with the pounding of horse hooves as the raiders tried to circle the house. The first of her labor pains began. It was much too soon, it was not six months yet. Trying to stay calm Osane began to sing softly to the children. Finding a deadly barrage of gunfire from the house the raiders tried to withdraw to the barns, believing they could attack from that angle.

Ander reached for the loaded gun his wife Edurne handed him. She sat on the floor with a box of shells loading the empty rifle from her husband in exchange for a loaded gun to her husband. They kept up a steady barrage of gunfire. As Ander looked out into the meadow where the raiders rode shooting at the house he saw a rider come close to the house. Intent on the destruction of the ranch the rider carried a burning torch. The rider's horse slipped under one of the many clothes lines strung up in the yard. Too late the rider could not avoid the clothes line as it caught him under the chin and dragged him from his horse.

Horrified Ander watched as the rider became almost decapitated struggling on the heavy wire clothes line. At that time another outlaw began another run at the house. The injured rider lay in the yard under the swinging wire line, unmoving. The raiders had not been able to penetrate the ranches defenses.

The raiders gathered for another run at the fortress. The largest group circled as close to the river as they could and made their start. One of the riders that was drunk separated from the group and raced his horse closer to the house. Suddenly the horse and rider disappeared thorough the slanted door of the cave. The scream of the horse echoed around the walls. It regained its footing and escaped back through the broken door. The drunken rider stood blinking his eyes trying to realize what he was seeing. A young girl and two kids sat on a bench at the back of the cave. Candle light reflected from the jars of canned foods along the wall.

Wiping his face on his shirt sleeve he began to advance to the back of the cave in an unsteady walk. His whiskey fogged brain finally recognized a defenseless woman. Osane took the pistol from the pocket of her skirt and fumbled trying to cock the gun as another pain hit her. When she looked up the leering drunk was more than half way to her and the children. He had begun to remove his suspenders as he staggered towards his victims. Taking the gun in both hands Osane shouted for him to stop. The man appeared to not have heard as he advanced one staggering step at a time. Osane shouted a second time for him to stop. The two children began crying. The man kept advancing towards his victims. Just as he reached to grab hold of her Osane pulled the trigger twice both shots hitting the man in the center of his chest. The ring of the shots reverberated around the cave as the drunken man fell at the feet of his frightened intended victims.

The rider that had warned the house had also warned the other guards. The raiders were met with sudden deadly gun fire that caught the outlaws by surprise. The family had been expecting the raid since people had a tendency to forget that the Basque people understood some English, they however conversed in their own language. One of the raiders had bragged of the intent to burn down the Etxebarria-Abaroa ranch. One of the guards had overheard the outlaw and warned the sheep ranchers.

His wife safely in the cellar with his brother's children, Yosu returned to his rooms on the south east corner of the house. That side of the house took the first onslaught of gunfire. Returning the raiders gunfire Yosu fired from the window of the bedroom and picked up the second rifle kept there. He did not see the snipper on the roof of one of the outbuildings but he felt the bullet that spun him around by the impact. The bullet struck him in the right shoulder deep into the bone where it shattered the bone and traveled into his body. The impact staggered him. He managed to keep his balance by grabbing onto the foot of the bed to steady himself. He had seen where the shot came from and returned fire with deadly accuracy. He had little pain, not yet but he had been wounded enough times to know that would not last. He jerked the pillow case from the bed and shoved it under his shirt into the wound.

◆

By the time the fight was over which by most standards was short, Yosu had lost a considerable amount of blood. His father found him on the floor as he went to check on the family for any wounded. Benet had a grazed shoulder wound that his wife Amaia was able to take care of but Yosu needed a doctor, the bullet was lodged in such a position that to probe it blindly could drive it deeper, even into his spine or a vital organ. His father Ander alerted the family he could not remove the bullet they would have to wait on the doctor. The men had sent a rider for help to Gunsight for the doctor as soon as the raid had ended, it appeared he could not get to the ranch soon enough.

Suddenly a shadow came through the broken door as the children's father Benat came down into the cellar. He had seen the horse and rider go through the cave door. He pulled the dead man off to the side of the cave. He gathered his two children to him as Osane stood up she crumpled onto the floor leaving a large pool of blood on the floor.

Benat scooped his sister in law Osane up with his good arm and ran into the house. He was met at the door by his wife Amaia who quickly assessed the unconscious woman and told her husband to take Osane to the cot in the spinning room. Amaia called for Balere and the two

204

women attempted to try to make Osane comfortable and to stem the blood flow. Amaia went to the herb closet and returned with comfrey also known as black wort often used to stop excess bleeding. It was clear to both women Osane had lost her baby, now all they could do was try to keep Osane alive. Balere sent Amaia to see if anyone else had been hurt. She returned to the spinning room with the news that Yosu had been shot and it appeared he too was bleeding very badly. Amaia took some comfrey and returned to Yosu and Osane's bedroom giving it to Edurne to be used on Yosu.

An old long ago remedy for bullet or arrow wounds was to let the wound fester then remove it, but Ander had seen too many wounds turn to gangrene to trust his son's life to such methods. He could only pray the doctor would come right away. They would keep the wound open to drain and to try to keep Yosu quiet.

By morning bruising had already set in to the gunshot wound and there appeared to his father to be few to no choices to remove the bullet. Yosu woke to a world of pain, his entire body hurt and the shoulder wound felt as if it were on fire. Getting him onto the bed had been painful but keeping the wound open and cleaning the bed left him limp and exhausted, feeble as a new born kitten. By the morning of the second day his pulse was slight and fever had set in. He tried to rouse himself to set up, he wanted to go to Osane, but the fire and pain blazed hotter than Hells fire. He had overheard the whispers that Osane was hemorrhaging He broke out in sweat and became light headed and dizzy, the room spinning. The more he moved the more risk he put himself in for spreading the infection and moving the deadly bullet.

He asked about the condition of his wife, and was told she was put to bed. He drifted in and out of pain filled conscience, his cheeks became hollow and pain etched deep grooves around his mouth showing he had an enormous amount of weight loss in just a couple of days. His face was white, bloodless and as the pain got worse he closed his eyes, shuddered and bit down on his lower lip until it bled in an attempt to stifle cries of pain. His father Ander and mother Edurne would not leave his side. His aunt Balere and sister in law Amaia remained with Osane as she struggled with losing their baby and fought for her own life.

A rider raced to the town of Gunsight for the sheriff and doctor. It was two days later when they reached the ranch. Among the wounded and killed were two raiders one of the U.S. Marshalls recognized. The Marshall had asked Sheriff Beldon to send two of his deputized men to the Basque ranch. Beldon sent deputized Gavin and Mark to take the place of two of his deputies. It seemed to Beldon there was trouble all over central Nevada. Dead was Bill Johnson deposed owner of the Bar J and Tom Baker owner of the Half Moon who died later.

When the riders from the ranch returned they also brought the bad news that the doctor was miles from town delivering a baby and was not expected to return for at least two or maybe three days. One of the men had made a paste of herbs containing betony and woundwort. When Ander removed the makeshift bandage he saw the wound had begun to turn deep red and the shoulder and arm was swollen. There was a long red line going down the arm surrounded by a border of red. Gangrene! A certain death sign unless the damaged limb was amputated and the bullet deep within removed. There would become the familiar battlefield stink of rotting flesh and the putrid wound would be followed by death. Death was caused by a failure in the circulation of the blood to the injury.

◆

The U.S. Marshall with help from Gavin and Mark rounded up the raiders that had been caught or otherwise unable to retreat were tied and held in one of the barns. The Marshall later talked to Mark and Gavin. "Looks like the apples did not fall far from the tree. Now we know where the young ones Spike and Joey got their ideas of the sheep men. Both their fathers were killed in the raid. Gavin recognized Zeb Strader as the man killed when his horse ran under the clothes line.

The riders tied up at the porch and entered without knocking. Kemen had ridden day and night until he found the doctor. They reached the ranch four days after the raid. As Doctor George Crispen approached the wounded man he was certain the man was dying. The stench of the wound, a familiar battlefield stink of rotting flesh and putrid wounds told the doctor there was not much hope of recovery, death was inevitable. Suddenly the doctor was transported back to his service in the War Between the States some fifteen years past. He had been a young intern stationed with an older doctor. He was shocked at the clarity of the remembrance.

The wound was now a swollen discolored mass of flesh. The gangrene was spreading with its familiar diabolical speed. The skin was a deep raw red. It would soon take on a dark bronze color then turn black as the body rotted away from inside. The doctor knew what he would find under the bandage.

Speaking to the patient he got no response. Yosu appeared to have aged much in the last days. Being unconscious was the only relief from the pain that had etched deep grooves around his mouth. Hollow cheeks showed more weight loss daily since the injury. His face was pale, bloodless. The shoulder poultice over the wound was oozing a foul smelling pus. When the bandage was removed there was more swelling than the doctor could believe would have been, his chest had begun to blister turning black. A long red line surrounded by a border of red down the arm, it was wider than a day ago Ander told Dr. Crispin, another sign the deadly gangrene was unstoppable. He could not remember one case where the patient lived when wounded as badly as this man was.

As he examined the wound he was shocked that the wound was caused by a musket loaded mini ball. After extensive probing the doctor finally retrieved the mini ball. He was flooded with memories from the War Between the States when he was assigned to a base hospital. Memories of the smell of the putrefied wound as the result of gangrene that seemed to always follow the armament. The ball it's self was a conical hollow based lead bullet with a hollow base that expanded when fired from a musket muzzle loading rifle. The round ball tended to remain in the flesh and often took a winding path through the body breaking bones in the process. The result was almost always amputation and most likely death. It had been invented by a French Captain named Mini and was used extensively in the Civil War. Being hit by a mini ball was a constant thought of soldiers of both Union and Confederate armies.

The doctor turned to his other patient. As soon as he saw Osane he knew this patient too was going to die. The girl had too great a blood loss to recover. Osane slept very little, constant pains and sweating, her skin became so white that it looked transparent she was so fragile, as unsubstantial as morning mist. She had begun vomiting to the point of convulsing.

———◆———

Osane remained in a semi conscience state while all the time the hemorrhaging continued. Balere and Amaia had thought it wise not to tell her that Yosu had been shot or how bad his wound was. Her condition continued to worsen, she was fragile and cold. Two days ago she had begun constant vomiting, this continued. Now at times she showed few signs of life. It was difficult to tell if she was breathing.

On the fifth day after the raid, young Osane entered into eternal sleep. Balere and Amaia wondered how or if they could tell Yosu he had lost his wife and their unborn child. Closing the door to the dead girl's room they turned down the hall to the kitchen where Ander and Edurne waited for the doctor to finish with their son. As Balere and Amaia entered the kitchen it was apparent to the elder Etexebarria's Osane had lost her battle for life. The four made the decision to remain silent.

The following morning in the dark hour before dawn Yosu died. The doctor sat on one side of his bed, his mother, father and brother on the other. In one fell swoop the Etxebarria family had lost three members of their family all due to the greed of a few. There would be no exacting price for the crimes against the raiders as there was no absolute proof who caused the deaths. They believed Yosu had shot his killer. A man with a musket rifle had been found near the barn. Osane had saved the children and herself from the drunken raider. That was the only consolation for the family.

◆

Gavin and Mark again made the ride to the Etxebarria-Abaroa ranch to attempt to gather more information from the ranches herders. The war had to stop and it could only be stopped by each person trying to get along with his neighbors and bringing those caught to justice. Nevada was a rich state and there was indeed land for all. Men who were greedy had to be held accountable for their actions. The new Governor had ordered more U.S. Marshalls to the territory, men who had no axe to grind and their only agenda was to uphold the law. The way of life had changed much since Gavin had come to the valley, he had begun to think there was nothing new to do and then silver was discovered and again the land was the value. He thought to himself that perhaps it would be easier to tame the range war than to get Gideon and Isobel to stop fighting, hurting one another and their children.

On the way back to their ranch they came across a herd of sheep Mark had never seen before. "Gavin those sheep are different. I have never seen any like them before."

"Those are Merino sheep one of the Marshalls told me about them, they have special wool more like hair. This special wool when woven is much sought after by the immigrants going into the mountains. Next time we are at the post at Fort Grant look over the woven jackets on display. They are very warm and beautifully made." Thinking of what Gavin had told him the two men rode towards home in silence.

44

THE LADY IN WHITE

The lioness and her two half grown cubs slid through the shadows under the trees coming within a quarter of a mile from the lake they stretched out, their long tails flicking side to side, yellow eyes watching as the woman walked from the large house to the barn then retraced her footsteps back to the lane past the house and down to the lake. It was easy to see her as she was dressed in a white flowing gown. The lioness had not made a kill for several days and the calf she killed had been devoured by her cubs. She needed to make a kill tonight.

The full moon spilled light across the valley. The faces on the cattle flashed white as they grazed. The cats would have liked to go into the herd for one of the yearling calves. They had tried before but the ranch had black and white herd dogs that ran free. And three or four of the dogs presented a real danger to the cats. Each cat had had a go at the dogs at some time. When in a pack with two night riders there was no hope of killing a calf still they watched the ranch and the cattle.

One of the night riders came from the north end of the lake. When he saw the person walking towards the lake he turned his horse and rode back the way he came. He was certain it was the elder Mrs. MacDougall. These days it was not unusual for her to walk at night. Everyone on the ranch was aware of her condition and how her folly had caused her to become pregnant. They were aware also if the attempt to ruin her husband by accusations of rape against him until a diary was discovered that proved he was innocent. Forty minutes later the riders met and rode into view of the big cats. The dogs stopped and whined staying close to the men and horses awaiting instructions.

The riders heard the low growl of the cats lying in wait in the trees for a stray grazing calf. They took their rifles from their saddle boot and laid them across their laps. Like their horses and dogs they had no desire to tangle with the big cats. The Indians believed the cats were part human. A few years past Gavin MacDougall's wife had been killed by a cat attacking her horse. Many of the ranch hands refused to go into the Medera Mountains and never overnight. Whether or not there was truth or even half-truth to the stories it gave one pause to wonder.

The rider finished his ride at the south end of the lake. The figure in white was standing on the bridge that crossed the narrow end of the lake where it ran into a stream down the valley. The rider turned and retraced his route back around the lake, passing the other rider. This small horse herd was special. They were the very best the Broken Anchor had to offer and was payment for some of the Palomino horses recently received from the Montoya-Luna ranch in southern California. The Broken Anchor ranch now raised prize horses that were highly valued and in demand. The Montoya-Luna riders would arrive in a day or two to take the herd south. The cattle were sold to a rancher in Montana as breeding stock and the money from this herd alone would pay the ranch expenses for the year. It would be a few weeks before he arrived to have the cattle shipped north.

Isobel had never felt so desolate in her life. She had more money than she could spend in two life times. She could buy anything she wanted. Except the one thing she craved-love. All her money could not buy her love or fill her life with happiness and free her from the loneliness that closed around her like a dark dank cloak. She was more afraid of trying to rid herself of this baby than she was of giving birth. She had heard the horror stories of women dying trying to abort an unwanted child. Isobel felt humiliated, angry, abandoned, desperate and foolish. How could she have been so deceived as to get involved with someone to the point of becoming pregnant? Through all these thoughts she never once thought she was to blame. She first blamed Gideon then each of her children.

She was paying for her folly of trusting others, only Philip might have stuck by her. But Philip was no longer among the living. She had no one. Mark had married a girl that Isobel still refused to meet, Arabella had discovered the truth of her affair and now refused to even talk to her. Stephen had gone so far as to investigate her and had discovered she had an affair. How could he hire detectives to spy into his own mother's life? Lorelei had died while in some distant territory caring for children of rabble. The worse blow of all was that Gideon had won. Arabella and Stephen had both made amends with him when they discovered the truth. She was truly alone. And now this baby, she hated the way her body was changing. Once the baby was born it would always be a reminder of how she had been deceived and no one would be able to forget her indiscretions. A plan began to take shape in her mind. After all she really did not have anything to live for. She just knew she was tired of fighting, she did not want to raise a baby, she wanted out, out of life, out and away from the people who betrayed her, and out of this mess she was in.

◆

Up on the side of the mountain the cats watched as the white robed body sank below the water. The lions each in turn rose stretched and started to the lake in the valley where the wild horses came to drink. There were too many people and dogs here for their liking and a young colt would do as well as a calf.

An hour and a half later when the riders reached the bridge there was no sign of the person who had been there. They crossed the bridge and each continued to circle the cattle and horses.

The following morning as the sun began its meteoric rise over the mountain four of the Broken Anchor riders were headed for the outlying range. They would check the herd they had been gathering up in the north end of the valley and start them back towards the ranch. One of the riders saw something white floating on the lake. Turning off the road he rode along the bank to the north end of the lake. The other riders joined the first rider, and the older of the men knew before they took the body from the water what they would find. The ranch was a small community in its self and everyone on the ranch was aware of what went on at the big house. The riders had seen Isobel walking and knew she was unhappy. The older rider sent one of the men to the house to bring a wagon to carry the body home. It appeared the Broken Anchor was going to have to face another tragedy and Isobel MacDougall had put an end to her misery.

———————◆———————